# WITH THESE WORDS

## THE THINGS UNSEEN

K. LASHAUN

# BEFORE YOU DIVE IN...

With These Words is book #4 of The Things Unseen Series, and a continuation of book #3, Beneath the Silence. I highly suggest reading that book before before diving into this one.

## TRIGGER/CONTENT WARNING

This book contains mention and/or depictions of angst, child neglect/abuse, sexually explicit content, violence, gaslighting, profanity, and murder/death.

# PLAYLIST

Listen on Spotify

Bad Side - Nyla
Don't You Worry - Kelly Rowland, Lord Quest
Change - Rachel Kerr
Lose - R.A.D.
Love - Tree
Loving You - Kate Stewart
Say Less - Colette Lush
Heaven on Earth - Roann, Jordan Hawkins
Ready is Always Too Late - Sinead Harnett
Yeah You - King Sis
Fussy - MALIA
That's My Man - Shavaun Marie

# PROLOGUE

***Eden, Age 11***

"WHERE ARE YOU GOING?"

My mother's alto had my feet skidding to a halt in the door that separated the kitchen and living room.

Nervousness flooded me as I turned, bracing myself for whatever I'd done wrong. "Ma'am?"

A thin, arched brow lifted higher than the other as she folded her arms. One blunt-tipped nail aimed towards the dining room where all five of us had just finished a meal of spaghetti, garlic bread, salad, and pound cake. "You just gonna leave the table a mess?"

My neck jerked before I could stop it. I couldn't believe she was making me clean up *again*. "What about Benji and Madi? They haven't washed a dish in *months*." I was lying because Madi, had *never* washed dishes and it had been at least a year since Benji had to do anything besides exist in this house.

Her eyes flashed with anger. The same anger that always seemed present whenever dealing with me. Seconds later, she closed the distance between us, not stopping until the tip of her finger grazed my nose. "Did I tell them to clean up? Or did I tell *you*?"

My hands fisted on the back of the chair, trying to push down the urge to hit something. Whenever I felt wronged, overlooked, mistreated, or neglected, that impulse threatened to take over. At school, I was a regular in detention and in-school suspension because of the emotions I could never seem to control.

"But it's always me!" I was tired of being the only child in the house with chores or responsibilities. "Benji is gone with his friends all the time and Madi doesn't do *anything*. We share a room and I'm the only one who cleans up. She makes the biggest messes, but I get in trouble. It's not fair!"

She sighed as if I put the weight of the world on her shoulders. "*Life* ain't fair so you better get used to it." When I scowled at that stupid response, she tapped the tip of her finger against my nose as a warning. "Take your ass in the kitchen to clean up. And once you finish, go to bed since you have so much to say."

She walked off before I could respond.

It didn't really matter because arguing was pointless. I was the only one who recognized the difference in treatment. Whenever I brought it up, my parents called me a spoiled brat rather than a frustrated child who was tired of being her older and younger siblings' maid.

With a scowl still in place, I stomped to the table, slamming dishes on top of one another before dumping them in the sink.

Seconds later, footsteps thumped across the floor and I was yanked before I could turn on the faucet.

"*Slam another dish in my house.*"

My lids narrowed at my dad's threat, jerking against the tight hold he had on my arm. When I couldn't shake free, my anger boiled over and I was opening my mouth, saying something that I knew would earn me an even harsher punishment.

"This is mama's house, not yours. She's the only one who works and pays bills, remember? You just *live* here, like me, Madi, and Benji."

Shock rendered him speechless before he shoved me and lifted his hand. I flinched and slammed my lids closed, bracing for the slap. But when nothing happened, I parted my lids, bucking my eyes after spotting my older brother standing next to our dad, holding the arm that had been making its way towards my face.

"Let me handle it, Dad. I'll talk to her."

My dad's gaze swung to him, sizing Benji up. "You better because her mouth is going to get her fucked up."

With one last glare that I returned, he stormed out, probably going to the den to sit in front of the television like always.

"Stop being a *menace*." Benji teased playfully after he was gone. "That smart mouth is going to keep you in trouble, baby girl."

Instead of redirecting my anger towards him, I smiled with every ounce of my adoration. In a house where I felt like the enemy, I latched onto the one connection that didn't leave me disappointed. My brother was my whole world and I knew he felt the same way when the face that was nearly identical to mine beamed right back.

Our bond was ironic because my brother was mean. A *bully*. I'd seen firsthand how he interacted with other neighborhood kids but he'd reserved the small bit of softness he had for his family. But most of all, for me.

Shaking his head with a laugh, he elbowed me aside, moving towards the sink and adjusting the dishes much more calmly than I had. "I'll wash. You dry."

Nervously, I flicked my gaze to the door, expecting my mother to come in and scold me. Every time Benji tried to step in and take the load off, instead of fussing at him, she called me lazy and claimed I was pushing my responsibilities off on my brother.

That accusation set me on fire every time and my anger would explode, only getting me in more trouble.

Like a team, we worked side by side, finishing the cleanup much quicker than I would've alone. My anger would've slowed me down as I mumbled under my breath about the unfairness of it all.

Once the last dish was dried and put away, I turned to my brother, unable to stop my question from bursting free. A question that I'd been thinking about for a while but had been too scared to ask.

"Why don't Mama and Daddy like me?"

His brows shot up. There was no way he hadn't noticed how he and Madi were handled like royalty while I got the treatment of someone who'd come over uninvited and refused to go home.

"They love you, baby girl." I smiled at the nickname. No one else had ever given me one so I felt extra special since it came from my favorite person.

"They love me because they have to." I responded, dropping my smile. "But they don't *like* me. You don't have to pretend not to see it. It's *obvious*."

"I don't know about that." He denied, then poked me in the ribs when I rolled my eyes. A low snicker left his lips when I squirmed. "I don't know what Dad's issue is, but I heard mama on the phone one time. She said you're just like her. She sees herself in you but you fight back. You don't just take it when people hurt you. You have a voice but she's too scared to use hers." He shrugged like what he'd said was no big deal. "I just think she's jealous of you."

I'd talk to my best friend, Mo, about it later to see if she could help figure it out because none of what he'd said made sense. But Benji was older, wiser, and would never hurt me, so I believed every word, even if I didn't fully understand. He'd always had my back. He always stepped in whenever our parents started in on me. Especially during the times when I was blamed for something that Madi had done.

Out of everyone in this house, I knew that no matter what happened, I could always count on Benji.

Nothing, not even the people who created us, would ever break the bond we had.

The two of us were each other's best friends and we always would be.

# 1

# EDEN

"You still with us, Eden?"

Each of my muscles stiffened as I forced my wandering mind back to the conversation. Since being summoned nearly forty-five minutes ago, I sat in irritated silence, frankly not in the right headspace for yet *another* meeting. After becoming the newest addition to VP Sports, I've spent more time seated in conference rooms and listening to people with *way* more money than I had making decisions about my career. What I'd rather be doing was fulfilling my actual purpose for being here... *competing*.

"You sure?" Eboni, my new sports manager slash agent asked with a shrewd gaze.

Now that the attention was on me, discomfort had me settling deeper in my seat, fiddling with the tiny stud in my right nostril. "Sorry. All of this is still new and it's taking a minute to process."

Which wasn't a lie. Despite being signed months ago, I was still uncomfortable.

Being Eden from White Grove was, at times, a burden. And slipping back into my role as Menace from the 400s also came along with its issues. But at least they were *familiar*, unlike whatever the hell this was. I'd been thrown headfirst into a whole new world that I wasn't sure I was cut out for.

A world of cameras, lights, scrutiny, fame, and notoriety. A world of networking, interviews, and non-stop meetings with executives, assistants, and agents. A world that scared me more than stepping in a ring or octagon ever would.

"That's understandable." Eboni said, flashing a sympathetic smile towards me then to the duo sitting across from us.

Out of all the interviews I'd sat through when searching for an agent, she'd stood out.

While the others had been nice, she'd been no-nonsense in her approach. Brutally honest and blunt, speaking as if already hired.

*"I'm going to be frank with you." She'd said, crossing one thick thigh over the other. "You're good, Eden. Actually, you're exceptional. You have a once-in-a-lifetime, generational talent. But you're rough around the edges and not palatable enough to appeal to the masses. You need polishing and that's where I come in. You're going to work with an image consultant. I'm going to put you through public relations training." Then she leaned forward, meeting my uncomfortable glare head on. "This is a new path you're about to take. One that's probably the scariest thing you've ever done. And it's going to take time. But if you're open to suggestions, open to change? It'll also be the best decision you've ever made."*

Her unwavering confidence had sold me and we'd started work immediately. And over the last few months, she'd done exactly as she said... polishing me, working with me, getting me the necessary training to become the household name she envisioned.

Like now, sitting in a meeting with a well-known company that wanted me to pose for their new women's athletic wear line. The buzz around my signing still hadn't died down and Eboni was setting me up to capitalize off every part of it.

Seemingly satisfied with my response, they continued tentative negotiations, and I resumed checking in and out of the conversation.

Instead of what was going on right in front of me, my mind kept drifting to my underground fight tonight.

My current schedule was jam-packed, barely giving me a moment to breathe. Between conditioning, meetings, training, appearances, and fighting underground, I wasn't sure how I managed it all.

Hell, the few times I was able to get the boys, my time with them was limited, at best.

"And the contractual obligation?" Eboni's no-nonsense tone pulled me back into the present. "Are you requesting specific promotional obligations from her outside of the initial shoot and appearance at the launch? Or are you looking for something long-term?"

I tuned out their answer, unsure why the hell I was even sitting here when I had a million other things to do. Things *she'd* tasked me with. The checklist I was working through before getting a chance to enter an MMA contest seemed to get longer by the day.

At this point, I wondered if I'd even get the chance to compete before my prime years passed me by or I injured myself fighting underground.

Once again, Eboni noticed I was distracted and tried to pull me into the conversation. Instead of giving her what she wanted, I smiled and nodded absently, which earned a glare from the stunning, plus-sized woman.

It was obvious to everyone in the conference room that I wasn't truly listening. And not an ounce of guilt plagued me when I checked out again once they started tossing around terms like royalty provisions, exclusivity clauses, and brand equity.

It wasn't until I heard, "We'll be in touch," that I jerked back to the present, standing along with Eboni to shake hands.

Minutes later, only the two of us remained and I braced for the questions I sensed coming.

"Are you sure you're okay, Eden?"

I propped a hip against the edge of the table. "Why did I have to be here for this?"

An uncharacteristic snort coming from her had my lips lifting. "I was attempting to be transparent, like you asked. I wanted to make sure you were part of the process from beginning to end, that way there's no doubt or questions later."

Though I had asked for that after the fiasco with my former manager, Jesse, I continued staring with a blank expression, conveying my annoyance.

One of her rare chuckles emerged again. "Might as well suck it up. We have a meeting with Monica right after this." She checked her watch then lifted her brow. "Well, in about an hour and a half. Can I trust you to show up if I allow you a break?"

Despite her teasing, there was a bit of warning in her tone that stretched my smile. Eboni *hated* how easy it was for me to fall off the grid.

I was rarely on social media and preferred keeping to myself.

Hell, I was normally as surprised as everyone else after seeing the new posts uploaded by the marketing team.

My phone was normally on vibrate or silent and at times, I even turned it completely off when I was doing work for the 400s or fighting underground. The last thing I wanted or needed was anyone in *this* world catching wind of what I was up to in my *other* world. It had been made abundantly clear in my contract what would happen if I competed elsewhere.

But for the sake of getting Eboni off my back, I nodded, unsure if I'd be able to keep my promise.

---

"ARE WE READY TO ACCEPT?" Joy, the jack-of-all-trades for VP Sports Management spoke, scribbling like always in the little notebook she carried around. Like Eboni, she was stunningly beautiful.

Rich sienna skin tone, bright eyes, and a megawatt smile she loved to flash. But where Eboni was closer to my height and plus-sized, Joy was taller, pushing six feet, and toned from a collegiate career of running track.

Their appearance wasn't the only area where the women differed. Joy was bubbly, warm, and inviting in a way that was almost innocent. But Eboni was a skeptic. A *boss* who didn't mind ruffling feathers if it benefited her clients.

She might be hard and sometimes pressed the gas when I wanted to stomp the brakes, but she had my back. Pushing her clients forward was her number one priority and nothing would stop her from achieving whatever goal she had in mind.

"I don't see why not," Eboni responded to the question about my competing in an exhibition match.

"Let's slow down a bit." Monica, the talent development manager, interjected with the familiar snark that had grated my nerves since our first meeting. "I understand that Ms. Foster is used to competing eight to twelve times per year. But at *this* level, the focus is quality over quantity. We can't just throw her against *anybody* like she's used to."

I tensed from the weight of her insult.

There wasn't a damned thing wrong with my *quality* considering I'd never lost. On any level. True, some fights in the small circuits might've been beneath my skill set. But competing in a male-dominated sport meant I took what I could get.

If not for the *quantity* of fights, I might not be sitting in this chair right now.

"Are you insinuating there's something wrong with my client's quality, Monica? If so, please make it known so we can address it here and now. Rather than in a passive aggressive email later."

Joy and I locked eyes. The comical way her brows shot up nearly had me losing control over my laughter. Though I wouldn't consider her a friend, we'd bonded over our shared amusement of Eboni's *kick-ass and take names* demeanor.

It took only a moment before Monica conceded, rolling her eyes back to me. "Where did you get the bruises?" I'd forgotten to cover the worst of them after my underground fight last week.

"You forgot what she does for a living?" Eboni interjected before I could.

This time, Monica didn't spare her a glance, staring me down as if she knew the truth. "I find it pertinent to remind you that any kind of physical activity or competition must be approved by management."

They'd told me that right after signing, stating it was a liability and I risked being dropped if I broke the rules.

I was forbidden from doing anything that might endanger or risk injury which meant I'd had to give up on private lessons and self-defense clients.

I was still in talks with sponsors and hadn't competed in months, which had my funds looking a little low. If not for the meager earnings from the 400s fights, I wasn't sure I'd be able to make rent next month.

"Looks like I'm right on time."

I tensed at the smooth, familiar tone, taking a minute to compose my nerves before lifting my gaze to Verse's commanding form in the doorway. The air in the room suddenly got thick, filling up with the power that effortlessly seeped from his pores.

As he greeted everyone, I stared directly in his face, waiting for whatever emotion would cross his features when those dark eyes met mine.

"Eden." He finally made it to me, holding that intense eye contact. His hand stretched out and I stood to grip it, refusing to back down despite the absolute uncertainty coursing through me.

He held mine a moment longer than he'd done everyone else's, giving away nothing but mild curiosity as he searched my gaze.

"I heard you were in the building today." He offered, finally releasing me. Instead of sitting, he remained standing on my side of the large oak table. "Just wanted to drop in and speak." Tremors wrecked my lower gut from the sheer intensity of his stare but I managed a shaky smile.

He said nothing for a long while, not breaking eye contact even after Monica cleared her throat.

The ability to stare without caring about the discomfort it caused was a trait he and his best friend seemed to have perfected.

Finally, after I feared water was about to spring above my lids from the pressure of holding it, he looked away. "I've interrupted long enough and my fiancée is not a very patient woman." The thought of Garryn and our tentative friendship we'd developed in St. Leesburg caused another ache. Once or twice, she'd texted after the trip, inviting me to lunches that my schedule hadn't allowed me to attend. But none of that mattered now. Since the severing of my relationship with Hakeem nearly eight months ago, I didn't expect to hear from her or *any* of them again.

Verse flashed another of those confusing glances my way before leaving, taking that overpowering cloud of intensity with him.

The second he was gone, Monica resumed discussing what I could and couldn't do. But her words sounded like they were coming from the end of a long tunnel. Now, anything concerning my career moved to the back of my mind while a certain, mostly silent, six-and-a-half-foot man pushed to the forefront.

Just seeing his *friend* caused thoughts of Hakeem to resurface. Thoughts I'd fought to keep buried since we called it quits.

"Eden. *Eden.*" I flinched at Monica's tone, jerking my gaze upwards after realizing I'd been staring at the tabletop. "Are you listening? That's like the fourth time you've zoned out today. I understand this might be a bit more advanced than what you're used to, but it's necessary if you ever plan on competing."

I let her slick ass *a bit more advanced* comment roll off my shoulders, pasting on the smile they'd taught me to flash. "Sorry. I'm listening."

Monica's lips parted to offer another passive aggressive remark but Eboni jumped in before she could. "How about we break? I need something to eat anyway since I skipped breakfast."

Monica's displeasure was obvious. But she knew she was

outnumbered when both Joy and I agreed. "Fine. One hour." And because she couldn't seem to help herself, she pursed her lips and looked at us over her glasses. "And *not* a minute more."

---

I REMAINED in the room while everyone else left for lunch.

Unable to stomach food right then, I stared out the floor-to-ceiling windows with folded arms, overlooking the beautiful skyline. Worry about tonight's fight continued to dominate my mind. I was still dealing with soreness in my ribs after *last* week.

Soreness that was taking longer than normal to heal.

Despite the severe pain I'd been in, nothing had been broken. According to the doctor, all I needed was rest to give my body time to heal before I took it through the gauntlet again. But that was something I constantly found myself in short supply of.

*Time.*

"You sure you're good?" I'd heard the steps coming down the hall but hadn't bothered to turn. The security in this building was airtight so I didn't worry about potential threats.

"Yeah." I said to Joy, glancing over my shoulder. "Just got a lot on my mind."

"I understand that it's all new." she offered, moving to stand beside me. "And I might be out of line for saying this but I just want you to hear me out. You're about to *ascend*. You're about to turn into a household name. And before it's all said and done, you're going to be on cereal boxes, commercials, and billboards. You'll be the inspiration behind a lot of brown girls' black history projects."

My teeth raked over my bottom lip nervously. I didn't want to be anyone's role model. Didn't think I was deserving of it. Not after everything I'd done.

My past was tainted. Hands stained with the blood I'd spilled and dirt I'd done. But instead of confessing any of this to Joy, I kept my expression neutral, grateful she didn't need a response to keep going.

"If you can't tell, I'm a bit of a fan." A sheepish smile transformed her gorgeous features in a way that had one tugging at the corner of my lips. "I saw a clip of you online about a year ago and it was the most *intense* thing I've ever seen." She scanned me with awe, making me squirm with discomfort. "You don't just go out there, pummel somebody and leave. There's a *beauty* to what you do. Almost like ballet." At my incredulous expression, she laughed. "Don't get me wrong... it's violent and bloody but you're also... graceful with the way you move. In tune with your body in a way I've only seen in dancers." Her slim hand came to rest on my folded arms, squeezing lightly as if we'd known each other forever. "When you're out there, you look like somebody who is fully living in her purpose. Somebody who understands what their calling is and decided to not only meet expectations but *exceed* them."

Noises from the hallway had her turning to greet Monica and Eboni as they returned. "Everybody ready to go?"

Long after the second half of the meeting resumed, Joy's words lingered in my mind.

Compliments about my career were normally in reference to my ability to spill blood. My natural penchant for violence. The power and skill displayed in my punches and kicks.

No one had ever described anything I'd done as *graceful*. And I'd damn sure never been compared to a dancer.

But before I could stop it, the flattery settled in, coating that place of insecurity, and taking up residence. God knows it wouldn't last long but I'd hold on to that compliment with both hands, letting it temporarily heal some of my broken pieces until someone came along to shatter them again.

"I'm sorry I need to meet with who?" I interrupted, catching Eboni off guard. Unlike the first half of this meeting, I made sure to follow the flow of conversation despite my wayward thoughts.

"A real estate agent."

"For?" A slight tilt of my head accompanied the question. I didn't recall discussing a new home with anyone. Hell, my funds were so low that affording the one I already had was growing more difficult by the day.

But my question was met with silence and I realized I must've missed some vital part of the conversation. I was the only one who seemed confused but I refused to care. Instead, I crossed my arms, waiting for someone to say something.

"You're now Eden Foster. The first female athlete to sign with VP Sports Management. You're one of *three* black women to receive a PFC invitation. Every part of your life is about to be elevated and we're starting with your address." Eboni paused as if giving me a chance to respond. But when I didn't, she forged on. "No offense but living in White Grove does not align with the woman you're about to become. I understand that's where you're from and you'll probably be leaving family behind." My heart sank at the thought of leaving Isaiah and Jayce *behind* but I remained focused. "The last thing we want is for you to be tempted by bad influences or put into a situation that could ruin your career before it fully starts."

Again, she paused, but I didn't have an argument ready. As much as I hated to admit, she was right. But there was one question I had before agreeing.

"How exactly am I supposed to afford this *new address*? Unless you signed endorsement deals behind my back and didn't tell me about it yet."

That hardness in her expression eased long enough for a small smile to peek through, revealing the slight gap between her two front teeth. "No paperwork has been signed, I promise."

"VP Sports owns several condos throughout the area for this very reason." Monica interjected. "We don't want our athletes to be tempted into doing anything illegal for money while working on their career. The first few weeks and months are the most difficult so one burden we can take from you is the stress about finances."

Now that was shocking and extremely... thoughtful. A lot of

athletes who first sign onto sports management agencies are fresh out of college and broke as hell. If they'd been involved in anything before, the temptation would be at its highest as contracts are negotiated and the money hadn't been deposited yet.

"So... Do you agree? We can go through the portfolio and schedule a tour so we can get you moved in as quickly as possible."

Yet again, I felt like some of this was going at warp speed while other areas moved in slow motion. But I saw no reason to turn down the opportunity being presented, so I agreed. Eboni seemed shocked by my lack of argument, but I genuinely didn't have one. There'd be other things to push back or fight tooth and nail for, but this wasn't it.

As if sensing the agreeable mood I was in, she launched into the next topic.

A photoshoot.

This time, I parted my lips to argue, but she kept going before I could get a word in. "Think of it as a pre-launch. It's been a few months since you signed with VP Sports but people's attention span is short and you haven't had any fights."

My flattened mouth and lifted brows conveyed my urge to say *at no fault of my own*, but Eboni kept going, unbothered by the attitude I'm sure was obvious all over my face.

"I can't make you do anything you don't want but I can strongly suggest things that I know will benefit you and your career." Eboni said with a nonchalant shrug. But I saw right through that bullshit. She had just as much riding on my success as I did. So, if it came down to it, she'd drag me kicking and screaming to that damn photoshoot if she felt it was necessary

Again, I didn't have a genuine argument so I nodded, hoping I wouldn't regret it later.

"Perfect." She chimed in. "Now, let's discuss the personal stylist idea you shot down last time."

*Fuck me.*

# 2

# HAKEEM

"Another one?"

I nodded at the hovering server, accepting the half-full glass of dark brown liquor. She'd worked our section all night, eagerly depositing drinks in my hand each time I drained the glass. I took another sip, pretending not to notice the concerned looks exchanged by the other people in the section. The people who knew me best. The ones sprinkled throughout the place Verse had rented to celebrate Gia's fortieth birthday.

I'd always tried to steer clear of any substances that could alter my state of mind or cause me to lose control. But since my... *breakup* with Eden, I'd been sipping more frequently.

I hated the person my mom became when she was under the influence. But for once, I understood. Inebriation was a great distraction. An escape from reality to a place where everything felt good and nothing really mattered.

A place where every unwanted emotion faded away to nothing.

But I knew I'd have to limit my intake soon. Especially if I didn't want to spiral.

I was the son of two addicts and knew it was a slippery slope that I didn't want to go too far down.

But with Eden, I'd learned how to *feel*. I'd learned how to care for someone beyond my platonic relationships. Without even trying, she'd taught me so many things about myself. Things that had opened my eyes to what I'd missed out on. Things I'd refused to entertain because I thought them unattainable.

And now that she was gone, I felt... lost. Simply going through the motions. A lonely boat floating in the middle of a rocky ocean, searching for its anchor. Craving the stability and calm she'd brought into my life.

"*Alright.*" Gia snapped on approach, hips swaying beneath a figure-hugging, gold dress that matched the theme of tonight. The color flattered her deep brown skin, turning heads as she passed.

She must've gotten her fill of teasing her ex-husband, Israel. Despite the temptation that she'd been swaying in his face for much of the night, the unflappable man merely smirked and shook his head, indulging her like always. I'd wished they'd put themselves and *us* out of our misery and just fuck already.

"Enough of this broken-hearted shit. I can't take anymore."

No matter how hard I'd tried, there'd been no hiding the effect of my separation from Eden. The knowledge of the secrets she'd willingly kept and our parting afterwards hurt. Like *hell*.

"What happened?" She questioned after dropping heavily in her seat, scooting over until less than a foot of space separated us in the booth. "Because if it's Eden's fault, I'll fuck her up for you."

For the first time tonight, I chuckled, tilting my head. "You know she's *professionally* trained, right?"

"And I'm from Uptown. I'll MMA her ass right to sleep." She fired back with a drunken giggle.

Both of us knew she wouldn't fare well in a physical fight against Eden. Especially if the version of her who showed up was the scrappy, uncaged one I'd witnessed at the underground fight.

But physically harming Eden wasn't the point Gia was trying to make. I could read between the lines and realized, in her own over-the-top way, she was just making it known that she was in my corner. That she'd go to bat for me and would even face certain defeat on my behalf.

Though I'd never put her in that position, I appreciated the sentiment. It felt good every time this special group reminded me they had my back through thick and thin.

"Seriously, Keem. What happened? You went from being up her ass nonstop to not even *mentioning* her or those boys."

I'd withheld the full truth because they knew, better than anyone, how deep my hatred for the 400s and anyone associated with them ran. At one point, the mere mention of the organization was enough to send me down a rage-fueled path.

And I hadn't wanted them to hate her because of their loyalty to me. I hadn't wanted to permanently change their opinion. Because, deep down, I still held out hope that we'd find our way back to one another.

If that happened, there'd be a lot of shit that needed to be discussed and resolved. But nonetheless, my want and... *need* of her hadn't eased one bit. Even with everything I'd learned.

"*Hey, y'all.*"

I was saved from answering when Birdie approached. For as long as I'd known her, she'd been a firecracker like her older sister and enjoyed being the center of attention.

So, the second she walked over, Gia and I both leaned forward, sensing her out-of-character mood. Birdie didn't have a shy bone in her body. Which was why the avoidance of direct eye contact and nervous wringing of her hands put us both on alert.

"What's wrong?" Gia asked before I could.

Birdie shrugged, eyes immediately falling to her lap after squeezing between us, just like she'd done as a kid. Her head rested on Gia's shoulder while her arm looped through mine.

Ever since she was a stubborn toddler who refused to take no for an answer, she'd stomped all over my boundaries, much like Gia had, until her need for physical touch and affection no longer bothered me.

"B." I muttered, nudging her with my elbow.

"Don't yell at me." She responded, making Gia chuckle. Though I hadn't raised my voice, she'd recognized the demand in my tone. "I'm *fine.*" She continued with another lazy shrug. "Just... a long day. This guy's been giving me a hard time."

Gia scooted to the edge of her seat, ignoring her sister's scowl when Birdie's head fell off her shoulder. "What kind of hard time?" she demanded.

Her gaze fell again and the lack of response made the urge to do *something* come on strong.

A problem, one that I didn't have a single detail of, had appeared and my first instinct was to fix it.

"I didn't come over here for that." She snapped, rolling her eyes before jabbing a finger in Gia's direction. "I came to tell you happy birthday." Then she turned on me. "And to check on you. To see if you're okay."

My even expression contorted into a scowl and I raked my fingers through my beard, conscious of the gray strands mixed throughout that seemed to appear overnight. "Why is everybody asking me that?"

There was no hiding the annoyance in my tone but like always, Gia was unbothered. "Because you won't tell us shit. But we'll come back to you." Her immaculate brows arched high as she returned the glare to her sister. "Now, what kind of hard time is this guy giving you?" Birdie parted her lips but Gia threw up a hand, stopping whatever she'd been about to say. "And don't play in my face. Because if you do, I'm bringing Verse into it."

Their brother's laid-back demeanor might fool many people but we knew how relentless he could be, just like I was, when looking out for those we loved.

I'd tried to tell him hundreds of times before that men like him *paid* people like me to handle their dirty work. But despite the celebrity status and wealth he'd accumulated over the last fifteen years, that man still held traces of the VP from Uptown in his DNA and wouldn't hesitate to get his hands dirty if he felt it necessary.

"It's not as big of a deal as you're making it." Birdie grumbled. "He just... doesn't respect boundaries. And he's... handsy."

"Fuck you mean, *handsy*?" I questioned, clenching my fist around the glass. I nearly missed her response because of the blood rushing in my ears.

"He just... hugs a lot and makes inappropriate comments. And he likes to say that I'd never be where I was if not for Verse being my brother." Her head dipped with shame as if she'd believed the bullshit he'd spewed. "But no one there even knew he was my brother until after I got the job. I *swear*."

"What's his *fuckin'* name?" Gia snapped, squinting her lids.

Birdie waved off the question. "I can handle it. Don't prove him right by sending Verse in to handle my problems. *Please*. I'm just going to keep my head down and do my job. He doesn't matter."

Gia's entire expression contorted, and her lips parted but before she could say a word, her gaze lifted to mine. I gave a subtle headshake in return and the anger immediately drained from her expression, replaced by a satisfied grin. That look alone meant she knew I would be stepping in, despite what Birdie had requested.

"Okay." She patted Birdie's leg placatingly. "I'll stay out of it."

After getting Gia's promise, she turned to me, expecting the same.

But I merely stared back, refusing to say a word. I wasn't going to lie nor was I was going to budge on my plan of making sure her work environment was free of... *whatever* the fuck was going on.

"Keem." She pleaded softly, trying to tug on my emotions. But I wasn't Verse or Gia. That wouldn't work on me.

So, I continued to hold her glare with a blank expression until she huffed. "I'm going to take your silence as a yes. Okay?"

I snorted, finally returning my gaze to my half-finished drink while Gia snickered. "We both know what that means." She teased, still chuckling as she stood, already swaying her hips to the beat. "Hakeem is going to do whatever the fuck he wants."

---

MY LIDS SPRANG OPEN.

I remained still, allowing the awareness of my surroundings to return.

The faint tap of my secretary's nails hitting her keyboard down the hall. The steady humming of the minifridge in the corner of the room. The low voices of guards and other employees traveling through the walls and floors beneath me.

I'd done it again. *Zoned out.* Ventured to the dark recesses of my mind. The side I felt creeping closer, teasing with its presence. Threatening chaos if I ever let it take over again. The blood that would flow like a river if I freed him.

*Reaper.*

The alter ego that I'd let rule my early twenties. The alter ego that had always been willing to do what others were too scared to, without thought or care of the consequences. Brief *appearances* from Reaper had occurred over the years, but I'd depended on the numb silence I lived in to keep it at bay. It had served as a suitable prison that allowed me to maintain control over my once volatile temper.

While with Eden, I'd experienced a much-needed respite from the turmoil. She'd been my place of peace. Which was why I still struggled with the fact that eight months had passed since the last time I'd spoken to her.

Two hundred and forty-two days, to be exact.

And despite our parting words, I couldn't stay away. Not *fully*. I'd picked up the habit of watching spots I knew the 400s frequented, hoping to catch glimpses of her. A few times, I'd spotted her leaving the warehouse where she was still foolishly fighting underground.

Each time she crossed the parking lot, her head remained on a swivel, searching the darkness. But her efforts were futile because I never made my presence known. Not like before.

Each time she walked out, I tried to harden my heart against whatever emotions that might flare up. And each time… I failed.

Especially on the nights where she looked especially defeated. Despite adding another win to her record, she appeared sad in a way that was hard to witness. Moving with dejection that made it obvious she still carried the weight of the world on her shoulders.

She had cracks in her shield, revealing the vulnerabilities beneath that she tried so hard to hide. The same vulnerabilities I'd damn near begged her to trust me with but hadn't been given the courtesy. And even with the distance between us now, I couldn't resist wanting to step in.

I *fixed* shit.

I kept the people I loved safe.

I found solutions to problems.

That was who I was at my core. A protector. A person who'd go to the ends of the earth for anyone who meant something to me. And despite the ink she'd stained her skin with years ago, despite the secrets she'd kept, I still had the urge to step in and right every wrong in her world.

The only problem was, how would I handle being around her if she insisted on keeping things the way they were? Watching her walk away was hard enough the first time. I wasn't sure if I was cut out to do it again. I wasn't sure if I could handle bridging the gap between us, even if only to help. I couldn't be around her on a platonic level. Not if I wanted to keep my sanity.

Quicker than I'd expected, she'd become my reason for everything. And that feeling hadn't abated in the slightest.

That's why these eight long months of silence was killing me slowly.

To help fill the time, I'd fully embraced my CEO role. A man who *hated* corporate life and office politics now spent most of his time in suits and seated behind a desk, desperate for anything to keep his mind and body occupied.

Then, long after the sun had set, I finally returned to the stillness of my home. The same home that now seemed desolate and depressing without the life and light that she, Jayce, and Isaiah had brought into it. But now that I'd gotten a taste of what it was like to have pleasant noise reverberating around my mind rather than the darkness and chaos of my past, I craved it more than my next breath.

"Need anything else from me, Mr. B?"

Grateful for the distraction, I rolled my shoulders, taking a moment before jumping back into work mode. Even after years of watching Verse bust his ass behind the desk at VP Entertainment, I still despised this.

Politicking, fake politeness, and pretending with clients would never feel fully comfortable.

People talked… a lot. And I… *didn't.*

Every meeting—whether with potential clients or staff—could be cut in half if people left out the filler conversation and got to the point. Exchanging pleasantries made me uncomfortable but conducting meetings with people who shrank at my scowl wasn't effective either, so I felt stuck.

But, like always, Krystal came through.

A friend of hers had been looking for work and I'd just so happened to be in desperate need of a secretary. I'd expected another woman who faded into the background, tolerating me until another, *better* job offer came through.

But Terrica had come in like a hurricane on day one, taking charge and giving me a sense of order that not even Krystal could. She was neither intimidated nor fearful. If anything, she found my disposition—which she called *grumpiness*—amusing.

I'd tried to keep her at arm's length, but the woman was bossy and nosy as hell. All day, in between being the most efficient secretary slash assistant, she somehow still found time to overshare details of her personal life while trying to dig into mine.

Despite my hatred for sitting behind a desk, with her help, embracing my CEO role was slowly becoming more natural. The kinks I'd experienced after being involuntarily retired as Verse and Garryn's bodyguard—to my fuckin' dismay—had seemed to work itself out.

"Nah." I finally answered.

When I looked up, my heart stuttered for a moment, taking in the bright yellow pants she wore. Even now, I couldn't see that addictive color without thinking about *her*.

Unconsciously, I swiped my thumb across the tiny sun on the inside of my right forearm. Weeks ago, after a night of overindulging, I found myself at a tattoo parlor, requesting a tiny addition to my ink.

The next morning, when I realized what I'd done, I didn't experience any of the regrets I thought I would. Instead, I went back and had them add shading to the rays of the sun, forcing that tiny image to stand out amongst the other ink.

"You like 'em?" Terrica asked in her cheerful tone, popping out a hip in what I guess was supposed to be a pose. "Yellow's my favorite color."

My eyes flicked up to hers, scanning her features, waiting for a spark of attraction. Terrica was a beautiful woman, no doubt—long, bone straight tresses she wore to her waist, chestnut brown skin, hazel eyes, full lips, and a curvy figure she knew how to accentuate with the right outfit.

But despite the appeal, I felt absolutely nothing.

Sometimes, I tried to convince myself that I was obsessed with the *idea* of Eden more than feeling anything for the woman herself. I'd told myself that all I needed to find was someone who could spark my interest and I'd be able to move on.

But so far, that hadn't happened. Women I once might've propositioned for casual sex, women who looked like Terrica, no longer appealed to me. Which made me wonder if I'd ever find someone who stirred my attraction the way Eden had.

"I've learned that silence is your way of displaying your grumpiness but even I'm a little weirded out by your face right now."

Still not releasing my scowl, I moved from behind my desk, not bothering to tidy the papers scattered across it because the wide-eyed woman watching from the doorway would only reshuffle them.

But I didn't complain. I'd never achieve Terrica's impressive knack for organizing so I let her have free rein over my office and files, surprisingly trusting her despite only hiring her three months ago.

"Taking a long lunch." I grunted, this time checking my watch, debating on walking the blocks to the studio where Birdie worked or hopping in my truck to drive.

"What's wrong?" she asked, crossing her arms over the billowy neckline of her white blouse.

"Going to check on a friend." I supplied reluctantly. She wouldn't let me leave until I gave her nosy ass something. "Debating between walking and driving."

One of her thin brows lifted. "Is this a peaceful checkup? Or a Mr. B is going to throw his weight around and scare people? Because if it's the second, then I need to know if I should start looking for another job?" Her tone was so matter of fact that if I hadn't gotten used to that amused glint in her gaze, I would've thought she was dead serious.

"I'm joking," she finally said with a giggle. "But seriously, it's ninety-something today, I'd suggest driving."

I gave her a small nod since she'd finally said something useful.

"Don't know how long I'll be gone." I said, which told her to hold down the fort until I returned.

She nodded at my unspoken command, shifting to allowing me to pass before following towards the elevator. "You have that two o'clock with Fitzgerald Benjamin Sharp."

I froze, finger hovering over the down arrow as I looked over my shoulder. "Who the *fuck* is Fitzgerald Benjamin Sharp?"

Her lips twitched and she bit back a smile. Thank God she didn't intimidate easily. Even when my temper or bad mood got the best of me, she beamed like she'd just won the lottery and carried on with her day. "The very important, prestigious, alcoholic, *hot mess* son of Senator *Theodore* Fitzgerald Sharp."

That sounded vaguely familiar but until recently, I hadn't interacted directly with clients. There were loads of people who worked on the floors below who managed that stuff.

Only extremely *difficult* clientele required to meet me before deciding to use our services. They wanted to throw their weight around but many quickly learned the hard and embarrassing way that I didn't give a damn about who they were. Nor was I easily intimidated.

"I don't—"

"Though I understand your reluctance to meet with him," she cut me off before I could tell her to cancel. "Think about HB Corp and the potential exposure. You're contracted with governors, mayors, and everything in between. But a senator? That's *big*. This could open even more doors for you." She was right. And I didn't want to admit that shit. Especially not to her. But my continued silence once again brought amusement to her face. "Though I'm only a measly assistant in the empire, I think you should listen to me."

"I'm always listening to you because all you do is *talk*."

She parted her lips to respond and I knew if I didn't make my escape, she'd keep going until the meeting started.

So, I stepped away from the elevator, moving at a brisk pace towards the stairs. "I'll be back by two." I called over my shoulder, not turning around to give her an opening to run her mouth even more.

"Alright." The amusement in her tone had my shoulders tightening with tension. "*Enjoy your lunch, Mr. B.*"

---

THERE WAS A LOT GOING ON.

People rushed all over while lights from high-quality camera equipment flashed constantly.

Women in power heels and men in sharp suits barked orders into phones, obviously the agents and assistants of the models being photographed. To my right, a refreshment area was set up, equipped with a fully stocked bar and a vast array of food that was going untouched.

And for the last half hour, I'd watched it all from my quiet corner of the large studio, trying to get a sense of the environment.

There were so many people moving in and out of the rooms that I honestly faded into the background, likely mistaken for one of the other bodyguards as they waited for their charges to finish.

But despite my awareness of everything going on, I was here for one reason. And so far, while I remained hidden, I hadn't liked what I'd seen. The Birdie I knew was nowhere to be found, hidden beneath a quiet, withdrawn version of herself. Photography wasn't her passion, but fashion was, so she worked with the wardrobe specialist on set, flitting from room to room, assisting in whatever they required of her.

Today, she wore shorts, an oversized tee and a ball cap pulled low. The jet-black wig she'd favored recently was pulled back in a stern ponytail, devoid of the heavy waves and curls she'd sported the last time I'd seen her.

Shoulders tight with tension, she looked almost scared as she approached the sharply dressed man standing near the middle of the lobby.

Out of all the big-mouthed people in the building, his voice was the loudest. He shouted and barked orders at everyone standing near him before zeroing in on Birdie a few feet away.

A small, calculated grin briefly touched his lips before he schooled his expression.

"*Presley*." His emphasis on her last name stood out, especially when he'd just used everyone else's first name.

Already, I was making my way along the perimeter of the massive room, slowly closing the distance. I grew irritated at the way her shoulders hunched around her ears. He said a few indistinguishable words that had her giving a reluctant nod. Seconds later, his hand settled uncomfortably low on her back and she flinched.

All pretenses of staying unseen fled and I was crossing the room at a quick pace, not bothering to excuse myself as I bumped into several people along the way.

Some uttered nasty words under their breath while others kept it moving after one glance at my face. And through it all, the man's focus remained solely on Birdie, unphased by the increasing discomfort he caused.

Once I was close, my hand shot out, gently removing her from his grip before tucking her against my side. Her initial reaction was a fearful gasp but when she realized it was me, her tight shoulders sagged with relief.

The man donned a polite smile, one that was obviously phony and pissed me off.

"I don't believe we've met," he said, sticking out his hand. "I'm Bernard Hampton, the creative director."

I kissed the top of B's head, never breaking eye contact. "Hakeem."

"And you are?"

"Brother." I said, gripping my palm in his. Before he could pull away, I squeezed, enjoying the painful twist of his expression. "And *protector*." I emphasized, watching coolly as his lips tightened. Donning my own fake smile, I leaned forward and whispered. "Was this the filthy hand you wrapped around her? Or the other one?"

"*Keem?*"

My bulk blocked Birdie's view of our hands and his pained expression. "Give us a minute, B."

"*Keem.*" This time, my name was a plea. One that begged me not to ruin this opportunity.

And I wouldn't.

I knew what this meant. Knew that she'd been busting her ass, working her way up the ranks without the power and influence of her last name backing her. I'd never jeopardize that. But this threat needed to be delivered because I wouldn't accept another day of her walking around like the shell of a woman she'd become.

"I got you. *Bernard Hampton* and I are going to have a chat. Just the two of us."

Despite the protest I could see all over her face, she walked away, flashing concerned looks over her shoulder the entire time.

Once she was out of sight, I returned my gaze to him, keeping the phony smile in place.

Adrenaline rushed through me at the opportunity for violence. The beast inside licked his chops, stretching languidly from his rested position, eager to come out of retirement.

I'd spent too many years being dormant.

"Which hand do you like the least?"

"You can't..." He jerked his neck back, eyes going wide. "What?"

"Which hand do you like the least?" When indignation settled on his features again, I tilted my head. "Be grateful I'm giving you the opportunity to choose which one I break. But my generosity is limited. Choose fast."

"Break?" His tone was shrill and nothing like the authoritative one he'd used minutes earlier. "I use my hands every day. *Both* of them."

"To be inappropriate with unwilling women. I know. I *saw*."

I squeezed the right one, preparing to crush it, smiling at the shift of delicate bones beneath my grip.

"I will sue the shit out of you."

This time, my sigh was filled with exasperation. He looked helplessly around the room at everyone who was too absorbed in their own world to even notice what was going on. "Look at me." I waited for his gaze to meet mine. "I don't fear lawsuits. I don't fear jail. I don't fear the police." I leaned forward. "I don't fear *death*. So, there's nothing you can threaten me with."

My grip tightened, crushing until the bones nearly gave way. "It took me less than a week to find out everything about you, Bernard. About your wife and her catering business. The private school your daughter goes to. Or the multiple times you've settled outside of court because of sexual harassment allegations. I know about your debts. I know about the shady deals you've made. I even know about your kinks that you live out at the sex club in Jonesboro."

His eyes bucked, pain temporarily forgotten.

Axel's grandfather hadn't called me the best for no reason. Despite my size, I was proficient at slipping in and out of places unseen. And there were a select few guys who worked at HB Corp that I'd brought on because of their similar skill set.

The man standing in front of me had been tailed nonstop for the last seventy-two hours and had no clue. I'd uncovered that much dirt in just three days. I could only imagine what I'd find out if I was willing to dedicate a month to the job.

"I'm a man capable of blowing up your entire world. A man who'll destroy you and everything you love without regret." He took a tiny step back but I followed, still refusing to release his hand. "If I find out that you've gotten out of line again with Brianna or any other woman... there's *nothing* that'll keep you safe from me. *Nothing*."

A pathetic nod had me considering breaking the hand but I knew I couldn't feed the beast too much. He'd get greedy, demanding more than I was willing to give. So, I stepped back before I lost control, scanning the room to make sure we hadn't drawn attention. And we hadn't. Everyone was still too distracted by the hundreds of other things going on.

The second I released him, Bernard made a quick escape, fleeing down a short hall that Birdie emerged from seconds later. Confusion contorted her features as she glanced at his retreating back before meeting my gaze across the room.

As I turned and headed towards the parking lot, her soft footfalls increased in speed behind me.

Once outside, the beaming sun heated my skin beneath the sleeves of my button up and I could already feel sweat forming near my temples.

"Everything okay?"

Before responding, I surveyed the parking lot for threats, coming up empty. Once satisfied, I dropped my gaze to her fake smile and tense shoulders. "Feel like I should ask you that."

She nodded, hugging herself before tilting her head. "How long is he going to stay alive?"

When her familiar sassy smile peeked through, I laughed. "As long as he keeps his perverted little hands to himself."

Her tongue swiped across her lips. "He'd gotten bolder lately. Threatening my position and I was scared to say anything. I didn't want to run to y'all to fix my problems again. I also knew if I reported him, my word versus his wouldn't hold much weight."

"Your words will always hold weight." I snarled. "Especially with us. Ain't no reason for you to be uncomfortable and harassed on your job. I could've handled shit way before it got this far."

When she slammed into me a second later, I nearly stumbled. Even after all these years, she still hugged me like her life depended on it. Like she'd done since we were kids. And just like then, I leaned down to kiss the top of her head.

"Thank you. For stepping in, even when I told you I didn't want it."

"That's what I do, B. What I'll *always* do."

# 3

# EDEN

"WHAT THE *HELL* have you done to yourself?"

I laughed despite the pain I was in, unbothered by Eboni's harsh tone.

My near loss at the warehouse three nights ago left me more bruised than I realized. Instead of normal wear and tear, I sported a nasty black eye and collage of bruises scattered across my arms and torso.

"Training."

"Um hmm." Eboni hummed skeptically. "You couldn't lay off the intense training until *after* the photoshoot?"

"You think they can make me pretty?" I teasingly asked instead, knowing the makeup artist's skills would be tested with the job of covering up the mess my opponent had made of me.

"We might be able to work with this." The unbelievably stunning woman standing behind Eboni said with a smile. She'd been introduced as the mastermind behind the entire shoot. "You're *beautiful.*" She praised, scanning my frame almost clinically. I shook off the discomfort from her compliment, too interested in what she had to say next. "But there's a bit of darkness to you. *Ruggedness* that we don't want to polish or cover up." Again, she paused, taking in the nails on my fingers and the hair that had been installed.

I'd been raking my fingers nonstop through the long, black tresses that framed my face in soft waves. For so long, I'd only worn braids or my natural hair that this felt awkward and... *foreign*. But I had to admit that it looked damn good, even with the busted face.

"You'll still get coverage to hide any minor blemishes." The creative director said with authority, watching me with that intense glare. "But I'm leaving the bruises. They'll give that grit I'm looking for."

Then she whirled, stalking towards the man fiddling with camera equipment a few feet away. Once she'd relayed her message, she sashayed back in my direction. That false confidence I'd displayed when walking in was fading fast.

This was my first big photoshoot where I'd grace the cover of Sports Unlimited magazine. A follow-up interview was scheduled two weeks from now once the photos went live.

"We're going to get you over to makeup." She said gently as if sensing my mounting panic. "Then we'll take a few practice shots just to get you comfortable in front of the camera. I have a very intentional vision in mind today so just bear with me. I promise to try to make this as painless as possible." Her teasing smile eased my nerves just a bit. "So... you with me?"

I flicked my gaze around, finding nearly every eye in the room focused on me, waiting for my response. "Yeah, I'm with you."

As she walked away, a giggle emerged from the corner where Joy and Jayce played.

I know I should've dropped him with my mom but the time he and I had together was already limited. Hell, he'd even been at training yesterday, playing in a corner so I could keep an eye on him.

Another giggle brought a big smile to my face that quickly faded when a flash went off.

Eboni and I both flicked our gazes to the photographer who was slowly lowering his camera. "Just a test shot." He said before flashing a wry grin. "But that was the first genuine smile I've seen since you walked in. If I need to, I can set him up right behind the camera if it keeps that grin on your face."

"Stop flirting with my client." Eboni said when all I could do was blush, making him laugh before he held up his hands innocently and returned his attention to the equipment.

Shit. I hadn't even *realized* he was flirting. Was I that out of practice?

"I wanted to go over a few things before you get set up." Eboni moved on, business-minded like always. "First, here are your keys."

I hadn't even visited the place I'd be moving into soon.

Instead, I'd picked from the selection of photos shown by the real estate agent. They'd given the option to schedule a walk-through, but I'd been too nervous, too afraid to become attached to something that might fall through before it became mine. But the lease had been signed and the keys were in hand. Yet, I still found myself struggling to wrap my head around it.

"Joy scheduled a moving company to come by Friday. Since you're free most of that day, you'll be there to tell them what needs to go where." Her eyes were scanning the phone in her hand, completely oblivious to the panic attack I felt on the verge of. "Also, the charity event. I don't have you scheduled to participate in the tournament but you'll make appearances throughout the weekend and attend the gala that Saturday night."

Her head tilted, as if she was considering something before flashing her sharp gaze back up to mine.

"Do you want a date?"

I snapped out of my stupor, contorting my features in a frown. "Excuse me?"

"A *date*." She repeated simply. "For the gala. If you would prefer not to attend alone, we could arrange for someone to escort you." I don't know what she saw in my expression but whatever it was made her burst into laughter. "It's more common than you think."

The thought of a stranger going with me to my first VP Sports event caused my stomach to turn. I had a hard time trusting people and knew that I'd spend most of it gauging my fake date's motives and sincerity rather than enjoying myself.

"I'll pass."

That knowing smirk she loved to flash appeared before she nodded. "Let me know if you change your mind."

"I won't."

"How do you feel about your fight? You think you're ready?"

The subject change caught me off guard before I shrugged. "Of course." As if the conversation between Barry and I had been heard, Eboni had let me know about an upcoming tournament. Though it had been nearly a year since I stepped in a ring professionally, the fight itself wasn't what worried me. That was honestly the only thing I truly felt like I could conquer no matter the circumstances.

It was all this other shit that kept me on edge.

Now Eboni's gaze was fully on me, trying to see past the high walls I'd built. But despite how damn good she was at reading people, this was not something she'd accomplish with me. "I'm good, really." Then I flashed my phony smile and gave the go-to excuse that always seemed to work. "Just trying to take it all in. My whole *life's* changing. It's a lot for anyone to handle. But I got it."

Eboni wasn't easily fooled. That shrewdness she was known for was on full display as she squinted. "You know my job is also to be here for you. Right? I'm the one you're supposed to come to if something is up. If something's wrong, my job is to fix it or find someone who can." Her words closely aligned with those spoken by a certain man many months ago.

A man who'd told me that he was the nigga who *made shit happen*. And during times like these, I wished for his level of confidence.

Despite the darkness of his past, Keem fully embraced who he was... good and bad. He might not be the most eloquent person but he didn't hide who he was. You either accepted him or you didn't, neither of which affected his behavior in the slightest.

On the other hand, I'd built my entire existence on the approval of others. Damn near everything I'd done was to receive praise or favor from those I wanted to love me in return. Even the career I dedicated so much time to had started out as a way to bond with my brother. It was only after he'd switched his attention to another sport that I decided to stick it out rather than joining the basketball team like him.

"You sure you're good?" At Eboni's concern, I automatically pasted on a smile that both of us knew was fake.

"*Eden*!" My name being called by the makeup artist captured our attention, saving me from a response. "*We're ready for you*."

I attempted to walk away but stopped short when she gripped my forearm. "Eden, I can't help you if you don't talk to me."

*Jesus*. I'd heard those words before too. From Mo. Hakeem. Hell, his best friend had made a similar plea only a few days ago.

So many people claimed they wanted to help me and make things better. But I'd been burned before. Time and time again, I'd put my trust in the wrong people and paid the price for it.

Now I was skittish. Wary and mistrustful of damn near everyone, just like that horse Hakeem favored at the Sanctuary.

There were only so many times a person would take a punch to the face before they started lifting their arms in defense. Only so many times a person could be torn down before they locked themselves away and hid the key so no one else had the power to do it again.

I was that person. And I was terrified that my need to keep my secrets and protect myself would have me looking back thirty or forty years from now at a long, lonely existence of my own making.

---

"YOU KNOW THEM?"

I kept my gaze on my phone, frowning at yet another unanswered text that I'd sent to Isaiah before following the direction of Joy's gaze.

Across the parking garage, Crow and Rome waited next to my car, watching with familiar taunting grins that I was quickly tiring of.

"Yeah." I said with a fake smile. "Friends of my brother." I couldn't even bring myself to lie and say they were friends of *mine*. Not when I knew whatever had brought them here had the potential to ruin my day.

Her curious gaze switched between them and me, hesitating to turn onto the next aisle towards her own ride. "You, uh... you need me to stay with you?"

This time, my smile was genuine. She was so sweet and caring. Obviously the two men raised her red flags but she still wanted to stick around so I wouldn't be alone.

Unfortunately, Rome and Crow cared less if witnesses were around. And the last thing I needed was someone at VPS catching wind of what I was doing in my spare time. If the higher-ups learned that I was breaking my contract every other week, my career would be over before it started.

"I'm good." I supplied, hoping she didn't see past my smile to the truth. "I asked them to meet me here, so I didn't have to drive all the way to their place. I'll see you later, okay?"

Not giving her time to respond, I squared my shoulders and strode quickly towards the two men, grateful when her footsteps grew faint in the opposite direction.

When I was a few feet away, Rome licked his lips, stroking his gaze slowly over my skinny jeans, peach V-neck top, white blazer, and matching heels.

An outfit I never would've chosen for myself, especially on a casual day filled with meetings. But Naima, my new *stylist*, advised that the last thing I wanted was paparazzi or fans catching me off guard or in compromising situations. She'd gone on to add that if my name was going to be linked to hers, I wouldn't be caught dead in my normal casualwear.

The fact that anyone even *cared* enough to snap a photo of me still didn't make sense. To the outside world, I was Eden Foster, the first female athlete to sign with the prestigious and ever-expanding VP Sports Management. The public wanted access to my world and I had no idea why they found me so interesting. I still felt like a regular person from White Grove trying to live out my dream.

Eboni's inbox was flooded with interview requests along with invites to events that I once dreamed of attending. People who I'd never met wanted my name linked to theirs even though I hadn't done a damn thing since the ink dried on my contract.

This world where the right connections could make or break you was proving to be more challenging than competing in the octagon.

"You look good, baby." Rome's gleaming grill flashed as he raked his top row of teeth over his bottom lip. "*Different.*"

"Why are you here?"

Crow narrowed his lids while Rome laughed under his breath. "You're late on your payment."

"My payment?" I frowned before smoothing away the irritation on my face and flashing a warm smile at Joy as she waved and drove past. "The fuck are you talking about? I fought last week and won. Barry is keeping almost *all* my winnings... I'm not late on *shit.*"

Crow pushed away from the car. "Watch your mouth."

I didn't even glance his way. "Tell your lapdog to shut the fuck up while adults are talking."

Immediately, Rome's hand shot out, catching Crow before he could step towards me. "She's good, man. *Chill.*"

Crow sucked his teeth, keeping that beady-eyed glare on me but I paid him no mind. Still thrown off by the so-called *payment* I was late on.

"You're supposed to fight every two weeks. But you've been training with them." He hiked his chin towards the VP Sports building, face contorting as if smelling something foul. "So, you've been inconsistent which means you owe us a payment to make up for that lost income."

"That wasn't the agreement."

"The agreement is whatever we say it is."

The smug smile he sported had me taking a step closer, getting right in his face. "You and your little bitch over there can tell Barry I'll fight next week as planned. And he'll deduct his portion from my earnings after I win, as *planned*. But I'm not paying him or you *shit*."

That smile I once loved grew before deep laughter rumbled out. "You know I love when you talk your shit... but is that really the game you wanna play with us? Because I'm sure Madi and I can find somebody else to keep Jayce this weekend."

That threat was getting old. And *tired*. I was sick of him and everyone else thinking I'd always bow to their demands. "Rome, I'm in the Pit more than I'm working on my actual career. You're pocketing more of my earnings than I do. *And* you'll be getting a portion of my pay when I start professional fights. What else do you want from me?" My voice elevated, becoming desperate as I asked. "What *else* do I have that you can take?"

"*Everything okay over here?*"

The three of us tensed and whirled at the same time, spotting Verse in the backseat of a blacked-out SUV quietly pulling up beside us.

His expression was earnest as he opened the door and stepped out, but there was an underlying steel to his tone that had both men straightening, immediately becoming alert. I didn't know a lot about Verse outside of him being rich, hopelessly in love with Garryn, and Hakeem's best friend. But I'd heard rumors, seen the articles about him having a less than squeaky past.

And Hakeem was tight-lipped so all I'd been able to do was speculate. But he'd always given me a sense of danger that was more subtle than Hakeem's.

His two security guards stepped out right behind him, completely silent and still, hands resting on the guns attached to their hips.

*Shit.*

I did *not* want Verse or his employees getting involved. The last thing I needed was to give Keem more ammo if something happened to Verse because of my past.

"We good." Rome spoke, dropping his smile. Now, his face scrunched with irritation, aimed at Verse who looked completely unbothered.

The man in question met his glare head on then smiled before turning to me. "C'mon, Eden. I'll give you a ride. I need to talk to you about something, anyway."

I stiffened under his intense stare but kept my smile in place. "Oh, you don't have to do that, I drove." I thumbed towards the two men blocking the path to my car. "And I can come by your office later or tomorrow if you want to..."

My words trailed when his smile dropped. Rome had taken a step towards me and Verse did the same, which meant so did his security.

And I was caught in the middle. A terrible place to be if this went south.

The annoying heels on my feet and the too little purse I carried meant the only weapon I had was a stupid can of pepper spray attached to my key ring. My gun was in the glove compartment of my car since no weapons were allowed on VS Entertainment's property.

And if anybody tried to sneak past with one, like I'd done on my first visit, there were metal detectors and armed security at each entrance to ensure that didn't happen.

"You want to finish your conversation with these gentlemen? Go right ahead." Verse instructed as if I'd asked permission. Then his hand slipped smoothly in the pocket of his white VS Maxx joggers. "But when you finish, I'll be waiting right here because you're riding with me." I parted my lips to remind him again that I'd driven but he cut me off. "Your car will be delivered to your home within the hour."

Finally, he returned that intense glare to Rome who practically trembled with anger. He didn't like being one-upped but knew in this situation, Verse had the advantage.

"So..." Verse continued conversationally. "Are we leaving now? Or you want to handle... *whatever* this is first?"

I'd probably pay for it later, but I moved towards his truck, ignoring Rome and Crow's glare.

Reaching the door that was already open, I stepped back and waited for him to get in first. He merely lifted a brow until I got the hint and climbed in.

Once the door closed, the truck peeled off then it was just us in an uncomfortable silence that I honestly hoped lasted until I got home. I did *not* want to explain what he'd just witnessed. But luck was not on my side when he turned in his seat just enough to fix those dark, intense eyes on me.

"You want to fill me in on what that was about?"

---

"UMM..." I stammered, unsure what to tell him.

There were *so* many things that I wanted to avoid happening—like losing my contract or having my double-life exposed. Nothing good would come of involving Verse in the mess of my life so I played it off like I'd perfected for years.

"They're friends of my brother. Checking on me since he's in jail. They do that sometimes."

The silence that followed would've had me squirming if I hadn't learned how to keep my composure under pressure. The man sitting on the opposite end of the backseat watched me through thin slits, teasing his bottom lip with his top row of teeth, causing the deep dimple in his cheek to crease.

Verse Presley was too much. Too self-assured. Too handsome. Too *intimidating*.

"Eden..." He began then paused as if weighing his words. "I'm not a man fond of wasting time. Nor do I appreciate when people play with my intelligence." He hefted his chin in my direction. "Your roots might've originated in White Grove, but mine started in Uptown. And those roots are *deep*. Deep enough to recognize when two niggas from the 400s are standing in front of me. So, let's try that again... what the fuck is going on?" I tensed but said nothing and he chuckled. "I have a vested interest in you and your success as the newest athlete to sign with VP Sports. If there's anything that might hinder that, I need to be made aware. *Immediately*."

"Is that what this is all about?" I turned enough to prop my knee on the seat, abandoning the proper posture I'd learned during one of the many etiquette classes I'd been forced to attend. "Just trying to protect your investment?"

He waved his hand in a so-so motion. "Yes and no. I'm a businessman and it would be stupid to ignore red flags that might affect said business. Especially if they're right in front of my face." He leaned closer and I stiffened. "But more than anything... you've got my boy's heart. Whether the two of you get back to what you once were is up to y'all but I made a promise to him in St. Leesburg. That I'd protect you and your nephews like you're one of us. And I can't do that if you're hiding shit. I can't *help* you if you don't tell me what's going on."

I crossed my arms protectively over my chest, abandoning his gaze to look out the window. I didn't trust my words. If I started talking, all the shit I'd buried would unearth itself. Rushing out with the force of a geyser after being repressed for so long.

The debts, the fights, the 400s and my past. The shit with my family. This confusing space I was in with Hakeem.

It would all come spilling free and I couldn't risk him using it against me. I couldn't risk him using my moment of weakness as the evidence that would snatch my dream out of reach before it fully began.

Not when so much had been sacrificed to get here.

So, I kept quiet, watching the passing scenery of downtown Sienna Falls, thankful he didn't push for more.

What felt like minutes later, we were pulling up to my building and a large hand bumped my arm as one of his drivers waited for traffic to clear.

When my gaze jerked upwards, he wore one of his infamous charming smiles as he slipped a sleek, black business card into my hand.

"If you need anything... if Jayce or Isaiah need anything, don't hesitate to reach out. No matter the time of day, I'll be there. And if I physically can't, I'll find someone who can."

I flicked the card over, reading the information printed in gold font before snorting. "Not sure Garryn would be okay with me *reaching out at any time*."

He laughed, flashing those deep dimples again. "My baby knows she has nothing to worry about. So, if she sees your name, or any other woman's name on my phone, there won't be an issue."

"Are you going to tell Hakeem?" I blurted before I could stop myself. "About what you saw today?"

"I think a better question is, are you? Because you should. Let him in on what's going on. Maybe he can help. *We* can help."

I snorted again. "That man does not want to see or hear from me, trust me."

That secretive smile widened a bit as he shrugged. "I'm not too sure about that."

The awkward silence that followed would've been the perfect opportunity for me to make my escape. But I hesitated, flipping the card between my fingers as I built up the courage to ask, "How is he?"

Satisfaction took over Verse's expression, as if he'd been waiting for that question. Thankfully, he didn't call me out on the way my voice had softened considerably. Instead, he just shrugged. "Hakeem is... *Hakeem*."

Even without more explanation, I knew exactly what he meant.

Hakeem was stoic and closed off in most situations, so I could only imagine his controlled expression that rarely revealed anything, shutting everyone out.

I just hoped he was faring better than I was since our separation. Because despite how it might seem on the outside, I was gutted and barely holding it together. Spending way more nights crying myself to sleep than I'd ever admit aloud.

"He's not saying much." He turned to face me across the backseat. "What happened between you two?"

I tensed because I'd thought for sure that Hakeem would have let them in on what happened. Then again, the man was as skilled at secret keeping as I was, so I wasn't surprised to find out that even those closest to him had been left in the dark. "What happened between us... *happened.* It was good while it lasted. And I want to leave it at that."

I pleaded with my eyes for him not to ask more and when he seemed to concede, I finally reached for the door handle.

"Eden." I froze at Verse's tone before facing him. "Promise me that you'll stop suffering alone."

I flinched before I could stop myself. "Wh-*what?*"

"Garryn was the same way. So damn independent because she didn't think she had anyone in her corner. She thought she had to fight everything alone. She was too prideful to accept help from anyone. And it took time to overcome that." He chuckled almost reflectively as he shook his head. "*A lot of time.* But now she knows that she has people in her corner. People who'll fight for her and with her. Just like you do. You just gotta let 'em in."

"Even Gia?" I asked teasingly, hoping he didn't spot the water threatening to flood my lower lids.

God, I could only imagine what that felt like. Having not just one person, but an entire *group* who'd ride for you at a moment's notice.

A *family* who genuinely cared about your wellbeing rather than focusing on what you could for them. Or how you benefited them.

Outside of making it to the PFC and being what Jayce and Isaiah needed, that was what I'd wanted more than anything. What I'd *craved* for so long before writing it off as a pipedream. That might be how things worked in the Uptown crew, but my reality was a solo one.

And that's how it would have to remain.

Again, he watched me silently, zeroing in on the dampness in my gaze that I'd failed to blink away. His conflicted thoughts flashed across his face before he seemingly decided to have mercy on me.

A slight chuckle flashed that tempting dimple again that

would've made my knees go weak if I wasn't already partial towards his best friend. "Gia has a lot of mouth and can come across as hard but it's out of love and loyalty. And I promise if the situation arose, she'd be in your corner too. She took you and those boys in as hers in St. Leesburg and that's not something she does lightly."

I held his gaze then flashed a shaky smile, pretending not to see the disappointment flashing across his face. "Thanks for the ride."

This time, he simply nodded and slid from the car, walking around it to open my door. "Your car will be here within the hour."

Then he flicked his gaze around the complex that I'm sure was a far cry from the luxury he was used to before turning his gaze to mine with a nod.

"Take care, Eden."

# 4

# HAKEEM

"Mr. Biggers, I look forward to utilizing your... *services.*"

There was no mistaking the suggestiveness in Darla's tone. The middle-aged beauty was a socialite whose power and influence were as well known throughout the tri-city as her timeless beauty and affinity for younger men.

Though I didn't consider myself *young* since I was knocking on the door of forty, Darla was fifty-nine, two whole decades older than my thirty-nine. But the tight body, youthful features, and sharp fashion that flattered her curves made her seem much younger.

Our meeting had lasted half an hour, ten minutes longer than I normally preferred. But she'd kept flirting, unable to take a hint that I wasn't interested.

She was beautiful. Hell, she was *gorgeous*. But despite her physical appeal, Darla was about three inches too tall and three shades too light.

There was no stud in her right nostril, and her bottom lip wasn't quite heavy enough. It didn't curve in that tantalizing way that I'd grown obsessed with.

Her exposed arms were slender but not toned and muscled. Her honey skin was also free of ink, more specifically a certain tattooed sleeve that covered one particular woman from wrist to shoulder.

Darla Winfrow wasn't *her*. And she never would be, no matter how much sexual appeal she possessed, or how seductive her tone was. I'd already had a once in a lifetime thing and no one else could ever compare. Or even *pique* my interest because every part of me still belonged to Eden Foster.

So, despite the cute pout in her bottom lip or the *come-fuck-me* eyes she'd given our entire meeting, I turned down the woman without an ounce of regret.

"*HB Corp* looks forward to working with you." I said shortly before standing from my seat and gesturing towards the door.

She looked stunned that I hadn't taken the bait, but quickly schooled her expression, flashing that lascivious grin. Her hips swayed as she gathered her purse and moved towards the door. Again, she sized me up, gauging if it was worth shooting her shot again. But before she could, I nodded towards Terrica who stood in the doorway, waiting to escort the woman to the elevator.

"Terrica will provide you and your team with the information needed to set up services."

Her gaze finally left me, flicking to my secretary. Free from the pressure of her stare, I rolled my shoulders in discomfort at the tailored jacket draping my torso. Despite my current discomfort, I pasted on a smile that I was positive looked more like a grimace and closed the door behind them before Darla could proposition me again.

Once alone, I paced like a caged animal, fighting back everything I'd buried in my mind that told me I didn't *belong*. That I was undeserving of the blessings that had come my way despite all the things I'd done.

It had been surfacing more often, especially after things ended between me and Eden.

I'd been angry by what I'd learned about her past but more than that, I'd been disappointed in myself for how I'd reacted. As a person who had been judged by his past more than most, I should've given her the benefit of the doubt. I should've given her another chance to explain, no matter how many opportunities she'd had before then.

It wasn't like I'd been completely forthcoming about everything I'd done, especially while working for Axel and his grandfather. Hell, not even Verse and Gia knew *everything*.

I could've expressed my anger without going to the extremes. It was no wonder she'd wanted nothing to do with me when I tried to take her home after that last interaction in the parking lot. I'd threatened and treated her exactly how she hated... dismissively. I'd done to her what everybody else who'd let her down had and that bothered me more than anything else.

She hadn't deserved that but I was still too big of a coward to approach her.

Shit, even if I built up the nerve after all this time, what the fuck would I say? I wasn't known for my wit or charm so all I had was *me*.

The silent, grumpy asshole who sometimes struggled to form a sentence when under pressure. She'd seemed satisfied with my less than stellar qualities before. But now, with all the shit between us, I wasn't sure if that'd be enough. If I *was* enough.

Growing up, I'd developed what I considered... *flaws* in my personality.

According to the therapist Verse and Gia forced me to see, because of the dysfunction of my childhood. I rarely formed attachments with things or people. Because I'd been deprived of so much for so long, whether mental, physical, or emotional, I trained myself not to need or want anything or anyone.

So, when the time came that I found things and people I wanted to keep around, my protection and sheltering of those things went... overboard. And just because space and time had passed between me and Eden, that incessant need for her hadn't abated.

If anything, she ran across my mind now more than ever. I'd taken advantage of having her around and now that she wasn't, I struggled to find a new normal after my previous one adjusted so quickly for her in the first place.

That was part of the reason Gia gave her such a hard time early on. Not because of anything she'd actually *done*. But because, deep down, underneath all the hard layers, was the Hakeem Gia had first met. The little boy who couldn't manage his emotions. The teen who engaged in fights and allowed himself to be hurt just to *feel*. The young man who could only find peace when doling out violence.

Gia knew every day was like walking a tightrope. One wrong move, one tiny misstep could send me hurtling back down in the darkness I'd barely escaped from.

But Eden had soothed that chaotic part of me. She'd quieted the chaos in my mind, filling it with all the sweet parts of her that she kept hidden from the world.

And now that I don't have that anymore... didn't have *her* anymore, I feared the next time I battled the demons of my past... I'd succumb to the power they still held over me.

---

"EASY, GIRL."

In a tone that was low and soothing, I murmured words of comfort to the skittish, injured horse on the opposite side of the fence.

After a storm three nights ago, the stubborn animal I'd bonded with, Midnight, had escaped her enclosure after a tree had fallen on a section of it.

It hadn't taken Pike and the other caretakers long to find her but during her escape, she'd managed to inflict a deep cut on her left flank.

The vet had been on standby with the tranquilizer, anticipating her wild and volatile reaction to anyone getting too close. While she'd been under, they repaired the fence and mended her leg. But now that she was back in her own pasture, she pouted like a teenager and tossed her head around when anyone tried to check on her condition. The vet had given me instructions on how to care for the wound since no one else dared to enter her area.

Now, after a back-and-forth dance that lasted an hour, I was inside the corral and changing the dressing on the wound while inspecting the stitches, pleased that no sign of infection was visible.

I'd been grateful for the opportunity to do something *different.*

Life without the variety of following Verse and Garryn around was boring as shit.

On the days when my schedule was packed with meetings or training with the guards, it was tolerable. But days like today, where there'd been nothing to do, it settled in how... *lonely* my existence was.

Pent up adrenaline that had nowhere to go left me feeling jittery and unsettled. It was as if time slowed, creeping by at a snail's pace just to spite me.

Sometimes, I considered making a trip to A&K Sports Complex to burn it off. Then again, that wouldn't be too smart. I'd run the risk of running into *her* and with the mood I was in lately, that might lead to doing something stupid. Like hemming her up against the closest wall and taking my frustrations out in the most pleasurable way possible.

Between her thick, toned thighs.

The familiar sound of one of the carts The Sanctuary used to travel around the property had both me and the majestic animal turning towards the source. When she stomped her feet and brayed loudly, I stepped back, having only a second to glance at the dressing around her wound before she took off. Her velvety coat and jet-black hair seemed to shine under the rays of the sun as her powerful muscles bunched each time her hooves hit the ground.

She didn't seem to be too hindered by the injury.

It wasn't until she disappeared behind her favorite patch of trees that I hopped over the fence, meeting the familiar face that I hadn't seen in almost two weeks since Gia's birthday.

*"I've been told I need to come check on you."*

My face contorted as I eyed Verse unfolding his frame from the vehicle. He wore one of his customary two-piece tracksuits with his hands shoved deep in the pockets.

Once I made eye contact, the smile that built on his face was slow and teasing... light in a way that I envied. He'd found his other half. Found the woman who completed him.

Found the person who made him look forward to going home every night. And it showed in every aspect of his being.

There was no mistaking how in love Verse was because the peace and contentment that came along with it was evident in everything he did. There was a distinct gleam in his eye that heightened whenever he spoke about his fiancée. It was even worse when she was around.

"Did you come to be on some gossipy shit?"

Verse snorted, keeping his steps measured until he stood right next to me. "If it snaps you out of the funk you've been in, then hell yeah. We can spill all the tea."

I lifted a brow. "Spill the tea?"

He shrugged without care. "Every time I'm in the room with those damn G's, I feel my balls shrink a little bit." *Gia and Garryn.* Ignoring my surprised snort, he kept going. "Nigga, Gia asked me how her shoes looked with her outfit. First of all, why did she think I was the person to ask that shit?" His face contorted and I bit back a laugh. "And why the fuck did I tell her *it's giving bad bitch*? What does that even mean?"

The laugh I'd been holding back exploded from my chest.

"*A'ight*. You giggling a little *too* hard." Verse chided as he rested a shoulder against one of the fence posts. "You ready to talk about this funk you've been in?" All remaining traces of my humor faded as I cut my gaze in his direction but he merely shrugged. "I'm smart enough to realize that it's because of a certain MMA fighter I had the pleasure of seeing yesterday." I tensed in anticipation. Desperate for the tiniest bit of insight into her world rather than the pieces I'd observed from afar since our breakup.

When he didn't say more, I sucked my teeth. "Fuck you, Verse. How was she?"

That asshole side of him flashed a brief smile, knowing he had me right where he wanted. Desperate for information. "She looked... tired. Overwhelmed. Uncomfortable." Then he gave a little chuckle as if remembering something. "But still tough as shit. She held my stare like she was daring me to say something. Like she was challenging me to scold or condemn her. Probably about something I don't know *shit* about." He paused, tilting his head. "She asked about you."

My heart did a flip-flop. *What the fuck was that*? "What did you tell her?"

"That you were being a mean, miserable son of a bitch and she needed to come see you ASAP because we couldn't take much more of it."

My glare intensified as I stiffened. "You said *what*?"

His laughter was both a relief and annoying. "Nah... I just said you were being you and not telling us anything." He paused a beat, weighing his words. "Obviously, you miss her. And from what I saw, she's lost without you too. When you find a connection like that, you don't just let it walk away without good reason. So, what happened?"

I'd held on to this shit for eight months. Been *miserable* for eight months without telling a single soul about what had bothered me.

Maybe it was time to unload it.

Maybe Verse could help me make sense of it all.

Maybe he'd agree with my actions after finding out or maybe he'd condemn me for walking away prematurely. For not fighting harder for her when she'd said we had an expiration date.

Whatever his reaction may be, I was ready to get this shit out of my head and off my chest.

I wasn't a man of many words so I got right to the point. "She's 400."

The shift in Verse was immediate. Gone was the slow-talking, teasing version, replaced by *VP* whose lids narrowed and nostrils flared. "She's *what?*"

"400." I repeated. "Deep in that shit, too. Used to enforce for Barry, even fucked with his nephew for a while."

Verse stared silently but instead of the shock I expected, understanding evened out his features. "Hmm."

Finding out that Eden, *my* Eden, had been an enforcer for the organization I'd vowed to always hate had caught me off guard. Which was why I hadn't expected this reaction from him. The one person who understood more than most how fucked up and conflicted this whole thing would make me feel.

"What?" He looked away after my question, which only raised my suspicion. "*What is it,* Verse?"

A long sigh broke free before he groaned. "I'm really turning into a gossipy ass nigga." Any other time, I might've laughed but we were talking about Eden and I was feeling anything but humorous. "When I was leaving, she was in the parking lot with two of them. A big dude with a grill and a thinner man. Weird ass face."

"Long nose and big eyes?" He nodded his confirmation. "Rome, her ex. Barry's nephew. The other is Crow, his right-hand."

Now, the shock I was expecting moments earlier appeared. "How the hell did you end up falling for somebody in the 400s? And how did she even get involved in that shit?"

I shrugged. "She's *been* one. But somehow, they let her leave a few years back. But they've sucked her back in. Got some shit on her. Big enough for her to make questionable decisions and risk her career."

"Like what?" he asked, leaning forward.

"I still don't know *everything* but she's still fighting underground. *A lot.*"

"*Shit.*" He ran his thumb back and forth across his bottom lip. "How involved are you?"

I couldn't help the snort that burst free. He knew me. Knew that I'd insert myself right in the middle of chaos if I felt the need.

Consequences and danger be damned.

"Right now?" I paused to shrug. "Not at all. We didn't end on the best of terms."

And before he could ask for more details, I told him. About Axel sending me to her underground fight. About how I'd snuck into her place undetected, waiting with an unloaded gun.

About the threats I'd made and her devastation after. Then I told him about approaching her not even a week later and her shutting me down. Through it all, he remained silent, watching with a mounting intensity that caused the hairs on my arms to stand.

Once I finished and he still hadn't said a word, I felt like a kid again... waiting on my brothers to give their opinion on a questionable choice I'd made.

I'd had the utmost respect for them. And their approval was all I'd needed to keep me going for years until running into Verse and Gia. And at this moment, I wanted his honest opinion on something I wasn't too proud of.

"What do you want?"

I hadn't expected that question. "What?"

"What do you want? To do with her? To do with this whole situation?"

"To make it right." I said as if the answer was obvious. "To fix all of it so she can actually enjoy the career she's fought hard to get." My words trailed, debating on releasing the thought I'd been trying to keep buried deep. Then, after a moment of consideration, I decided to be honest. "I want to bury every one of them niggas for the old and new." I leaned forward. "And that's exactly what I'll do if it comes to that."

"You remember last time, right?"

His question threatened to bring up memories but I pushed them back, refusing to give them the power they once held over me.

"I'm not going to try to talk you out of doing anything. Because I know you and how you get once your mind is made up." I nodded but he kept going, leaning forward and matching my glare head on. "But be *careful.* And come to me if you need me." I was already shaking my head before he finished. "*Fuck.* You and that woman of yours belong together, I swear. Stubborn and prideful as hell." He grumbled. "Garryn ain't got shit on y'all." I snorted. "Stop always thinking you're out on an island by yourself. You're *not*, alright?" His hand settled on my shoulder, squeezing it lightly. "Come to me if you need me, a'ight?"

Then, because I knew he'd never let it go, I agreed. "Yeah. *A'ight.*"

# 5

# EDEN

Lights from passing buildings illuminated the dark interior of the SUV, giving brief flashes of the flawless features of the two women accompanying me.

Joy practically bubbled with excitement, which would've spiked my anxiety if not for Eboni's unflappable confidence and calmness to balance it out. We were mere minutes from arriving at the long-awaited VP Sports charity gala.

I felt like a kid on my first day of school, stomach knotting with nerves and eyes bouncing all around, trying to take in all the sights before I entered a new adventure. Everything leading up to tonight had been stressful but worth it.

This was my first big outing as a VP sports athlete and the pressure seemed to mount the closer we got to today.

Last week, I met with my image consultant to go through the options for tonight's wardrobe. I'd wanted to take a backseat role since no one had ever accused me of having a strong fashion sense. But when she'd pulled out the mid-thigh length dress in my favorite color, I'd been unable to resist leaning forward.

Spotting my interest, she'd immediately ushered me into the back to try it on, shrieking with excitement once I'd emerged. Compared to some of the other options, it was simple. A strapless, sweetheart neckline that clung to my curves and had simple embellishments that highlighted my hourglass shape. If I'd thought the dress looked good on me before, it took my entire look to another level once the makeup team finished and the inches of jet-black extensions were styled into cute waves. For once, I felt like those jaw-dropping women on social media that others raved about.

I'd always felt like I was *attractive* but not a breathtaking beauty. Not like Gia, Garryn, Mo, or even Madi. They possessed those attention-grabbing looks that had the power to stop people in their tracks. And tonight, with the hard work that had been put into my appearance, I felt deserving of that same attention. Of that recognition.

But despite the beauty of my outward appearance, on the inside, I was a mess. Nausea rolled violently in my gut while my heart fluttered. It took every ounce of the same control I used in the ring to not fidget in my seat or bounce my knee to release some of that anxiety.

"We're here."

The deep voice of the driver had me tensing even more, glancing out the tinted windows to the line of cars waiting to pull up to the red carpet outside. "You ready?"

Instead of the confidence I hoped to inspire, my answering nod caused Eboni's face to drop with worry. Getting into a ring or cage with hundreds or even thousands of people witnessing me pummel my opponent didn't cause even a tenth of the nervousness I felt right now. The only thing keeping me from fleeing in panic was telling myself that I'd likely fade into the background amongst all the other big-named celebrities in attendance.

Joy patted my exposed knee in a show of support. Her wide, contagious grin was on display while her irises practically sparkled with excitement. "You got this, girl," she encouraged with her always-optimistic attitude. "You're Eden *freakin'* Foster."

Not wanting to seem rude, I returned her smile even though I had no fucking clue what being *Eden freakin' Foster* really meant. To me, Eden Foster was an overworked, underappreciated fighter and aunt who was quickly approaching her breaking point. But in this universe, where the big and famous dwelled, Eden Foster felt like an inconsequential onlooker. A phony whose invitation to the in-crowd must've been a mistake.

Earlier, while getting dressed, I'd voiced those same thoughts to Mo. And being a friend who hated when I put myself down, she gave me an earful for feeding into what she'd called my imposter syndrome. She'd told me that I had to get over my feelings of inadequacy and whether I felt like I belonged in this world or not... I was *here* and needed to make the best of it.

Other than walking away and disappointing everyone who'd put so much work into me at VP Sports, there wasn't much that could be done about it.

"We're next." Eboni announced, adjusting her full breasts in the low-cut dress before checking her makeup.

Photographers began snapping photos wildly before we'd fully come to a stop. Once again, my stomach tensed with panic but I still pasted on the smile they'd shown me. The smile I practiced in the mirror and hoped was alluring and not creepy like it'd been in the beginning of my PR training. I'd had no clue how much could be assumed based on a simple smile, but the thumbs up I received from both Eboni and Joy assured me that I was fine.

While our driver got out and rounded the black SUV, I took a moment, allowing myself to go to that cold, empty place of numbness. It only took a second since I'd damn near lived in that desolate existence for the last eight months.

And, as expected, the anxiousness and panic faded, right along with the tiny bit of excitement I'd felt from even being invited.

"Okay..." Joy whispered. I'd barely heard her through the layers of protection I'd packed on mere seconds ago. Layers that would get me through tonight without incident. "*Showtime*."

AN HOUR AFTER STEPPING INSIDE, my cheeks ached from the strain of maintaining that phony ass smile.

Every time I wrapped up my greeting with a big-named executive or investor in VP Sports, they introduced someone else. I was quickly starting to resent the smile that felt permanently etched and I wondered if my face would be capable of returning to normal once the night was over.

The one thing that kept me going was Eboni's proud and boastful expression. She'd watched closely when we first arrived, waiting for any mishaps or moments of panic. But after the first few introductions went off without a hitch, she relaxed, looking like a proud mother witnessing her child flourish.

It made me uncomfortable and pleased all at the same time.

Having someone feel pride in something I'd done right felt completely foreign when all I was used to hearing was what I'd done *wrong*.

"Eden." Eboni called right after I'd turned from chatting with a woman whose name I already forgot. That conversation had been surprisingly pain-free and one I preferred to continue rather than bouncing around the room being shown off like the shiny new toy that VP Sports had acquired. "This is Thomas Gentry, Owner of Gentry Financial." Eboni continued, indicating towards the black, middle-aged gentleman. "Thomas, this is Eden Foster."

My internal alarms were blaring full force as he stepped closer. Before she'd even completed the introduction, his stare turned into a leer as his eyes greedily crawled over my frame, lingering on the swell of my breasts.

Without saying a word, he'd made my skin crawl.

Eboni must've sensed my discomfort because she stepped closer than she'd been all night, hovering just over my shoulder. But Mr. Gentry ignored her, too busy ogling the long expanse of legs I'd left open for his disgusting leer. I fought the urge to shuffle uncomfortably because that was likely the response he was looking for.

Instead, I waited for his outstretched hand.

The second I clasped it, he reached out with his other, cupping my waist and bringing me uncomfortably close, whispering in my ear. "You are... *exquisite*." His words sent a strong waft of the liquor tainting his breath across my face.

The urge was strong to slip my free hand between us and under my dress to grip the knife I'd strapped high on the inside of my thigh. But I refrained, not wanting to bring *Menace* into this environment. I needed to keep the two worlds where I existed separate because blending them could possibly ruin everything.

Instead, I pulled back enough to meet his gaze and squeezed his hand hard, crushing his fingers between mine.

Shock slackened his jaws as his eyes bulged before discomfort contorted his features. Immediately, he tried discreetly tugging his hand free but I maintained the grip, never breaking our stare. "*Nice to meet you, too*."

"*Eden*." Eboni warned lowly, wearing the same phony smile I did.

He flicked a pleading look her way before returning his gaze to me. I scanned every inch of his face with disinterest before I brightened my smile. "Enjoy the rest of your night." Then I released him, watching with pleasure as he immediately fled, cupping his injured hand against his chest, flicking glances over his shoulder until he disappeared in the crowd.

"That wasn't very nice." Eboni chuckled next to me.

"Should've kept his hands to himself then." I shot back, scanning the room before making eye contact with a woman around my age.

Her open smile and pointed stare let me know she was coming my way so I braced in preparation of another introduction.

"Eden Foster, I've been dying to meet you." She gushed, flashing a quick smile towards Eboni before gripping my hand in both of hers.

"My daughter is a martial arts student and a huge fan of yours. After she showed me a few of your contests, I can understand why!"

"Thank you." I blushed after her words, still unused to compliments from total strangers. More praise fell from her lips before she asked for a photo and I readily agreed. After Eboni took the pictures and I recorded a short video message for her daughter, she moved on.

While someone else walked up to speak with Eboni, I tensed for an entirely different reason. Ignoring the chatting duo in front of me, I scanned the spacious ballroom, unable to shake that tingling at the nape of my neck.

A familiar sensation that sent my nerves into overdrive.

Immediately, I scanned the room but came up empty. I started to relax before that instinct that had gotten me out of messy situations more times than I could count had me scanning the room again. Still, I saw nothing. But I knew *he* was here. Watching from his position that wouldn't be revealed until he *wanted* it to be.

"Eden?" The question in Eboni's tone had me turning back with a polite smile, realizing she'd made an introduction that I hadn't heard. Thankfully, she was quick on her feet. "This is all still so new to her." She said with a laugh, placing a gentle hand on my arm. "This is Boris, VP Sports's financial director."

I shook the man's hand and returned his greeting, nodding and laughing when appropriate. I even answered every innocently curious question he'd tossed my way.

But when the conversation wrapped up, I knew I wouldn't be able to recite a single thing we'd talked about. Not when it took every ounce of my willpower to keep my gaze on him and not my surroundings.

Not when I wanted to walk away mid-conversation and survey the perimeter of the room, searching every nook and cranny for the man I hadn't seen in months. But I fought the urge, suffering through introduction after introduction, constantly scanning, hoping to catch a glimpse of him.

But I never did.

And finally, when I got a break from the polite smiles and handshakes, I made my escape, needing to distance myself not only from the pressure of the night… but the pressure of having his gaze on me.

A gaze I wanted to meet head-on.

A gaze I wanted scanning me with the adoration it once held rather than the disdain I remembered.

A gaze that had the ability to soothe and set me on fire all at the same time.

# 6

# HAKEEM

She'd been surrounded since the moment she stepped inside. Not only because of her mounting popularity, but that yellow dress that clung to her was a beacon for every eye in the place. It hugged her curves, displaying that body she busted her ass for.

Thick thighs that had squeezed my waist when I was deep inside peeked from underneath, teasing me with memories from across the room.

Someone walked up to her and she beamed a fake smile, turning to greet them. Immediately, my gaze dropped to scan the plump curve of her backside and sculpted calves. I'd never found a woman's calves attractive before now. But with the thickening behind the zipper of my slacks, on her, it was a new favorite body part.

Standing behind her chair, she nodded at the woman who'd walked up, flicking a nervous glance around the room every now and then. I couldn't tell if it was because of her sixth sense when it came to me or if her voyage into this new world had her on edge.

Though she tried to hide it, Eden was like me. A predator that preferred to lurk on the outskirts. That preferred the comfort of darkness. But *unlike* me, she had a skill that deserved the spotlight. One that would catapult her to levels of success she couldn't even fathom.

All my thoughts came to a screeching halt and my bottom lip disappeared between my teeth when she slipped off her white coat, exposing the toned muscled arms and impressive ink that stretched from shoulder to wrist. Even now that I knew about the chain-link tattoo, it was impossible to notice amongst the intricate artwork.

Right after she'd completed that interaction, someone else walked up and that fake, polite smile returned. The placating one that wasn't big, bright, and didn't stretch her cheeks like the one she'd reserved for Isaiah and Jayce.

The one she'd reserved for *me*.

Finally, when she had a moment to breathe, her shoulders slouched and she eased from the crowd, slipping away from her agent and everyone else who'd demanded her attention. On the opposite side of the room, I followed, never taking my gaze from her until she slipped out a side door that led towards the gardens. I flicked a glance to TJ, signaling that I was stepping out. He nodded, keeping his gaze alert until Garryn and Verse arrived.

Stepping outside, I sucked in a lungful of the clean air, listening closely until I caught the click of her heels against the gravel. Keeping my steps light, I followed with a frown, wondering why she was going so deep into the gardens. Especially alone.

Then again, the two of us were probably the biggest threats on the property.

Finally, those faint clicks tapered off and I kept going until I spotted her. Her back faced me, cupping her waist in a self-hug that made me want to pull her into my arms. Those eyes that I wanted on me remained focused on the fountain that sent tiny droplets of water spritzing into the air.

She seemed to be lost in her own little world, so I continued observing, inching closer before purposely shuffling my feet on the gravel to alert her to my presence.

Immediately she whirled and had a gun pointed my way in one smooth motion.

Damn, she was gorgeous.

I didn't make any sudden moves, giving her a second to recognize me. Her eyes bucked and she lowered the gun, thought better of it, then jerked it back up. "That's the Menace side of you, huh?" I muttered.

Her flinch was barely noticeable. "Why did you follow me?" she asked and I sucked in a low breath after hearing her voice for the first time in so long.

"That's our thing, isn't it?"

This time, there was no mistaking the sadness that came over her. "Not anymore."

"Hmm." I muttered, shoving my hands in my pockets and strolling casually towards her. When I was close enough for the gun to press against my lapels, I merely lifted a brow, biting back a smile at her moment of hesitation as she slowly lowered it. Before she could change her mind, I closed the distance between us.

This time, she was the one sucking in a deep breath, lids fluttering as she inhaled. A burst of pride and possessiveness surged in my chest, knowing I still affected this woman. Just like she did me. Once our fronts were nearly flush against one another, I bent my head, lowering until my lips hovered just above hers. "Then what's our thing now, Eden?"

This was a moment I'd imagined so many times over the last few months. Being this close to her, having the opportunity to speak to her again. "I don't know what you mean." she muttered, fiddling with the waistline of her dress. "We don't have a thing."

I crowded her even more. "You believe that?"

Those eyes I couldn't seem to get enough of turned hard. Everything in me grew tight at the chill in her gaze. "We haven't spoken to or seen each other in months. You broke into my apartment and threatened me with a gun. Telling me to stay away from anyone you cared about. And I've done that. I've done *exactly* what you asked. So, what the fuck do you think?"

"It wasn't loaded."

"And that made it okay?" She paused, then took a breath. "Hakeem... I am walking on a tightrope in my life right now. I don't have the... mental capacity to deal with whatever you want from me." When I merely stared, she sighed. "If it's sex, I'm sure there are *plenty* of other women available."

Finally, I reacted, scrunching my face but before I could respond, the moonlight caught the jewelry on her wrist, making my chest grow tight at the sight of the yellow diamond bracelet I'd gifted for her birthday in St. Leesburg. I couldn't believe she still wore it.

Sensing my distraction, she followed the direction of my gaze then pulled her arm away, holding the wrist protectively as if I might snatch the jewelry right off her.

Little did she know, seeing it caused pride to surge in my chest. She might've believed that we were over but that little piece of jewelry gave me something I hadn't felt in a while.

*Hope.*

Then not even a second later, she dashed it. "We should just keep our distance and let things stay how they are." Then she gave a sad little shrug that hit me right in the solar plexus. "What we had was good, despite it all. Let's not ruin the memory of it by trying again when we always knew it was temporary."

Several moments passed. Moments of complete warfare in my mind as I battled conflicted emotions. I could respect her wishes and fall back while continuing my plan of handling her problems behind the scenes.

But she was *right here.* In front of me for the first time in a long time. And I wanted it again. I wanted it all the time and I was too selfish to give that up. I hadn't fought for her the first time. I'd accepted what she'd said and kept my distance despite every one of my instincts telling me to go to her.

But this time, I would listen. Those instincts had never steered me wrong before and I doubt they would start now.

"Please." She begged in a soft tone. Her hands rose to my shoulders, using them to assist in lifting onto her toes as she placed a soft kiss against my jaw. My hand immediately shot to her waist and she sucked in a low breath, cupping my cheek lovingly. She looked at me like she used to. Before everything had fallen apart. Before we'd both walked away from the best thing to ever happen to us. "Please leave things as they are. I can't... can't take on the weight of you hating me, too. That might be the thing that actually breaks me." A hollow ache spread through my core. She thought I *hated her*. "Goodbye, Hakeem."

Though I should've immediately contradicted her statement, I was stuck. Too shocked to do anything but watch as she dashed around me in those heels to return inside.

It wasn't until she disappeared that I snapped out of it and moved, following her at a quick pace. She wouldn't get away from me that easily.

Not this fuckin' time.

# 7

# EDEN

My hands trembled.

Not only from the shock of seeing him but the actual interaction. A man I was sure hated me had gone out of his way to follow me outside. And he'd seemed... *different*. In a way that I couldn't pinpoint, but it caused flutters in the pit of my stomach.

After fleeing the garden, too many people had been in or around the main restrooms, so I'd crept up the stairs that were supposedly off-limits to guests. During my search, I'd stumbled upon an obnoxiously decorated sitting room and a massive office that was the size of my entire apartment in White Grove before finding a private bathroom at the far end of the second floor.

The rushing water emerging from the gold faucet coated my wrists, cooling the warmth that just a glimpse of him had stoked inside me.

The bracelet that had caught his attention slipped down my arm as I shut off the stream. My stylist, Naima, had paraded a vast array of jewelry in front of me, hoping I'd select anything besides the simple, yet special piece that adorned my wrist anytime I wasn't in the ring or cage.

But I'd stubbornly refused.

I'd deferred a lot of decisions regarding my life and career to other people over the last few months. But that small decision, that small choice to wear this bracelet meant more to me than anything else. In this new, scary world that I was learning to navigate, I wanted something familiar to ground me.

Something to soothe me. Something to bring me comfort when my nerves tried to get the best of me.

And I'd been doing so good. I'd smiled when necessary and made small talk when I'd rather be doing anything else. Tonight had damn near been perfect and I'd actually been proud of myself for not coming unraveled.

But one glance... one encounter with *him* had rattled my cage and knocked me off kilter.

The door I'd closed behind me crept open and I tensed before pasting on a fake smile in case it was someone I needed to wear my mask for.

But when I turned, that smile faltered at the sight of him.

The gardens near the fountain hadn't been as well-lit as this bathroom so I got my first full view of the man I thought about way too much.

His big frame filled the doorway, shoulders set with familiar confidence. He knew he looked good in the tux that was tailored to fit every contour and bulge on his frame. That beard I'd caressed with my fingers had grayed even more over the last few months. It gave him an air of maturity, enhancing his appealing yet not quite traditionally handsome features.

Hakeem didn't need to have bedroom eyes and a sleek smile to be attractive. Simply being him, all six-and-a-half intimidating feet, was more than enough.

As he took a tiny step inside, I realized that the casualness he'd displayed outside was gone. In just the few minutes since we'd separated, his entire demeanor had changed.

Unlike before when an almost playful air had softened his hard gaze, his eyes now blazed with familiar lust that was also stirring low in my gut. Uncomfortable under his scrutiny, I parted my lips to say something but stopped when he closed the door quietly behind him.

He didn't utter a single word. Just stared unblinkingly. Watching like any predator did its prey—focused, intent, and narrowed-lidded.

Unfamiliar awkwardness paralyzed me. I wasn't sure how to act around him. I wasn't sure what to say because I didn't know how he truly felt.

Was he angry about my deception? Did he still resent my proximity to the men who'd murdered his brothers?

Maybe he'd been too upset at the time to remember how everything went down between us but I hadn't forgotten.

The distance between us, the hurt words spoken, the threats made... And despite it all, deep down, I still wanted him. I just wasn't sure if he truly wanted *me*. Or if the desire reflected in his gaze was for the body he'd never failed to praise when we'd been together.

With the curve of my ass planted firmly against the counter, I could only watch as he closed the distance. Each step he took was like a vice tightening my lungs until I realized I was holding my breath in anticipation.

Intense eyes refused to release me from their stare even after he'd stopped with barely an inch of space separating us. One of those big, calloused hands slipped up the outside of my thigh and I knew I'd hate myself later for the desperate moan that emerged.

He'd cast some sort of spell over me during our time together. A spell that had conditioned me to crave his touch. A spell that ensured only he had the ability to set me ablaze like this even from the smallest contact.

"You got any more weapons I should know about?"

That rumble from his chest sounded like... *home*. Regardless of the words or the hint of gruff impatience he couldn't stop from leaking into his tone, I immediately felt soothed and at ease. Calm in a way I'd been desperate for.

Thinking about his question, I flicked my gaze to the clutch resting further down the counter that held the gun I'd pointed at him earlier.

"No."

His lips twitched in that infamous half-smile as the hand on the outside of my leg slipped between us, trailing up the smooth skin of my inner thigh.

I gasped, widening my stance, inviting more of his warm touch before tensing when a sudden yank removed the pleasurable contact. The knife I'd strapped to my leg appeared inches from my face before he tossed it on the counter. I watched as it skidded across the marbled countertop, coming to rest not far from my clutch.

His grip returned to the outside of my thigh as he bent far enough to whisper in my ear, "*Liar*."

Smooth lips and the soft hairs of his beard brushed lightly against my cheek and neck before hovering above mine. "You are fuckin' beautiful, you know that?"

The unexpected compliment had me averting my gaze. Why wasn't he giving me the cold shoulder? Why wasn't he reminding me to stay the fuck away from the people he cared about that were surely downstairs by now?

"Couldn't keep my eyes off you from the moment you walked in." Why was he being so *nice*? A low chuckle met my ears and I pulled back to witness it but his normal blank expression had already returned. "I'm never nice." He said, making me flush at the realization that I'd voiced the stupid question aloud. "I'm just not being mean." The hands on my thighs slipped higher, easing the fabric of my dress up until the seat of my panties were exposed. "You want me to be mean to you?"

God knows I deserved it for what I'd withheld from him but right now, I just wanted... gentleness. I wanted him to give me the side of himself that he kept closed off from all others. I wanted to feel *special* to him... even if only for tonight.

"No." I whispered back then bit my lip to smother a moan when his hand finally found the apex of my thighs. "I don't want you to."

He gave one of his infamous noncommittal hums. "Good. Don't know if I could, anyway." Just his thumb eased past the barrier of my underwear, swiping up my damp folds. "Not when you're this wet for me."

Lust for this man tightened my nipples and caused an almost painful clench in my abdomen in anticipation of what was next.

His hands gently cupped the back of my head, keeping his eyes on mine until our lips touched in a gentle caress. I dug my nails into the back of the hand lightly teasing between my thighs. An overload of sensation shot through my system as I pressed myself further into his touch, moaning in his mouth when that light touch turned intentional.

Glancing down, I watched that strong, scarred hand strum my clit like a seasoned guitarist. His other abandoned the back of my head to unzip my dress, lowering it until my full, bare breasts sprang free.

"*Keem!*" I whined, arching when his lips drew my dark areola into his mouth, surrounding it with liquid heat. His tongue swirled the stiff tip, lavishing it with his attention before moving to the neglected twin. His damp hand moved to the back of my thigh, lifting it up until my knee rested against his hip. The visible hardness through his pants pressed against my mound, thrusting lightly against me, teasing with what was to come.

I'd lost count of the number of times I'd touched myself to the thought of this. Teased between my thighs to the memory of just how intense the passion between us was. Plucked my own nipples as I remembered how he could just set me on fire with one simple touch.

Over my ragged breaths, I could hear someone downstairs speaking into a microphone. Their voices invaded our moment of privacy and I tensed, realizing that at any moment, we could be caught.

If someone decided to venture upstairs in search of privacy like I had, they could stumble upon us. But when the slow, torturous sound of his zipper sliding down filled the air, all I cared about was him. If someone did walk in, they could watch for all I cared because nothing would stop me from getting this. From selfishly taking this man between my thighs again.

"You know how many times I've imagined this?" His voice rasped with hunger, causing my hips to writhe in anticipation. His hands never stopped moving as he spoke, retreating far enough to push the waistband of his pants and underwear over an impressive erection that sprang free. The hot, heavy length rested on my thigh and I sucked in a low breath. He was bigger than I remember. Thick and veiny as a bead of arousal wept from the tip.

Instead of slipping my underwear off, he easily lifted me on the edge of the counter and shoved the thin fabric aside. The wide head of him nudged my clit and I moaned, widening my thighs further to accommodate. "So damn *tight*," he groaned, grabbing both hips in his big hands to help impale me further.

Pinpricks of ecstasy raced through my nervous system as he stretched me. I suddenly felt short of breath. Overwhelmed by the sensations as the burning heat caused my toes to curl.

He still wasn't fully submerged, giving me short, teasing thrusts. Even when we'd slept together regularly, he'd had to ease me into sex, giving my body time to adjust to the wide girth he wielded.

A low, keening moan burst free as my head fell back against the mirror and my hips arched. "Harder." I begged. One of my legs wrapped high around his hips, yanking him into me, enjoying the way pleasure and pain merged.

"I was trying to be gentle," He grunted, staring directly in my eyes, caressing my hips with each word. "But you don't want that. You never wanted it easy between us, did you?"

There was a hidden meaning to his words that I was too far gone to decipher. Instead, I licked my lips, feeling my shoulder curl in a moment of insecurity.

"You know I can't deny you." He continued, pulling me from against the mirror until my chest aligned against his. "Even now, you can ask for whatever you want and I'll move heaven and earth to make it happen."

Before his words fully penetrated the sexual fog clouding my mind, he buried himself inside to the hilt.

"Oh!" I wailed. The pleasure was... excruciating. It didn't make sense but I saw no other way to describe it. That fine line between pleasure and pain was blurred and I loved it. Loved that I felt safe enough with him to experience it.

"I'll give you whatever you want. Whatever you need... even the things you're too scared to ask for."

The sting of tears caused pinpricks behind my lids and I was thankful my face was buried in his neck so he couldn't see them. Hakeem was fully fucking me now. With deep heavy strokes that caused my building pleasure to peak. And all I could do was give myself over to it.

I clung to his shoulders, drawing him closer until not an inch of space existed between us. For the first time in so long, despite his bruising grip on my hips and punishing thrust between my thighs, I felt safe. Secure in that protective bubble of his.

"You gonna walk away again?" He pulled back far enough to meet my gaze as his deep rasp washed over my senses.

"You *pushed* me away." I reminded, hating the hitch in my voice.

"And I tried to rectify that..." He countered. "Then you pushed *me* away."

Neither of us had ever apologized for what caused the end of our relationship. And it felt like we were back at square one, wanting each other... wanting this connection but still holding back parts of ourselves. Parts we weren't sure the other would accept.

But words failed us both when my muscles clenched his shaft as his thrusts grew harder, rougher. Pleasure contorted his normally stoic expression and I felt my lower half tightening before I exploded around him. My nails clawed the fabric covering his back as my sharp cry echoed in the room. My walls spasmed around his still thrusting shaft and I felt a slight tremble in his big body as he lost his fluid rhythm. The collision of his hips slapping my damp skin grew louder until he choked out a groan. "*Fuck, Eden*." The sound of my name on his lips set me off a second time when the hot, jetted stream of his release warmed my insides.

Thank God I was still on birth control.

Despite his violent orgasm, he still thrust into me, not slowing his ferocious speed. The movements were so rough that my ass was slipping back and forth across the smooth marble.

Then suddenly he grunted and stilled, heaving breathlessly as his hands settled on each side of my hips while his forehead rested against my shoulder.

After a long silence, my discomfort mounted and I tried to disentangle myself but he stopped me and leaned back. Holding my gaze, he sank back inside and I gasped, realizing he was still hard.

I bit my lip to fight my moan which caused an immediate furrow in his brows as if he didn't like that. Slowly this time, *teasingly*, he resumed thrusting while his thumb swiped lazily up and down my slit.

My legs cocked wider, knees damn near touching my breasts. My lids fluttered closed and all I could focus in was the pleasure between my thighs as he slow-fucked me.

Mere minutes passed before I came again. This time, it wasn't an explosion of passion and heat like before. This orgasm was slow-building and toe curling. Like the subtle pleasure that lingered after a good stretch. But just like its predecessor, it left my legs trembling and body tingling with its lingering effects.

"How long do you have to stay?" I kept my eyes closed before they popped open at the light smack against my thigh. "*Eden*."

Words failed to compute so I shrugged. His lips twitched and I thought I would be blessed with another of those rare smiles, but it didn't happen. Instead, his tongue swiped his bottom lip as he spoke, eyes dropping between my thighs. "What's your address?"

I froze briefly, wondering how the hell he knew I'd moved but then I remembered who he was. This man was capable and resourceful in a way like I'd never seen before. "Why?"

He hummed, then pulled out a handkerchief. I followed him with my gaze as he ran it beneath the faucet next to my hip. Then, to my surprise, he set the cloth aside then bent at the waist, keeping his gaze on mine as he pressed a soft kiss on top of my mound.

Despite being pleasantly sore, I raised my hips, wanting his mouth just a few inches lower. I wanted his tongue swiping through the folds, teasing my clit in that way he did so well. But he pulled back instead, pressing the warm cloth between my thighs and wiping gently. I felt uncomfortable but thankful that his eyes were lowered. All his concentration was aimed downwards as he cleaned my folds, wiping away all evidence of our passion before righting the panties he'd yanked aside.

"Why do you think?" He finally answered.

This time, I was rewarded with a smile but instead of falling under its spell, I shook my head as regret settled in. It slowly drained from his face, replaced by confusion as I jumped off the counter, forcing him to take a step back.

"What's wrong?" His big hand cupped the back of my head, holding me in place as he kissed me, swiping his tongue gently across my lips. "You okay?"

"I'm sorry." I whispered. "I shouldn't have done that. *We* shouldn't have done that."

His neck jerked. "Why the fuck not?" I steadily avoided his gaze, grabbing my clutch off the counter. "*Eden*. What's going on?"

I gave myself a onceover in the mirror, making sure I didn't *look* like I'd had a quickie in the bathroom. Satisfied with my appearance, I turned to face the man watching me with confusion and some other unnamed emotion in his gaze. The intense attraction between us practically crackled in the air but I couldn't feed into it. I couldn't just fall back into this again. I couldn't set myself up to be hurt again.

I had to put myself and my emotions first, which meant getting the fuck out of here before I could fall under his spell.

That potent spell that still had the potential to easily pull me back under its power.

Walking right up to him, I cupped his cheek and smiled sadly, feeling my chest ache at what I was about to do. "I need to go."

"Eden... Don't..."

I rose to my tiptoes and pressed my lips against his. His hand cupped my waist and tightened, attempting to deepen the kiss. For a moment, I allowed it, reveling in his touch and taste. When that hand started to lower back between my thighs, I jumped back, severing the contact between us.

I touched my lip, savoring the taste of him before taking a shaky step back when he took one forward.

"I need to go." I said again, more as a reminder to myself.

"You don't have to." His tone was soft and so unlike Hakeem that I briefly considered it. Then I remembered the emotional agony I'd lived in since we parted. That pain had been indescribable. So, I latched onto that feeling as a reminder and it fueled the steps I took towards the door.

His harsh glare seared my back but I refused to look. I refused to give in to that temptation because it was a good chance that I'd stay if I held that eye contact.

"Goodbye, Hakeem."

# 8

# EDEN

***Age 17***

"EDEN!"

I ignored my *unofficial* trainer, Luke, as he yelled across the gym. Instead, I continued advancing towards the person who'd been making disrespectful comments since I stepped in the ring.

*Crow.*

My boyfriend Rome's best friend who'd had it out for me from the moment we crossed paths. And unfortunately for the beady eyed, thin-nosed boy, the feelings were mutual. I wasn't sure who he'd dealt with in the past but backing down wasn't in my blood. Which meant, more often than not, I let my mouth get me into shit that my hands had to get me out of.

This was another moment where simply walking away was the smarter choice but I couldn't let his slick insults continue to go unchecked.

"You got a lot to say for a man who spends his time fetching water for real athletes." The jab landed exactly where I wanted when his face tightened, fists clenching next to his side as he straightened from his bent position over the rope. Crow had longed for a career in boxing but never developed the skill to compete. After two vicious knockouts in the amateur circuit, they had relegated him to a supporting role that never failed to piss him off.

My smirk widened into a full-blown grin when he slipped through the rope and into the ring.

From the corner of my eye, I spotted Luke's exasperation because he'd already given up on trying to stop me. He knew me well enough to realize I'd already reached the point of no return.

If I backed down now, Crow would believe I was running scared and I'd *never* allow that thought to become a reality.

With one hand, he tugged the back of his shirt up and over his head, carelessly tossing it aside. He was tall and lean, yet still outweighed me by about forty pounds. But instead of fear or nervousness, all I felt was the excitement of knowing I was about to put him on his ass.

"Knockout?" I asked after he'd wrapped his hands.

Just like me, he exuded nothing but confidence as he nodded. The slick grins on the faces of the other men proved they thought his victory was a foregone conclusion. They would all be in for a *rude* awakening.

"Rules?" I asked, bouncing on the balls of my feet.

He gave the exact answer that I wanted while flashing a menacing grin. "None."

"Bet."

Then he attacked, coming at me wildly. Still sporting my taunting grin, I easily avoided contact, dancing around him on the balls of my feet.

For the first few minutes, we continued that same routine. Him attacking and me effortlessly avoiding contact. Rage settled deeper into his expression, warning of an impending explosion of anger.

But I didn't care. Despite my skill heavily outweighing everyone else who trained at the gym, I still had to work ten times harder to prove myself. So, whenever the opportunity arose for me to annihilate someone? I jumped on it.

"That's all, Crow?" I continued, smiling at the way he huffed but still couldn't land any significant jabs. "I know you can do better than that."

In a straight bitch move, his arm shot out, backhanding me across the face. My teeth dug into my lip and blood oozed out, dropping onto the white canvas. I was annoyed but didn't let it show. Instead, I backed out of swinging distance, swiping my forearm across the wound, observing the red streak before flashing a smile.

It was time to turn up the intensity.

"C'mon." I taunted, planning on ending the fight in the next few seconds. This had gone on long enough.

By now, I'd already proven my point. Though I was younger, smaller, and *weaker* in his eyes, he still couldn't fuck with me.

Like expected, Crow rushed me and in one motion, I ducked, feeling the air from his wild swing rush by. After stumbling past, he whirled to swing again, only to meet the full force of my fist.

He dropped like a sack of weights.

A chorus of *oh shit* rang out but I paid them no mind. Instead, I bent over Crow's prone frame on the canvas, catching his unfocused gaze before I smirked. "I think that counts as a knockout." His brows furrowed and I tapped his sweaty chest with my fingertips. "Good try."

Then I straightened, feeling the first sense of apprehension as I walked towards Luke. Now that I was coming down from the adrenaline high, I realized my next few visits to the gym would be hell. Luke despised showboating and bragging but I couldn't find it in me to regret what I'd done.

There were so many areas in my life where I was lacking. I hid many flaws beneath my tough exterior, but no matter what anyone thought of me, no matter how many hits my self-esteem took... the one area I was fully confident was in the ring. Whether boxing or MMA, I had a natural talent that made me want to constantly shout to the world that I was great at *something*.

There *were* people who saw the value in me and my skill set.

*"I wouldn't do that if I were you."*

Glancing over my shoulder, I tensed at the sight of Crow's angry glare. He'd gotten to his feet and scrambled to the edge of the ring. One of his hands was inside his bag, frozen in motion as if about to pull something out.

To his left, my older brother stood, gun resting a few inches from Crow's temple.

"Take your L." He continued in that rough tone that placed the fear of God in some men but provided comfort for me. "Barry would be pissed if I had to kill you and your boys because you couldn't handle losing to a girl."

*"Woman."* I corrected.

Benji's nose wrinkled in irritation, but still, he backtracked. "Losing to a *woman*."

"She fuckin' cheated!"

I snorted, causing Benji and Luke both to flash me *shut the fuck up* looks.

"You calling my sister a cheater?" His head tilted.

Crow might like to throw his weight around with me but knew better than to try that shit with Benji.

While the two glared at each other, I eased towards my bag in case I needed my own. But before I reached it, Crow lifted his chin, pulled his hand out of the bag and walked out without another word, taking his crew with him.

"I'm gon' follow them niggas in case they want to act stupid or something." Benji offered before leaving too.

Then it was just me and Luke. "You need to learn to control that." He snapped the second they were gone.

"Why?" I questioned, full of cockiness. "I can beat *anybody*. I'm not scared of shit. I'm *good*."

A disbelieving scoff rushed out as he braced weathered hands on lean hips. "You are incredibly stupid. You know that?" Luke's insults were as familiar as the tape I wrapped around my hands each time I prepared to fight, so I merely waited. "Everybody can be beat." He said with a disgusted glance at my busted lip. "Even by somebody that's not as good as you."

"But I have *skills*, Luke. I can hold my own, *even* on an off day."

"Trusting your skills, talent, and training is important. But it's equally important to trust this." He paused and tapped my temple. "Because that's always going to be your biggest opponent. Whether it's insecurity or, in your case, *overconfidence*." I rolled my eyes. "This up here can make or break you, little girl. You need to train your mind the same way you train your body. Train it to feel absolutely *nothing* when the time comes."

I didn't know how to feel *nothing*.

I'd always been a person who felt *everything*. Which had resulted in my parents calling me sensitive all the damn time. But I'd learned to use those emotions. They fueled me in the ring. I fought with every ounce of regret, anger, sadness, rage, and disappointment that cluttered my mind. I went at each opponent as if they were the one who'd personally offended me and it had worked so far.

But the thought of stepping in a ring and being a blank slate? Of fighting without the heaviness in my chest from the weight of all those emotions? I couldn't even imagine it.

"Can you teach me?" I asked quietly. "To shut it all out and feel... nothing?

For once, the harshness that lined his features eased as he eyed me. The intensity of it was stifling, as if he was searching to the depths of my very soul.

As if he was wondering if it would be worth it. And for once, I humbled myself and let the cocky facade fade away to make room for the real me.

The authentic Eden who, despite her affinity for using fists to solve problems, loved too hard and too easily, especially with people who made her feel less than.

Eden, who walked around like she owned the world, but went home to cry silent tears.

Eden, who'd allowed herself to be mistreated by boyfriends because simply having them around eased that bit of loneliness.

I dropped all pretenses and gave him the raw, unfiltered Eden who I tried to protect at all costs.

What he saw must've been convincing because he sighed, looking towards the ring with a bit of trepidation. "I can try. But it's going to be up to you whether it sticks."

Joy filled me but I merely flashed him a small smile of appreciation. "I promise. I'll do whatever you ask." I paused before speaking the next words, realizing I meant them more for me than him. "*I'll do whatever it takes.*"

---

AN EXPLOSION of pain shot through my entire body after a fist slammed my side.

My opponent approached and I misjudged her next move, lifting my arms to protect my face, foolishly leaving my entire core open for attack. Without delay, she swung again, driving it upwards, stealing my breath with the sheer power and force behind it.

I was making rookie mistakes.

All because I couldn't seem to calm my wayward thoughts. Mere days had passed since the gala. And instead of basking in the success of the night, I was deep in the heart of White Grove, battling in a grueling underground fight.

Winning was normally the only thing on my mind, but tonight, everything except my opponent had my synapses firing.

Even as fighters battled in the underground ring known as The Pit, I'd tried to recall the lessons learned throughout my career.

Lessons that helped build my fearless reputation. That helped maintain an undefeated record, both professional and underground.

But at the moment, I was failing miserably.

My muscles burned from overuse. My core ached from the hits it'd taken. Sweat poured from me in droves, dripping onto the mat, mixing with the droplets of blood leaking from an open cut above my brow. The splattered mixture stained the canvas pink, leaving a mess I'd slipped on trying to evade her powerful hits. And between my thighs was deliciously sore because of a man I was trying to force to the back of my mind. I was already fighting like shit. I didn't need *another* distraction to throw me off my game.

The crowd's indistinct murmurs quickly switched from excitement to confusion as my normally dominant performance was nowhere to be found.

*Fuck*!

Another blow to my side had me hissing and doubling over. Not wanting to miss the opportunity to beat the undefeated *Menace*, she aimed another well-placed fist across my face that sent me tumbling to the canvas.

Shocked gasps filled the air as most of the crowd stood to their feet, looking at the ring from their elevated positions, wondering if I'd rise again.

For a moment, I thought about giving up. Staying down until they called the match. I thought about tossing in the towel, literally and figuratively.

But then I thought about my boys, who I hadn't seen in weeks.

I had more than just me to worry about. Barry had made it no secret that he'd use them to keep me in line.

My opponent came at me full force, going in for the kill like a shark who'd smelled blood in the water. But I was prepared this time, rolling away from her attack and pushing through fatigue to launch to my feet.

The crowd roared with excitement. And for once, instead of tuning them out, I used the noise as fuel.

Used their joyous cries to fill the emptiness inside of me.

Used their excitement to fill the void where my self-determination once dwelled.

Without thought, I started swinging. Some were wild, missing their target while I delivered others with the vicious precision I prided myself on. The louder the crowd got, the harder I swung, increasing my accuracy each time until a swift uppercut snapped her head back before she collapsed to the mat.

But instead of getting up like I had, she stayed down, blinking at the overhead lights as if in a daze.

Immediately after my victory was declared, I slipped through the ropes and climbed from the ring. Heavy palms slapped my sweaty shoulders in congratulations as I maneuvered through the crowd. But I ignored them all.

I'd gotten what I needed to get over the hump that nearly stopped my victory.

Now that I'd succeeded, they were once again background noise as I walked with purpose across the massive room, stopping short at the sight of a familiar figure propped next to the door I needed to enter. "*Little girl.*"

Normally I'd crack a smile at the name Luke sometimes pulled out, much to my irritation. But I couldn't even muster up one for him. Not after such a close call.

All I could think about was what I'd done wrong and scold myself for the stupid mistakes I'd made.

Noticing my solemn mood, Luke pushed off the wall and shuffled closer. "You forgot how to block?" He asked in that tone that let me know a lesson was coming.

One I didn't want to hear. Hell, I was already criticizing myself and didn't need him adding to it. "Not in the mood, Luke."

His face contorted with a frown, unused to the cold, closed off version of me. Not with him, at least. Though his reaction bothered me, I remained steadfast, not giving anything away. I had to remind myself that I didn't have anyone in my corner. I didn't have friends or alliances in the world of the 400s and probably never had.

"That's why you looked like shit out there?" He asked, waving a dismissive hand over my body. "Because you didn't wear your lucky color?"

I didn't have to glance down to know what he saw. Socks, shorts, sports bra, and hand wrap—all black.

Somehow, I'd foolishly believed that wearing a sunny color every day would help replenish the pieces of my soul this organization and the men in it had stolen from me. But I'd stopped living in the clouds. My feet were firmly planted on the ground and all I believed in was reality staring me in the face. A grim reality that only seemed to grow bleaker as the days passed.

"I don't rcally carc."

"You're giving up?"

"What the fuck are you talking about?" I snapped, irritated that he was keeping me from getting upstairs. "Didn't I *just* win?"

"Not talking about the fight." He said cryptically and I rolled my eyes, not prepared for this riddled shit. "You're going to just roll over for 'em? Go right back to being an errand girl, willing to do anything just so someone'll like you?" He huffed. "That fearless girl who walked into my gym would be embarrassed at what she let herself be turned into."

His words hit their intended target, but I remained stoic, unmoved because I couldn't run from the truth. "Look at me, Luke." I said in a tone that had the skin between his brows creasing. He wasn't getting through to me and didn't like it. But I couldn't find it in me to care. I couldn't find it in me to care about much of anything besides ending this conversation. "Stop looking for any pieces of that girl you once knew because she's gone. My life now consists of training for the PFC, fighting in the Pit, and enjoying what little time I'm *allowed* with my nephews. *That's it.*"

Noises from behind the closed door captured both our attention and I moved towards it, not looking over my shoulder as I tossed out one last point.

"Keep the pep talks to yourself, Luke. Save them for one of your young trainees because I'm not interested."

---

AFTER TURNING my back on Luke, I opened the door to reveal a member of the 400s standing guard.

He leered at me as I passed but I paid him no mind, taking the stairs behind him two at a time, ignoring the way my joints protested each time they landed.

Another familiar face was coming down the hall when I reached the top. Benji's friend, Loc, eyed me with casual detachment like always. He was one of the few 400s who didn't seem to be at Barry or Rome's beck and call.

Honestly, Loc's role was never fully clear to me. I just knew he'd picked up the money and dropped it off to my then manager, Jesse, when they used to wash their illegal funds through my fights.

I'd never been able to get a read on him, even after all these years, because he wasn't a man of many words. He didn't linger once his job was complete and made little effort to win anyone over.

Loc was Loc and everyone knew and respected it.

"E." He greeted me in a low tone.

"*Loc*."

A hint of a smile appeared, then was gone a second later.

As the distance between us decreased, my head tilted to accommodate his imposing height. I kept his handsome face in my line of sight, not wanting to miss the small changes in his expression that would reveal his true thoughts.

He was like Hakeem. Keeping his cards close to the chest, guarding his emotions with an iron fist that would take an act of God to penetrate.

Sadness over walking away from Hakeem for a second time hit with a swiftness that caused my step to stutter.

Loc's gaze dropped to my sweaty legs before jerking back up to my face. "You good?"

I nodded, blinking rapidly. I was a bit surprised and embarrassed at the sudden onslaught of emotions overtaking me. I'd done such a good job of hiding the truth so far. No one was the wiser of just how heartbroken I truly was. Not even Mo knew about the nights I'd cried myself to sleep, missing the way he'd held me. The way he'd made me feel secure without saying a single word.

The way he'd made me believe that *more* was possible. Only to dash those hopes with a few well-aimed words.

Taking a fortifying breath, I slid closer to the wall, giving Loc the space he needed to pass. But instead of moving on, the arm closest to me shot out and captured my wrist in a tight grip, halting my steps.

Despite fatigue, my muscles stiffened, prepared to launch an attack or defend myself if the need arose. "Let me go." I said, keeping my tone even.

Ignoring the command, he pulled me close, leaning down until his forehead was mere inches above mine. "You need to tighten up." I bristled, thinking he meant my performance in the ring. Immediately, he shook his head, tugging on my wrist where he still held me. "Before you walk in there. They'll sniff that weakness out as quickly as I did."

"Who the *fuck* you calling weak?"

"*You.*" He shot back, crowding my space even further. "With your watery eyes and broken-hearted shit. Tighten the fuck up before they eat your little ass alive in that room. They feed on that."

None of these men knew how to deliver words with a soft touch. They only knew how to talk to Menace. And when that side of me was at the forefront, I could handle it because that was the world that created her. That was the world where she'd *thrived.*

But right now? I was Eden. And no matter how much I tried to hide or ignore it, Eden was tender hearted. Eden was sensitive. Eden was gullible and people pleasing.

Eden sometimes needed softness to balance out all the hard in the world she dwelled in.

And other than the boys, the only person who'd given it to me had been a man known for his hardness.

A man I'd *lost*.

"I got it." The wobble in my voice was unmistakable. Loc's brows furrowed just like Luke's had but I ignored him too, yanking away to finish my walk towards the closed door at the end of the hall.

Before pushing it open, I took a deep breath, glaring at the camera mounted in the corner before walking in without knocking.

Though I was aware of every person in the room, I pretended not to be. Instead, I sauntered in casually, fixing my gaze out the floor-to-ceiling windows that overlooked the first floor and had a clear, unobstructed view of the ring below where two women went at it.

Unlike the other club where I'd fought for years, this one solely belonged to Barry, opened and operated without the permission of Axel Knight. A man who rarely let anything slip past, which was why I didn't understand why he hadn't come in and shut the whole thing down already.

When I faced the room again, all three sets of eyes scanned me, taking in my bruised, sweaty physique as I waited. "Where is he?" I asked, not beating around the bush. I'd done as Barry commanded. Won the fight. And my reward, besides a meager portion of my earnings, was unobstructed time with Jayce. Time I hadn't had in *weeks*. With him or Isa. My texts and calls to his phone had gone unanswered and every time I reached out to Mona, she had an excuse about him being out or busy and unable to come to the phone.

Though I couldn't prove it, I was sure she'd received a visit or call from Barry and was too terrified to go against whatever he'd told her to do.

Barry's gaze lazily dropped back to his desk, scrolling on his phone. Crow glared menacingly from the white leather sofa, eager for any order that would allow him to move on me. That man probably woke up dreaming of ways to hurt me.

Too bad I'd never let him get the chance.

Finally, I met the unwavering stare of the third person in the room. *Rome.* While I remained still, his eyes roamed over me, slowly and sensually, before a slight grin revealed the grill gleaming behind his full lips. It was a shame he was so handsome, considering he was a piece of shit.

"How long ago did you sign this.... *contract*?"

I tensed at Barry's low tone, still not breaking the staring contest I was in with his nephew. "A few months ago." It was actually approaching nine months but I kept that to myself. "Why?"

"*Why*?" His tone was incredulous. "Because you haven't had a single professional fight since you signed that piece of paper. If I didn't know better, I'd think you were being iced out."

I didn't have an answer because I'd been wondering about the same thing. I knew that the big leagues would be different, but I *also* knew that summer was the most popular time of the year for fights. Two major tournaments had come and gone, yet I hadn't heard a peep from VP Sports about entering either of them.

But instead of expressing my concerns, I shrugged. "There's a lot of behind-the-scenes stuff I gotta go through. PR training and all of that. You can't rush it."

Barry's eyes narrowed with suspicion but before he could start back up, an angry cry emerged from outside the room. Recognizing the sound, I looked around curiously before the door I'd just entered flung open. Madi stood there, struggling to hold onto a wriggling Jayce who was in the middle of a tantrum.

Despite his upset disposition, my heart soared.

"*Jayce.*" I cooed, before biting down on my lip to keep my emotions from spilling free. Like Loc said, they'd sniff out the weakness and find yet *another* way to use it against me. So, I watched calmly despite my heart breaking at the sight of my baby struggling to get down out of his mother's arms.

"Let him go, Madi."

She rolled her eyes, flicked a glance at Barry before setting him down.

"*Tee*!" He cried, running towards me at full speed. Before he could slam into my sore legs, I lifted him, returning the tight squeeze he gifted me.

God, I'd missed him.

As I shifted my arms from his back to under his bottom, a rustling sound had my brows furrowing. Peeking over his shoulder, I pulled the waistband of his jeans out far enough to look inside. And what I saw had my anger spiking.

"Why the fuck is he wearing a pull-up?" I snapped. "A *dirty* pull-up, at that."

When Madi merely returned my glare with her own look of confusion, I sucked my teeth. But before I could say a word, Rome interjected, sounding as exasperated as I felt. "He's fucking potty trained, Madison."

"I *forgot*. Damn, cut me some slack." Then her gaze flicked to me. "You look like shit." I took three steps in her direction and she immediately backpedaled. "I'm out." Then she was gone, not bothering to say goodbye to her only son.

*Bitch.*

"How the fuck do you deal with her?" Rome grumbled in my direction, eyes locked on mine as if really expecting an answer.

I laughed in disbelief. "I'm sorry... When did we become friends? That's *your* baby mama. Don't complain to me about her."

He grimaced, pushing off the wall to move closer. "Why you always gotta take it there? You can't just let shit be peaceful between us?"

"*Peaceful*?!" My neck jerked backwards. "Rome, how dare you..." I paused when my hand swiped against the fullness of Jayce's pullup, reminding me of my priorities. Getting him clean was the most important thing, not explaining to Rome for the fiftieth time why we would never be *peaceful* again. "I'm not doing this with you. I gotta get him changed."

On my way towards the door, he blocked my path. Immediately, I took a step back, hating that I'd left my weapons in the locker room downstairs. I should've stopped by to grab at least one but getting to see Jayce had been the only thing on my mind.

"Damn, I'm just trying to say goodbye to my son." He said with a laugh. He enjoyed my wariness despite his bullshit words about us being peaceful. He enjoyed having any sort of control over me physically, emotionally, or mentally. Any way Rome could exert his power, he would.

"I can't get a hug?" Rome asked Jayce, who clung tighter to my neck when Rome placed a hand in the center of his back. Instead of softening at the touch, Jayce tensed even more and whimpered, making my stomach clench. "Really, little nigga?" This time, when Jayce refused to give in, he yanked so hard I nearly lost my balance.

Immediately, my eyes bucked and I reactively swung. It caught him off guard so his duck was mistimed and I connected. A sharp curse shot from his chest as he stumbled back.

Crow was on his feet not even a second later.

But instead of the anger I'd braced for, Rome laughed. Hard and loud, as if that was the funniest thing that had happened all day. "That's the Eden I miss." He still chuckled, swiping a finger to catch the trickle of blood leaking from his nose. "That's my fucking baby. The little passive bitch you've been lately doesn't do it for me. Not like *this* side of you."

My muscles trembled with the urge to hit him again but I didn't want to push my luck. So, I ignored his grin and tried to leave, stopping only when Barry called my name.

I peered over my shoulder, stomach tightening at the sinister smile on his face. "You enjoy your time with him, okay?"

Again, I didn't respond. Instead, I left their taunting laughter behind as I slammed the door. It wasn't until I'd retrieved my things from the locker room and was secured in the safety of my car that I took a full breath.

"Tee?" Jayce asked from the backseat after I just sat there, staring at the building where I was shedding blood, sweat, and tears on a nearly weekly basis.

"It's okay, baby." I started the engine. "Everything's okay. Everything's okay." I kept whispering the sentiment as I drove, hoping it would bring me the same level of comfort I was desperately trying to give to him.

# 9

# EDEN

I DIDN'T WANT to go inside.

For the last ten minutes, I'd sat in my car and glared at the neon yellow, white, and blue logo of Johnny B's burgers.

A place that normally brought to mind childhood memories of Benji and I using our allowance to share a milkshake. Or getting dismissed from school early for fighting and instead of going home to face my parents, I went to the restaurant in our old neighborhood. There, I waited in the back booth for Benji to get out so we could walk home together like nothing had happened.

Johnny Bs was a place that reminded me of the brief moments of joy I experienced in a sometimes unhappy childhood.

But today, instead of nostalgia, my stomach knotted with dread at the thought of entering and facing my mother. I'd kept my distance, communicating only if it revolved around Jayce or Isa. Despite the way she treated me, I couldn't avoid *missing* her. She was *still* my mother and I loved her.

Probably a hell of a lot more than she loved me.

Deciding I'd hid in my car for too long, I got out, not removing my dark-tinted sunglasses even after stepping inside out of the beaming sunlight.

An elderly Black hostess waited near the door, flashing a warm smile that I returned.

"Sit anywhere you like, sugar."

The polite, PR-approved grin I'd perfected transformed into a genuine one at the honeyed twang of her words.

No matter which location I visited, it always felt like home.

Moving past her with a nod, I maneuvered through the tables, briefly scanning faces and making note of them as I passed. Tension swept through me when I finally spotted my mom near the rear of the diner. To my dismay, my dad sat right next to her.

Why the fuck was he here?

She wore a soft, uncharacteristic smile that made me uncomfortable. One that made me want to turn on my heels and leave without a backward glance. But that side of me that didn't know how to back down from any situation kept my feet moving forward.

Stopping next to the table, I resisted the urge to ask them to switch sides so my back wouldn't face the door. But I bit my tongue, knowing I wouldn't be here long enough for it to make a difference.

So, I sat, holding her gaze, refusing to give in to the urge to break the awkward silence. Whenever my eyes landed on my mother nowadays, instead of hopefulness and a desperate need for acceptance, I felt sad and... empty.

As if the blinders had finally come off and I could clearly see how one-sided our relationship had been.

The waitress approached minutes later to take our order, giving us a temporary reprieve. Normally, I was a stickler about my diet but if I had to sit through this shit, I deserved something satisfying. Like a Johnny B's burger with secret sauce and a New York cheesecake milkshake.

I'd hate myself later, but for now, it was worth it.

Finally, after our orders were taken, my mom broke the silence. "I'm glad you agreed to meet."

"*Um hmm.*"

"Don't be disrespectful."

My gaze sharpened at my father's scolding. "Excuse me?"

"Not today." My mom interrupted before either of us could get started. She must've sensed that I was walking a tightrope, barely hanging on to my self-control. If he started with me today, I'd return every bit of his energy. "We're going to sit here and eat like a normal, functioning family." My unladylike snort earned a glare. "*All* of us, okay?"

"Alright." I agreed half-heartedly. Internally, I was estimating less than half an hour would pass before this turned into a complete shitshow.

Minutes later, my assumption was confirmed when my mom beamed over my shoulder. Rhythmic taps against the floor had my spine stiffening with each step until I heard, "Hey, mama. Hey, daddy." There was a pause as she rounded the table and sat next to me before grunting out a reluctant, "*Eden.*"

I should've known.

Refusing to acknowledge her, I held my mother's gaze. "What was the one thing I asked when agreeing to this?"

Her mouth parted as she lifted her hands helplessly. "Eden... don't be like that."

"What was the *one* thing I asked?" I pressed, refusing to back down like I would've before.

"Watch your tone, little girl."

Again, I ignored my father. His ass shouldn't be sitting here either. But since he was, I would pay him the same amount of attention he gave me growing up. *None.* "I know you didn't want Madi to come but that's ridiculous. She's your sister and it's time to squash this petty mess between you two."

Not acknowledging the second half of her statement, I stood. "I just wanted to make sure I'd made myself clear. Now that I know I did, I'm out."

"She's always so dramatic." Madi spat as if she truly didn't have a clue as to why I wouldn't want to be near her.

My thin thread of control was tested each second I remained so I grabbed my purse and turned, stopping only to pay the hostess for the meal that I didn't even get to enjoy.

I'd almost made it to my car before hearing my mom behind me. "Eden, this is too much. You can't even be in the same room as your sister anymore? You've let it get this far?"

My steps halted. I sucked in a breath. Released it, then sucked in another. When my initial rage reduced to simmering anger, I turned. "*I've* let it get this far?" I snapped.

"I'm just saying..."

"That it's always my fault. Right?" I interrupted. "Without even trying to understand shit between us, you assume *I'm* to blame." With my frustration once again mounting, I snatched off my shades, giving an unobstructed view of my bruises. "*Look at my face*! I'm busting my *ass* and risking my career for some shit I didn't even do. Did your innocent little Madi tell you that she just stood there and watched as her baby father and his boys pistol-whipped me? And she *never* checked to see if I was okay. She didn't say shit when they put guns to Jayce and Isa's head! So, excuse the fuck out of me for wanting nothing to do with a bitch who'll never care about anyone other than herself. I've given her more grace than she ever deserved and I don't have any more to give."

My mom watched with bucked eyes, taking in everything I'd had no intention of revealing. It took a few moments before the tears welled above her lids and she closed the distance between us to cup my hands.

My heart thundered as that stupid feeling of hope sparked to life. Was she finally going to see my side of things? Had the blinders finally been removed and she realized that despite what they thought, I was *not* the villain in this story?

"*Eden*, baby." She looked lost for words as her eyes darted all over my face as if just now noticing the evidence from my fight in the Pit. "I'm..." I leaned forward before I could stop myself, eager for her next words. "I'm sure you just misread everything that happened. Madi wouldn't do that. Not to you and *definitely* not to those boys."

The feeling that came over me right then was indescribable. It was as if my world had tilted on its axis and I was scrambling to remain upright. Even after all the other times of having my heart broken by this woman, she still had the power to inflict more damage.

To yank the rug from under my feet.

To reduce me back to the little girl who took on more than I needed to in the hopes of earning any sort of praise or attention.

But just like she'd gotten good at destroying me emotionally without trying, I'd gotten good at hiding my reaction to it. So instead of showing the devastation her words left behind, I fiddled with my nose ring and gave her a curt nod before moving past, only to stop when she gripped my elbow.

That moment of sympathy for my plight disappeared as fast as it had appeared, replaced by irritation. "This has gone on long enough." She scolded, having the nerve to look affronted that I'd tried to walk away. "This little attitude of yours is getting old. Okay? I get that you like holding grudges against Madi, but you gotta learn how to let stuff go."

Moments passed when my mouth hung suspended. Was she... *Nah.* No fucking way was I being scolded for not letting go of everything I'd just revealed.

With a rough yank, I snatched my arm out her grip, ignoring the way she'd stumbled. Again, I tried to walk away but her voice stopped me. "Okay, stay in your feelings. That's your business. But in the meantime, are you too pissed to help your mother? I need the air in my car fixed."

Disbelieving her nerve, I turned around. "What did you just say?"

"I saw your little boxing deal." I didn't even bother correcting her because it'd go in one ear and out the other. "I'm sure they cut you a nice advance check." When all she got was my shocked silence, she sucked her teeth. "You know I wouldn't ask if I didn't need it, Eden."

"Then ask your other daughter." I snapped back. "Better yet, ask that sorry ass husband of yours."

"*Eden...*" She said in a warning tone that I blew right past. Fuck that.

"Mama, I'm going back to what I said months ago. I want nothing to do with y'all outside the boys and this time, I mean that. Dad, Madi, and you too. Don't call me and definitely don't ask me for shit."

Her eyes bucked and she took a step back. "You're really disrespecting me like this? Your *mother*? Over a disagreement?"

"Just let her go, Mama." Madi said as she crossed the parking lot towards us. "Stop trying to make her be part of this family. She chose to be distant so leave her out here where she wants to be... *alone*."

When she was a few feet away, I faced her, pleased at her tiny step backwards. "If you know what's good for you, you'd stay far away from me. I'm feeling like I don't have shit to lose. And the day I feed into it, you're the first person on my hit list so tread lightly."

Her eyes grew wide before she schooled her expression. Then she allowed that stupid look to surface that meant she was about to say something that would test my patience. "You're just *jealous*. I had a baby with your ex! So what? It's *done*. Stop walking around like I'm supposed to bow down and kiss your ass for forgiveness. I've apologized before. I'm not doing it again."

Not acknowledging her speech, I sidestepped to leave, but she blocked my path. "Madi... get the fuck out of my way."

"No, because you're making everybody miserable and I'm sick of mama stressing about your ungrateful ass. You owe..."

Before she completed her thought, her throat was in my grip.

"*Eden*!" My mom yelped but I ignored her, holding my sister's fearful stare.

"I don't owe *shit*." I said in a tone that only she could hear. "Any debts I might've owed have been paid off tenfold. To the 400s. To this fucked up family. Or to anybody who dares to fix their lips and say those words to me."

That darkness that I thought I'd left behind resurfaced and the urge to squeeze until the light faded from her eyes became strong.

Which let me know I was losing it. I was losing *myself* amongst all the chaos and on the verge of reverting to that mindless thing that Barry let off the leash from time to time.

I *never* wanted to go back there so instead of leaving my sister with bruises to match mine, I released her and stepped back.

"This is my last time saying this..." I warned. My emotions warred between pleased and sad at the wary glances they exchanged after glimpsing the malice in my gaze. Neither of them had truly witnessed Menace in full form. But with each insult, jab, nudge, and taunt I took, she was creeping closer to the surface, ready to cause destruction without care or thought.

"If Isaiah or Jayce aren't the topic, do *not* reach out to me. By call, text, email, letter, pigeon carrier... it doesn't matter. Stay the fuck away from me. Understood?"

It took a moment, but they both nodded, still exchanging glances and communicating without words in a way that had never included me.

Before I let that add to the anger I felt, I walked to my car, climbed in, and pulled off.

---

"YOU FINALLY LEFT that Uptown nigga alone?"

My chest tightened at the thought of Hakeem, but I pushed it way down, keeping my expression composed. I refused to let Benji see just how devastated I still was about my situation with that *Uptown nigga*.

Just like every other time I came here, sitting in the visiting room of Thatcher Correctional Facility hadn't been high on my list of things to do.

But my brother called and asked me to come. So here I was.

If he still cared, I'm sure Hakeem would be disappointed to learn I'd shown up, even after our talks about extending grace and time to people who didn't deserve it.

Then again, he probably had already purged my existence from his mind and moved on from our little... *one night stand.*

When Benji realized I wasn't about to give him a response, he shrugged. "I talked to Ma the other day. You need to take it easy on her." When my brows shot up, he leaned forward. "Stop trying to make her choose between you and Madi. Whatever beef y'all have doesn't need to touch her."

I was so... *tired* of hearing that. Nobody ever *asked* her to choose. She did that all on her own.

"You know..." I began, tilting my head with a mocking smile. "You, of all people, know Mama is biased." I leaned forward, narrowing my lids. "I only care about the boys. They are my focus. So fuck whatever mom, dad, or Madi has to say. And if you agree with them, fuck you too."

"*Watch your mouth*!" He snarled, shoving to his feet.

I did the same, getting fed up with men who thought they could always tell me what to do and expecting me to blindly comply. "And if I don't?"

"*Foster*!" The guard near the door barked, slicing his shrewd gaze between my brother and me. Both of us were tight with tension, fists clenched in preparation of the other to make a move.

We'd never exchanged blows, except during petty squabbles as children. Back then, though we'd been angry, neither of us had actually tried to hurt the other. We'd loved one another too much for that.

But that affection was lost long ago and despite the chances of getting locked up with him, I was ready to do damage if he tried me.

"We got a problem over there?"

Both our gazes swung from the guard at the exact same moment, sizing each other up. He was bigger, taller, and likely stronger if the bulging biceps were any indication... but I had professional training and a simmering rage that had been threatening to explode. I liked my chances.

But at the same moment, we seemed to decide to keep the peace, wordlessly sitting but refusing to break the stare we'd locked ourselves in.

Finally, after a few moments, he chuckled under his breath. "That smart ass mouth and mean streak hasn't changed, huh?"

I didn't respond, still seething beneath the surface. That camaraderie between us was lost long ago. I wouldn't be sucked into the trap of him teasing me with our bond before snatching it away again.

Lips still curved upwards in amusement, he continued. "Look... you can focus on your career without the distraction of the boys. That's what you've always wanted, right? To be able to fully commit to your fighting? Now it can be your priority again."

I laughed too but mine lacked the humor that laced his. How can a person I once thought the world of know so little about me? "I'd walk away from fighting today, with no regrets, if I was forced to choose between it and those boys. They're my priority and they always will be. Getting to the league was a dream but those boys are my life, Benji. My *life*!"

He sighed, looking away, allowing the animosity to fade. "I'll talk to 'em, aight? Just don't start crying or no shit."

I rolled my eyes, unable to even muster up thanks. An awkward silence fell, and I tensed when his gaze returned to me, observing the bruises littering my face more closely. The ones lingering from last week's fight.

"I'm sure seeing me like this satisfies you." I said, arms crossed, posture defensive.

I expected Benji's agreement, but I got a squinty-eyed look that confused me. "You really think that?" He asked.

I snorted, rolling my eyes around the mostly empty room. "Benji, you have made it no secret that you hate me."

Anger rolled across his features like a thundercloud. "Don't say shit like that to me."

My neck jerked, surprised at not only the hostility but the words he'd spoken. "Then don't *fuck* with me. You know exactly what I'm talking about. When I first left the 400s, people didn't leave me alone because of anything Rome or Barry said. It was because of *you*. They respected you enough not to come at your sister. But the second they found out you looked at me as a traitor, too? That you didn't care about me? That little protection I had was gone and I became a target."

I fought the sudden surge of tears, not wanting to give that part of myself to my brother. He didn't deserve it. He hadn't earned it, not in a long, long time.

"That's why I called you here!" He snapped. "I'm trying to talk some sense into your silly ass. Trying to get you back in line because you've been going rogue. Not following the plan. You're bringing all this shit on yourself by refusing to *listen*. This *is* me trying to protect you."

I couldn't believe he'd fixed his lips to say that. "I'm just the traitor who abandoned y'all, remember? I'm not protected anymore."

"Yes, the fuck you are." He snapped, surprising me. "I specifically told them not to touch you."

I struggled to find the right words, positive that I'd misheard him. "Why would you do that?"

He sucked his teeth. "Don't ask stupid questions." That sounded like the Benji I knew. An asshole to the very end. "Why do you think?"

"That's what I'm trying to find out." I argued. "I'm not part of the 400s anymore and I'm not *coming* back. So, if you think you're going to manipulate me and my feelings, I'm not falli—"

"Because despite all the dumb shit, you're still my fucking sister, Eden." He cut me off, slamming a hand on the table that earned another glare from the guard. But my brother paid him no mind, too worked up to see anything but me. "You're blood, baby girl."

I flinched at the nickname I hadn't heard in nearly a decade. I'd known Benji, the boy. The younger version of him that I would've given my life for. But this was Benji, the man. The hardened prisoner. I didn't know this person so reading him and his emotions was nowhere as easy as it once was which meant I couldn't tell if she was being genuine. So, I kept my expression clear and tone neutral as I responded. "Did being *blood* matter when they pistol whipped me?" I leaned forward, lowering my voice so we wouldn't be overheard. "Did it matter when they threatened the boys and held guns to their heads?"

My statement was met with more silence. An eerie one that caused the hairs on my arm to rise.

Most of what I knew came from this man.

Most of the dangerous shit that I'd gotten involved in had been with or for him. We'd been an unstoppable duo that shared the same penchant for violence.

Before walking away, I might have been the official enforcer for the 400s, but I wasn't the only one who'd gotten my hands dirty. And while I'd thrived in that position, he'd worked his way up the ranks, damn near having as much pull as Rome before getting locked up.

He licked his lips again and looked away.

"B?" I asked, not liking the array of emotions flashing across his face.

He didn't immediately respond. Instead, his fists clenched while he shifted on the hard seats before taking calming breaths and returned his hard gaze to mine. "Just..." His words trailed as he frowned at the table. "Just stop whatever you're doing, Eden. Stop going rogue and do what you gotta do to keep the boys safe. You claim to care about them so much, then stop doing stupid shit that's putting them in danger."

His audacity was just as bold, frustrating, and hurtful as my mother's. But just like with her, I outwardly remained composed despite the painful clench it caused in my stomach.

"You saying this is my fault?" My tone was so low and even that it sounded foreign leaving my lips. "Madi stealing and getting in debt is my fault? The same debt I'm sacrificing my body for despite what that bitch and Rome did to me?" I laughed and leaned forward, making sure his gaze didn't stray from mine. "Y'all keep testing me, pushing me, *fucking with me...* trying to send me to the point of no return." When I stood, he did too, watching with slightly furrowed brows. For once, he looked wary and I was glad. "I'd hoped coming here today wasn't some bullshit but I was wrong. So, I'm about to tell you the same thing I told your mother and sister. If it ain't about those boys, I don't want to hear from y'all."

His face scrunched. "The fuck is that supposed to mean. You're done with us? Your family?" Then he gave that bitter laugh. "Turning your back on us? *Again*?"

"Let's face it, B. The family turned their backs on me a long time ago. The *family* wanted the benefits of what I did to support and hold it together but still treated me like an outcast. And I'm done with that. The only family I have is Jayce and Isaiah."

His lips flattened, lids narrowing to thin slits as a nasty glint flared in his gaze. A glint that warned me to prepare for a low blow, so I braced, coaching myself to remain unbothered. No matter what he said.

"Who you doing all this for? You ain't a leader or a thinker. You're a tool to be used when everybody else sees fit. You take orders because that's all you're good at. So, this *rah rah* shit you on right now means somebody done put the battery in ya back."

Fuck. Him.

"Who was it, E? That Uptown nigga and his people?" Another of those sinister laughs caused the hairs on my arm to rise. "You over there playing their little bitch now? Because everybody knows you'll do anything if they pretend to care about you. That's why you sitting here cutting off your real family? They sold you a dream of being a part of them or some shit?" His knuckles rapped the tabletop as he stood, smile growing wide with each second I remained silent. "How long you think that fairytale gonna last? Because no matter what, you'll never be one of them."

I held his glare, clenching and unclenching my fists under the table while fighting back tears, pretending not to be bothered by how dangerously close he'd gotten to the truth.

"But I still believe in family over everything. So, we'll waiting for your apology when you come crawling back after they drop your ass like the dead weight you are."

Then, before I could process his words or form a response, he left me standing there and all I could do was watch his retreating back while stewing in my feelings of inadequacy.

# 10

## HAKEEM

I HADN'T BEEN able to get that night out of my mind. I couldn't get *her* out of my mind.

The way we'd left things in the bathroom didn't sit right with me. The entire time she'd eased closer to the door, I'd briefly considered blocking it and forcing her to stay.

But I'd gotten a glimpse of the exhaustion in her gaze. The *pain.*

And I didn't want to add to it. No matter how hard it was to watch her flee from me. I had to let it happen because that's what she'd needed at the moment.

After a quick walk around the property to blow off some steam, I'd discovered her early departure. So I'd gone to check on Verse and Garryn and speak to their security before leaving, too.

Almost a week later, instinct had me leaving the comfort of my secluded home just before midnight, driving deep into White Grove. Dim bulbs along the wall were the only source of light around the perimeter of the dark warehouse.

Every other spotlight was aimed towards the cage in the center of the massive room.

The pungent scent of liquor, cigarettes, and body odor tainted the stale air, making it difficult to breathe.

Despite staying stationary in a corner of the room, a stumbling man who'd been tossing drinks back all night bumped into me. Immediately, I tensed at the contact, cutting my gaze in his direction. He tried to appear tough, meeting my glare head on and pulling himself up to full height. But I remained still, letting violence surface in my gaze.

I knew the unspoken threat was effective when only a second later, a soft sucking of his teeth met my ears before he stalked off.

*That's what the fuck I thought.*

"Damn."

That soft exclamation from the man standing not far from me had my gaze swinging towards the cage.

And there she was, moving swiftly across the floor, stepping through the opening in the chain-link without sparing anyone a glance.

A calming warmth flooded my chest, lifting the heaviness that sometimes settled on me when I got lost in my thoughts.

That curvy body I knew intimately was only covered by a red sports bra and tiny black shorts that fit more like underwear, hugging the plump mounds of her ass.

Standing there, she couldn't look more different than the woman I'd seen at the charity event.

She appeared fierce and *fearless*. None of the vulnerability or softness she'd shown in that bathroom was visible.

Despite being in hostile territory, I wanted to go to her. To grab her. To hug her. Never letting go until that hard shell cracked and exposed the woman I'd fallen for hiding beneath.

Even from this distance, I could see the tension.

Repeatedly, her jaw clenched and because of my obsession with watching her fights online, I recognized that she was in lock down mode.

Those big brown eyes were clear and focused, refusing to blink as she sized up her opponent. The bigger, yet obviously less confident, woman understandably looked nervous as she prepared to battle the hardened warrior opposite her.

Eden's stance was wide and intimidating, giving off the aura of someone several inches taller than her five-foot four frame.

She was beautiful. Devastatingly so.

The woman currently standing in the cage reminded me of the Eden I'd seen at A&K for the first time. No-nonsense, alert, and ready for everything coming her way.

My heart leaped into my throat when the calm, coolness she displayed before the match disappeared as soon as the bell rang. Pure, unfiltered violence replaced that focus and she went on the attack like a wild animal that had been unleashed. Unfortunately for her opponent, there was no referee in the cage to regulate.

These fights were underground for a reason. The list of rules was small and even then, exceptions were made. Damn near everything was legal and Eden... no, *Menace* was taking full advantage.

Loud, bloodthirsty roars filled my ears each time a clenched fist collided with flesh.

Out of instinct, I scanned the room again, trying to find the usual players.

Barry, Rome, and a few long-standing members of the 400s had their own section to themselves, overlooking the cage from their elevated positions.

They watched with hunger in their gazes. Like she was their prized horse in a race on the verge of crossing the finish line.

They didn't even look at her like a person. Or a living being with feelings.

They eyed her like a *thing*. A product they owned.

And watching them watch *her* caused dark feelings to stir. Ones that made me want to walk over and end every single one of them. But common sense told me I had to play it safe. It would be stupid to act rashly and have everything blow up prematurely. Especially if Eden, Jayce, or Isaiah ultimately paid the price for my actions.

Barry and the 400s held nowhere near the level of power that Axel did but they were still connected and had people who might retaliate if every person in a position of power within the organization suddenly came up... *missing*.

A chorus of *oooohs* had my gaze jerking back to the ring right when Eden took a fist to the face. My pulse raced but she kept fighting, blocking, and swinging as if the blow that would've put someone else on their ass was nothing.

It was as if she was so checked out, she didn't even *feel* it.

I leaned forward, separating from the wall when she took another blow to her side. But instead of protecting it, she exposed more of the vulnerable area and her opponent dipped to swing again. The same thing had happened at her fight two weeks ago and she'd taken a nasty blow to the side that left a still visible bruise on her dark skin.

At the same moment, we all caught on that Eden had purposely left that opening, baiting her opponent into taking that cheap shot. And like a streak of lightning, her knee shot up.

There was no doubt in anyone's mind that the fight was over when she made contact. After that blow to the chin, the woman went limp, eyes rolling upwards before collapsing on the mat.

Instead of the boisterous celebration and cheers other competitors gave in to after winning. Eden stared blankly at the crowd before exiting as swiftly as she'd entered.

Instead of relief at being the victor, the tension in her face grew tighter as she entered a door and closed it behind her. I moved closer to the exit, keeping that door in sight.

Minutes passed, maybe three or four, before she reemerged, this time with her bag and Jayce in tow. Like the protector she was, she cupped the back of his head, holding it down so he wouldn't be exposed to all the debauchery going on around him.

With jerky movements, she pushed through the crowd with a slight limp, favoring her ankle. Some people watched with interest while others merely offered congratulations. But she ignored them all, staying alert and glancing over her shoulder periodically as if expecting someone to rush out behind her.

Trailing silently, I followed all the way to the densely packed parking lot, keeping my steps light and frame hidden by shadows.

Despite displaying obvious paranoia, she was still distracted because not once did she notice my presence like she'd done at A&K. Something heavy weighed on her, putting a haunted expression on her face. An expression I didn't like one bit.

And right then, as I watched her taillights disappear around the corner, I made a vow to handle it so she could experience the peace she deserved. I vowed to stand in the gap and take the brunt of whatever had her acting so out of character, just like I'd done with Birdie.

Whether we became an *us* again wouldn't stop me from fixing her problems.

I was going to make everything okay for her and those boys, even if I had to sacrifice myself to do it.

---

"I MIGHT HAVE a one-sided beef with that bitch but she is *bad as fuck*."

A reluctant chuckle burst free after I shook my head, still glaring through tinted windows at the activity down the street. "What are you talking about?"

"Eden's fine ass!" Gia snapped as if annoyed she had to admit the woman was beautiful. "You haven't seen her pictures, yet? The ones from the sports shoot?"

My tongue swiped my bottom lip while I opened the *Snapshot* app. Birdie and Krystal created a page years ago, but I'd never used it. Hell, my profile picture was still the generic one assigned to all new accounts. I had no interest in social media and only kept it open to appease them.

Now, I was grateful I didn't have to go through the tedious task of creating a profile. After clicking Eden's page and not seeing any recent posts, I switched to the VP Sports page and sucked in a low breath.

Eden was... *breathtaking.*

In the three hours since the twelve photos were shared, she'd already surpassed fifty thousand likes. And as I swiped through the gallery, it was easy to see why. The photos highlighted the fact that she'd leaned out, dropping weight in certain areas and packing on impressive muscles in others. Muscles like the ones bunched in her mahogany thighs. The clothing she wore did little to hide the sickening figure I'd had writhing underneath me.

"You found them?"

I nodded. "Yeah." I cleared my throat after that came out hoarse. "*Yeah.*"

"I gotta give her credit, she looks good."

Good was *severely* underselling the devastatingly beautiful woman that was the focal point in the photos.

The first two were in a locker room. Ripped jean shorts covered her lower half while a white towel was slung across her shoulders, covering just the mounds of her breasts and leaving everything else exposed. Gloved hands dangled between her spread thighs as she glared at the camera. Her face was made up, enhancing her already gorgeous features despite the heavy bruising around her bottom lip and eyes.

There was another in a fitted, short red dress and matching heels that displayed her sickening curves as one muscled thigh crossed over the other. Her fingers looped through the fence surrounding the octagon as once again, an intimidating glare hardened her features.

I continued swiping, feeling *something* in my chest flaring to life. I wasn't sure if this unnatural reaction to her would ever ease. And I honestly wasn't sure I wanted it to. However short it was, our time together had been... *special.*

Out of the entire set, my favorite was the last four. In those, she was dressed for a fight. Mouthpiece, wrapped hands, sports bra, shorts, and hair pulled up into a tight bun. Impressive muscles appeared even more defined under her oiled skin and she had her game face on.

The one where her brows dipped slightly in the middle and the corners of her lips downturned with displeasure. Narrowed-lidded and glaring, it was as if she dared whoever was on the other side of the camera to try her. The glint in her gaze promised certain defeat for any challengers.

The last few were captured in the middle of executing a move. It was hard to pick a favorite but if I had to choose, it would be the one where she was midair, one knee lifted in a point while the other leg was extended.

"You got your hand in your pants, don't you?"

Gia's badly timed question jerked me out of my Eden-filled thoughts. "You are a pain in my ass, you know that?"

Her laughter filtered through the phone. "I'm aware."

"Hmm." I muttered, swiping through the photos once more before setting the phone aside and returning my gaze to the group of 400s outside the warehouse, completely unaware of the predator lurking not far away.

If I planned to free Eden from whatever hold they had on her, I needed to learn everything I could.

The easiest option would be just to go to Axel but any information he offered would come at a price. One I didn't want to pay unless it was absolutely necessary. So, for now... I chose to gather information.

While Gia rambled off instructions to her assistant in the background, I watched that ugly muthafucker Crow as he leaned against his motorcycle, rotating a toothpick from side to side. The jerky movements and impatience etched in his features proved he was waiting on someone and they were running late.

"G, let me hit you back." I mumbled, sitting up in my seat, zeroing in on a slight figure approaching on a bike. It was hard to tell whether it was a teen or small woman because a bulky hoodie hid their figure.

"Okay, bye." She responded distractedly, already resuming her conversation before disconnecting the call.

Crow's face contorted into an even uglier scowl as he approached the bike, pointing his finger to display his frustration. Whoever it was simply nodded and that seemed to set Crow off. He grabbed their arm and yanked hard enough for the hood to fall back.

My heart sank as I immediately recognized the person. *Isaiah.*

Still fussing, Crow grabbed something from behind his back and passed it to the teen who quickly stuffed it into the dangling bookbag.

Crow finally flicked away the toothpick, saying one more thing to Isaiah that caused his head to hang before they left in opposite directions. Crow's motorcycle roared as it zoomed down the block while Isaiah trudged along, pushing his bike.

Starting up my truck, I followed at a distance in case someone was watching. Once sure the coast was clear, I pulled my truck right alongside him.

He tensed before glancing over, eyes going wide with shock after spotting me through the open window. It lasted only a moment before his expression closed off into one I recognized. One I'd seen his aunt don more times than I could count.

I'd been so absorbed with my own feelings after the blowup between Eden and I that I hadn't considered how he and Jayce were affected. Jayce might have noticed my absence, but he was still young enough not to be too affected. But Isaiah and I *bonded*.

He'd opened himself up and shared things he'd probably never told his aunt before. Things I'm sure that had taken a shitload of courage to reveal. Like his hurt behind his father's incarceration and his mom who never seemed to have time. How he felt like a burden on his aunt because he knew she'd give her last so he and Jayce could have whatever they needed.

"Get in."

"Why?" His lids narrowed and I bit my lip to hide my smile. The kid had so much fucking heart.

"I'm not asking, Isa."

"*Isaiah*." He corrected, letting me know I no longer had the privilege of using his nickname. That my absence had removed any connections we might've made. "And I'm only getting in because I need a ride home anyway."

Biting back a grin, I got out and loaded his bike before pulling off once he buckled. Eyes on the road, I held my hand in his direction, palm up.

"Give it to me."

"Huh?" His tone was affronted but held a tinge of fear. "Give *what* to you?"

"Isaiah," I emphasized. "I'm not asking."

There was a bit of grumbling before he reluctantly reached into the front zipper of his backpack and pulled out something that nearly made me swerve off the road.

A fucking gun. Taurus 9 mm, to be exact.

"What the fu—" I cut myself off, taking a moment to calm my flaring temper. "Why do you have this?"

Instead of answering, he scowled. "Were you watching me?"

"I'm asking the questions."

His shoulders sagged and he sucked his teeth before slouching in his seat. "I gotta protect myself." Then his eyes glazed over and his lips trembled. "I gotta protect my aunt."

I took another moment, wanting to make sure I had the right words before speaking. Now was not the time to spew the jumbled shit that popped in my mind at the worst times. I needed to handle this situation delicately because despite my anger, I understood the helplessness he felt with the need to protect himself and his loved ones from danger. But just like with his aunt, I wanted to be the one to stand in the gap. To be on the frontline of whatever attacks they faced that made him feel like a gun was necessary.

"What do y'all need protection from?"

Briefly, vulnerability peeked through. Though it lasted only a second, I recognized the cry for help. "Can I get it back?" He asked instead, holding out his hand. "What we got going on ain't your business. You proved that already."

I frowned in confusion. "How?"

He tensed again before jerking his gaze away. "When you left... like everybody else does. She got hurt and she didn't have anybody to protect her. *Nobody* protects her! So I'm going to do it."

He didn't know that I'd damn near begged his aunt to let me in. To tell me what was wrong so I could help. I hadn't expected the affiliation with the 400s and could admit the way I'd handled it could've been better. But I wanted her to let me in but .

"What happened? How did they hurt her?"

"Why?" His face scrunched. "You from Uptown right? I can't trust you."

I wondered if Eden had put that shit in his head before immediately shoving the thought away. I knew better than that. From what I'd seen, she went above and beyond to protect the boys from anything 400-related.

"You really believe that?" I questioned, flicking on my right turn signal. "I know I fu— messed up by walking away. And if I gotta make up for that, I will. But you really think you can't trust me? You think I'll do something to hurt you, Jayce or your aunt?" I didn't show it but I was on pins and needles waiting for his response. My gut tightened as I braced.

If he believed I'd harm them, I couldn't stomach that shit. I didn't know how I'd come back from that.

"No." He grumbled reluctantly. "But that don't mean you won't leave her again when she really needs you."

I had to remind myself to look at the situation through the lens of Isaiah. A kid who thought the world of his aunt. A kid who'd had a front row seat to her struggles and probably saw her truly happy for the first time with me. And then the aftermath of it all when we came to an end.

"Look, Isa..."

"*They hurt her*!" His eyes grew wild and wet as he pounded his fist against his leg. "They threatened us and kept us apart. I haven't seen her in weeks!" He continued, letting his words fall freely. "They won't let us see her unless she wins at that fight club. I hate this!"

My anger swelled so fast it nearly choked me.

Eden was walking around with the weight of the fucking world on her shoulders. Yet she still found the strength to keep going. To get up every morning and do what needed to be done.

She constantly sacrificed and gave up so much. Her own feelings rarely mattered when making decisions. It was always for others and it made me feel sick to think that the only time she allowed herself to be selfish was with me. She'd known her secrets could possibly put an end to us so she kept them so she could enjoy what we'd had.

And at the end, I'd condemned her for it. I'd threatened her and walked away without a backward glance.

The rest of the ride went by in silence because I didn't trust myself with words at the moment. Not after what I'd just heard. Isaiah sitting next to me was the only thing keeping me from busting a U-turn and ending every nigga in that warehouse.

Starting from the top.

But unlike the first time I went on a rampage against the 400s, kids were involved. Kids whose lives would irrevocably change, no matter what action I took.

So, I pushed my bloodthirsty thoughts for revenge aside, using the rest of the ride to think.

Thankfully Isa's moment of anger left him calmer and more reserved, giving the silence I needed. Now he seemed more subdued. Drained and regretful of what he'd revealed.

But it was out now and there was no taking it back. Now, it was up to me to take care of the rest so he didn't feel like he had to.

"You still got my number?"

His wet, red-rimmed eyes swung to mine then back towards the complex I'd parked in front of.

"How'd you know I lived here?"

I didn't give him an answer. He didn't need to know I'd made it my business to learn everything about his aunt after our separation. Filling in even the tiniest blanks of Eden's life had become an obsession.

"Do you still have my number?" I asked again.

"Maybe."

The grumble proved that he did but I made a point in sending him a text just in case. A satisfied smirk lifted the corner of my lips when a faint ding emerged from his backpack.

"Call me if you need anything, a'ight? And don't worry about your aunt. I'm gonna handle that."

He hesitated with his palm hovering right over the door handle. "You gonna keep her safe?"

"I'm gonna try my best."

His expression hardened. "That's not enough." That wild look appeared in his eyes again as he bounced his gaze between my face and the door he wanted to escape from. "Promise me that you'll keep her safe. If you won't let me do it my way, then *promise* me you won't let them hurt her again." Then, for a second, desperation softened his gaze. "*Please.*"

There was no hesitation on my part. Though I hated making promises, this was one I intended to keep.

"I swear to you, I'll keep her safe."

# 11

# EDEN

***Age 19***

"SO YOU JUST STOOD THERE and did nothing?"

I crossed my legs to stop my fidgeting lower half. Normally, I'd try to be more composed but I couldn't. Not when the blood I'd spilled still felt fresh on my hands.

The urge to reveal the truth burned me from the inside but I pressed my lips together, nodding slowly.

"I knew you were simple-minded, but I didn't take you for *weak*."

Where I once would've exploded with uncontrollable anger at the accusation, I sat quiet, tensing each time Rome's arm brushed me as he paced back and forth. Mine were folded across my chest, eyes aimed at the floor as the silence coming from his uncle, Barry, set my nerves on edge. I loved Rome but I hated the control his uncle had over him. Therefore, I hated the control he had over *me*.

Especially in moments like these when I normally would have swung at the disrespect falling from his lips.

"Tell me what happened again." Barry ordered, not bothering to hide his dislike.

Instinctively, my eyes flicked to Benji but Rome yanked my chin, forcing my gaze back to his. "Don't fucking look at him."

"There were some guys at the party." I began softly. "One of them tried to talk to me and I turned him down. He didn't want to take no for an answer, so he tried to grab me." My stomach clenched in memory of the harsh grip that I'd thought I wouldn't be able to escape. "Benji ran over. Dude tried to pull a gun but his friend told him not to. Too many people were around. They argued but eventually moved on." I paused to wet my lips, trying to remember what Benji had instructed me to say. "Later on, we were getting ready to leave and they jumped him by the car." Everything up until this point was true. But now, it was time for me to do something I abhorred... *lie*. Just so my brother could get respect and credit for something he didn't do. "He reached for his gun again, but Benji pulled his out first and shot. Once they were down, we hopped in the car and left."

There was terse silence after I finished, and I wondered if I'd been convincing enough. I'd stuck as close to the facts as possible, keeping what I said simple so it would be easy to recall if I had to repeat it.

"And what were you doing?"

I lied again as I met Barry's gaze. "Nothing."

"So, you stood there and did *nothing* while your brother was getting jumped?"

Rome gripped my chin again in that threatening way he loved, glaring directly into my gaze. "You lying to us?"

I shook my head, keeping my expression earnest because I knew he could read me. It must've worked because seconds later, he sucked his teeth and pushed me away from him. Anger bubbled up at the rough, yet familiar treatment, but I knew not to go at him in front of his uncle. Rome knew it too because he smiled, fully aware that I wanted to attack.

Our relationship was toxic and violent but I loved him regardless.

He'd given me a home within the 400s and looked out for me in his own way. He was *family* and I was brought up on the mantra of family over everything. And nothing would come between that.

"Good job, B." Barry said to my brother, who puffed his chest out with undeserved pride. "Come and see me tomorrow at the warehouse. I might have a job for you." Then his expression soured as he turned back to me. "Get her out of my face." Benji turned to leave and Rome and I followed, stopping only when Barry called him back.

My boyfriend froze, looking torn between the two of us before he made his decision. "Go straight home. I'll see you later."

Again, I bristled at the command but followed his order, trailing silently behind my brother. The disappointment in the room was palpable and I knew I'd be paying for what they believed happened for quite a while.

It wasn't until we'd gotten a few minutes down the street that I burst into tears.

Unlike the lies I'd told minutes earlier, Benji was not the one who'd pulled the trigger. Those two men *had* jumped him by the car and when one of them reached for his gun, I pulled mine first. I was familiar with weapons. It was hard not to be when Rome kept them all over his place. But hitting a target at a shooting range didn't even come close to the feeling I got when the bullets from my gun entered those two men.

I froze afterwards, eyes bucking wide and stomach violently rolling with nausea as they collapsed. Before I could dwell on what I'd done, Benji pushed me into the car and drove off.

Less than an hour later, we'd been standing in front of Barry, lying about what happened because my brother was too embarrassed to admit the truth. I don't know how I managed to hold it together but now, the adrenaline was wearing off and my emotions were at war with themselves.

"Benji, I shot them. I *killed* them."

Instead of the comfort I was seeking, he pulled to a stop right in the middle of the road. With the same rough grip Rome had handled me, he yanked until I leaned across the center console, nearly nose to nose with him. "You didn't do shit, remember?" His hand squeezed my face. "I shot them, right? *Not you.*" I nodded, sniffing and swiping at my runny nose. "Toughen the fuck up." His words were mean and nasty. I'd seen him treat others like this but never *me.* I'd thought I was the exception but obviously not. "You want to be part of this shit? Then act like it. Don't bitch up."

I held his gaze, knowing he could see the flood of tears threatening to spill. And for a moment, one brief moment, his hard gaze softened and the Benji I loved peeked through. Then, as if it never happened, the hardness returned.

Without another word, he shoved me back into my seat and I used Luke's lessons to help me block off my emotions. I couldn't afford to be upset about what happened because in everyone's eyes, I was a coward. In their eyes, I'd let my brother get jumped by a rival gang without stepping in. Benji had earned their respect while I'd be viewed as the weak link that left him hanging.

Though none of it was true, I'd never tell them that. My brother had been working hard to earn their respect and I'd given him the perfect opportunity for it. Even if it was at my expense. Now I was back at square one, fighting to not be counted out simply because I was a woman.

But I'd earned their respect once. I could do it again. All I had to do was step up and be what they needed me to be.

What the *family* needed me to be.

That wasn't such a hard sacrifice to make when I knew they had my back, too.

---

A WEARY SIGH rushed from my lips as hot water cascaded down my shoulders.

I'd been inside the frosted, rectangular shower of the master bath for the last twenty minutes, washing away the stress of the day.

"*Call from... Mo.*"

The robotic voice coming from my waterproof speaker startled me when the R&B music I'd been listening to stopped. With a frown, I stepped out of the spray of the water to answer.

"Hello?"

"Have you called him?"

I sighed and shook my head, elevating my voice to be heard over the shower. "No." I'd spoken to her several time over the last two weeks about my... *run-in* with Hakeem. She wasn't the biggest fan of any reconciliation between us because of how things ended the first time.

"Do you want to?"

I scoffed, resting my forehead against the glass. "So bad..."

Leaving him after the charity event had been hard and I'd been craving his touch ever since.

"On one hand, I want you to reach out because I want you to be happy and I *know* he made you happy." I sensed there was more to her statement so I waited her out. "Can I be honest?" I could imagine the pursed lips and hiked brows as she spoke. "You and I both know you've been off your game. With everything going on right now, you honestly can't afford another distraction. Your first fight is coming up in *eleven* days. Your dream is finally about to come true. Stay *focused.* Don't let anything come in and distract you. Not right now. Not when you're so close. You need to focus on that fight. And I'm not too sure whether his presence will take away or add to your distraction." Hesitation on my part had her sucking her teeth. "What is it? Your ass ain't shy so don't start now."

I snickered. "What if..." I paused, then licked my lips. "What if fighting doesn't make me happy anymore?"

"Do you want to stop?"

I sighed. "I can't stop, Mo. I've put too much into this. It would be stupid to walk away now."

"What do you want, Eden?" She asked in a tone that had me bracing. "Do you even love fighting anymore? Or are you just doing it because it would feel like you've wasted all the time you've put into it? What do *you* want? What will make *you* happy? You've gotta ask yourself those questions and then go after it." I wasn't expecting the conversation to go this way but I was listening to every word she spoke. "You've got to stop sleepwalking through life. Stop letting shit happen *to* you. Stop putting everybody else and their problems first. Start looking at shit with the mindset of if this isn't going to benefit me, fuck it."

"Fuck it?"

"*Fuck it*." She emphasized. "You've spent too much time making sure everybody else was taken care of while neglecting yourself. You're in a once-in-a-lifetime opportunity and I don't even think you're enjoying it because of all the outside shit going on. It's *okay* to be selfish sometimes."

"I hear you." I muttered, wondering if I was truly capable of developing a selfish mindset. All I'd *ever* done was put myself last.

The buzz of my doorbell echoed through the room, saving me from forming a response. I frowned, knowing damn well I hadn't invited anyone over. As a matter of fact, I hadn't even lived here long enough to give anyone my address.

"Somebody's at the door." I mumbled, shutting off the water and climbing out. "I gotta go."

"Um hmm, bitch. Don't run from this conversation."

Unable to resist, I laughed while slipping on my robe. I already knew she'd let me have it later. "Bye."

A second later, the front door opened and slammed shut, sending me into motion. Just like in White Grove, I had weapons stashed throughout the condo and reached for one as I stepped into the hallway. Out of instinct, I walked on the balls of my feet as I crossed the floor, not wanting to alert whoever it was that I was coming down the hall.

With my gun aimed, I walked through the condo, clearing each room until I reached the kitchen.

Turning the corner, I froze at Rome and Crow leaning against my bar, sipping from the crystal glasses that had been a housewarming gift from Joy. Along with an open, very expensive, out of my price range bottle of limited edition 54th & Lennix Cognac from Verse.

"How did you get in?" I asked calmly despite the adrenaline and anger plaguing me.

"Must be losing your touch," Crow chuckled. "Or you've gotten too comfortable. Front door was unlocked."

I parted my lips to immediately argue, refusing to believe I was *that* careless.

Then again, I had been distracted and exhausted after the tough session I'd had with my trainer today. I honestly didn't doubt that I might have walked in without double checking. "Why are you here?" I asked, directing my attention to Rome, refusing to acknowledge Crow.

"Just wanted to let you know, I can still get to you, love." My ex said with a grin. "Even all the way out here." He took a small sip from the glass, then held it out, eyeing the brown liquid. "Might not fuck with that nigga but he makes a *damn* good bourbon."

Crow chuckled, pouring another glass.

I should've known they would never let me have a moment of peace. They felt like they owned me. Like they'd *made* me which gave them free reign over my life.

"They set you up with a nice place, baby. Might need to have a sleepover."

"*Rome.*"

"Crow, give us a minute." He said in a short tone that had his friend glancing at him in confusion. But Rome's gaze never strayed from mine as he suddenly turned serious.

He stood once the door closed, crowding my space. Instead of retreating, I stood my ground, frowning up at him, wondering what the fuck he wanted now.

"You still do it for me." He mumbled, then tilted his head expectantly. A rare show of tenderness and affection softened his hard features.

My nose scrunched before I laughed. "Am I... am I supposed to be flattered by that? I still *do it for you*?" I snorted out another laugh that had him grimacing. "I don't give a fuck about what I still do for you because you don't do a *damn* thing for me."

The brief softness fled, replaced by irritation as his hand shot up to grip my cheeks. He wasn't squeezing to the point of pain but the tight grip caused discomfort. "You're so ungrateful." He sneered, getting so close to my face that the rush of air from his breath caused my lashes to flutter. "Do you have any idea of what I do for you? How I've kept you safe? Kept you protec—"

His words trailed as his entire frame stiffened when the barrel of my gun touched his chin. I'd held his gaze, letting him vent while easing the weapon into position.

It took only a moment before familiar smugness returned. "You won't do it." He taunted in a sure tone. "You'll never pull the trigger. Not on *me*."

I returned his smile, holding his stare, enjoying the slow drain of his grin until what seemed to be *hurt* contorted his features.

"You'd actually shoot me if you could get away with it?" Then he dropped his grip on my face, rubbing the center of his chest with a pained expression. "You'd really shoot... *me*?"

"Without hesitation."

He searched my face as if hoping for an indication that I wasn't being truthful. But what he found had him taking a step backwards, which I followed keeping the gun tucked nicely under his chin.

"Eden. *Baby*. I know we've had our issues in the past, but this is our thing. We do this back-and-forth shit." He had the nerve to look affronted. As if I'd wronged *him* somehow. "You let that Uptown nigga and his people turn you against me to the point that you'd actually pull the trigger. On me?"

For a moment, I lost control of my composure, mouth dropping open in shock.

My initial thought was to explain for the thousandth time why I felt the way I did but I simply shook my head, not in the mood for his shit.

Instead, I removed myself from his space. Rome was truly delusional and I didn't need him reading into anything that wasn't there.

"Just go, Rome. I'm not dealing with whatever you're trying to do. Not tonight."

Still maintaining that look of hurt, he pulled out his phone, dialing almost robotically before lifting it to his ear. "Bring him in."

Minutes later, Crow returned with Jayce in tow. Like always, he scrambled down, running full speed towards me, slamming into my legs.

It had only been a few days but his head dug into my waistline, as if he'd grown taller.

"Hey, big boy."

His head lifted, chin propping against me as he beamed a wide smile. That same wide smile that got him whatever he wanted.

Surprisingly, Crow left without tossing any insults or sneers my way. But Rome crowded my space once again, resting one hand gently on my waist as he kissed my temple.

When I immediately tensed, his grip tightened as he spoke in a tone low enough that only I could hear.

"You and I both know Madi isn't fit to be a parent. Jayce sees you as his mother, baby. He misses *you*. He cries all the time when he's with her. He won't talk. Barely eats or sleeps."

Despite being a manipulative bastard, I knew this was one time he was being truthful. I could see the evidence of Jayce's neglect each time he returned to me. The bags under his eyes and ravenous appetite. The almost excessive clinginess and near paranoia each time I left the room. The full-blown tantrums or out-of-character silence he portrayed when it was time for him to go back with his parents.

My baby boy was suffering. And it killed me, knowing I was helpless to do anything to stop it.

"He needs you." He continued in that deceptively gentle tone. A tone that had rarely been directed towards me during our relationship. "And I'm willing to let you have him all the time. I know you have your fighting and training and shit but when you're free, he can be with you like always."

"In exchange for?" I asked, knowing the price would be one too steep to pay.

"Bringing your ass back *home*." That soft, gentle tone turned harsh. "Stop fucking around like you don't know you're going to be right back with me. I don't know how many times I have to tell you that. We're in this forever. Eden. Fuck all that dumb shit. You're *mine*."

My stomach tensed at having unlimited access to Jayce dangled in my face again. But going back to Rome, giving myself to him couldn't happen. I was still picking up the pieces of my life, my sanity, and my self-esteem. All of the progress I'd made would be lost if I gave him that power over me again. So I pushed back the tears that threatened to fall at the words I *had* to say. "I'll have him back on Monday, as planned."

His big frame jerked, neck rearing back in disbelief that I'd made that choice. He searched my gaze, desperate for any hint of hesitation. When he didn't find any, he scoffed and turned away, running a hand repeatedly over his waves.

Even though I hadn't been intimate with this man in years, I still recognized that my decision hurt his feelings. He never expected me to choose the current arrangement over getting back with him and having full access to Jayce.

And as bad as I wanted more time with my baby, I just couldn't do it.

Rome sniffed then did it again, clenching and unclenching his fist in the way that let me know he was trying to suppress his anger.

Then that grill flashed as he donned a smile that didn't reach his eyes. "*A'ight.* I'm not gonna push you right now. You need your space and I'll respect that." He nodded towards his son who hadn't looked at him once while clinging onto me. "You can keep him for a while." When I bristled in anticipation of some ridiculous demand, he chuckled. "You can relax. I'm not going to make you do some crazy shit. Despite what you think, I do care about my son and know that being with you is what's best for him."

I didn't miss the distinction in him saying he *cared* about his son, not that he loved him. But after knowing the man standing in front of me for nearly half my life, I doubted whether he was capable of loving anyone.

He couldn't. Not if he was so willing to hurt the people he so-called loved.

"Crow's going to reach out soon. It's about a meeting Barry needs you at. Make sure you answer, *a'ight?*" When I merely pursed my lips, he sucked his teeth. "Work with me, Eden. *Fuck.* Even though you give me shit, I'm going against my uncle's orders again. For you."

When he pointedly stared at his son, I huffed out a breath, skin crawling at having to play nice. "I'll *answer.*"

He nodded once, scanning me again then returning his gaze to mine. His lips parted as if he wanted to say something else but he stopped himself, never glancing at his son again as he left.

Once the door closed, Jayce finally pulled back and I squatted, grinning when he cupped my cheeks and kissed my nose. "Hey Tee."

I laughed to smother a sob, pulling him into a tight hug that he eagerly reciprocated. "Hey, my love."

"I cried a lot." He said in such a sweet tone that it broke my heart. "Because I missed you."

"Aww, I missed you too, baby." Then I kissed his face repeatedly, grinning at the explosion of giggles. "I missed you *soo* much."

# 12

# HAKEEM

"You fucking with Menace again?"

I froze halfway into my seat, narrowing my gaze at Axel. Did he have someone tailing me or Eden? I wouldn't put it past him. Axel always did whatever the hell he wanted with little thought or care about how anyone else felt.

"Why?" I asked instead, refusing to give an answer. Especially when I didn't have one. Would I classify our recent encounters as *fucking with her again*? No. But did I have every intention of fully reinserting myself back into her orbit?

*Absolutely.*

The brooding man across from me didn't answer my question either. Instead, he twisted the monitor on his desk in my direction.

On the screen, a video played. It showed a dark figure climbing out of a black SUV and approaching a familiar restaurant. Before stepping in, their head twisted around, observing the quiet street. Then, after a few quick movements, they bypassed the locked door and stepped inside.

Axel clicked a few times and another video appeared, this one showing the back office of that same restaurant where a middle-aged man sat behind a desk, working by lamplight.

Moments later, the figure stepped in the doorway, gun out and aimed at the man who froze. They wore all black, hat brim pulled low, blocking most of their face. An oversized hoodie covered their torso while baggy sweats tried to hide the feminine figure underneath. The hood pulled over the hat kept their features hidden from the camera but I'd had damn near every inch of that body in my mouth at some point. Even with all the cloak and dagger, it took only a few moments to realize that the hooded figure was Eden.

The same Eden who'd been shaking hands with some of the elites in the entertainment world not that long ago. The same Eden who sometimes came off as shy moved with utmost confidence.

Audio didn't accompany the video, but I could make out the movement of the man's mouth. A second later, she backhanded him and he launched at her. I found myself leaning forward, watching them tussle. It didn't take long for Eden to gain the upper hand, throwing vicious blows at the face of the man who outweighed her by at least fifty pounds. The last blow knocked him on his ass and she straddled him, pressing the gun right between his eyes.

Immediately, the man pointed across the room. She quickly leapt up, keeping her head lowered while searching the drawers, gun staying trained on him the entire time. She must've found what she was looking for because she stuffed something in the pocket of her hoodie before facing him again.

More words were exchanged and she fired a warning shot, hitting the lamp and submerging the room in complete darkness. By the time the man had scrambled to his feet and turned on the light switch, she was already gone.

I knew something was wrong with me when I felt a stirring in my groin. Despite annoyance at *what* she was doing, seeing her like that... so commanding and ruthless, called to the darkness inside me and the spark of lust from earlier returned.

I didn't want to alert Axel or War to the lustful thoughts clouding my mind, so I leaned forward, pausing the video myself.

"Tell me, Hakeem." Axel said in a deceptively calm tone. "Who do you think that was in the video?" He knew better than to expect an answer, so he went back to the first video, pointing at the name of the restaurant. "You recognize this neighborhood?"

Of course, I did. Pop's Place was a staple in the Red District, an area run by the Redz, a bitter rival of the 400s.

"All it took was two or three plays before I realized who it was. How long do you think it's going to take them to figure it out?"

Eden had done everything right. She'd kept her face hidden. She wore baggy clothes to disguise her figure and she'd kept any tattoos or distinguishable markings covered up.

For anybody else, that would've been enough. But for her, the sole woman in an arena where mostly men dwelled, it wouldn't be hard to narrow down the list of suspects.

"Ain't too many women in this shit, Keem. Especially with hands like those." He paused, waiting for me to say something but I didn't. I was too busy working the situation out in my mind, brainstorming ways to get her out of the brewing shitstorm unharmed. Axel wasn't too fond of being ignored so I wasn't surprised when his frown deepened. "What's stopping me from giving them the go ahead to put a bullet in that bitch?"

Before he could blink, I had the collar of his shirt fisted in my grip. "Watch your mouth."

A light tap against the back of my head revealed War had his gun out and aimed my way. I hadn't heard him move but didn't acknowledge him. All my focus was on the man who had the power to send everybody in the tri-city after Eden.

"Whatever the fuck she is or *isn't* doesn't matter to me. What matters is her shaking down shit that ain't in her jurisdiction." He spoke through clenched teeth before sighing. "You mind letting go?" I held on a moment longer before releasing his shirt. We both resumed our seats and he flicked an irritated glance my way while smoothing the wrinkled material.

"My job is to keep peace, balance, and *order*. And I've done it successfully." A dry laugh rumbled free before he continued. "The last time shit got crazy was when *you* went on a suicide mission trying to take out the 400s by yourself." All traces of humor disappeared as quickly as they'd appeared. "You might get a free pass with me, Keem but don't think that means everybody you know will too."

I knew Eden's reason for being in that shop had something to do with the debt she felt she owed the 400s. But what I couldn't make sense of was Barry's motivation for moving on that territory.

Anyone who was aware of the two organizations knew they didn't get along and had been dueling it out just as long as White Grove and Uptown had. The smallest disagreement had the potential to set things off. So breaking in, beating up the owner, and taking money from one of the staple restaurants in their community would incite a full blown war if Axel didn't stop it from happening.

"I'll be working my own angle to find out what the hell Barry is up to but in the meantime..." He paused for his usual dramatic effect before continuing. "Find out what the fuck she's doing, why she's doing it, and put a stop to it. I don't care what Barry is threatening her with. Keep her ass out of shit that doesn't concern her. This is my *only* warning."

I bristled at the command in his tone but held my composure. I understood his frustration and when it came to Eden and this situation, I shared it a bit. "I'll find out."

"You better because you don't want me to step in. Get that shit under control or I will."

"I *said I'll* handle it. You just keep the heat off her back until I do."

"Excuse me?" Axel frowned. "I'm giving you the opportunity to save her damn life and you're making demands of me? Telling me what I need to do?" He laughed incredulously then looked at War. "This nigga has *nerve*."

"Don't act like you're doing me any favors. You owe me just like I owe you."

"But I don't owe *her* shit."

"If you want to keep the peace, then you better treat her like you do. You know what I'm capable of. You know what I'll do if somebody comes for what's mine."

A grin stretched his cheeks and I clenched my fist, fighting back the urge to punch that smug look right off his face. "Oh she's yours again? When did this happen? Because from what I remember, you fucked that up."

If I was being completely honest, I knew she'd been mine during our separation, just like I was hers. She'd never stopped being mine and this time around, I'd do things better. Be better for her. I'd be exactly what she needed so that if trouble did come, she knew I was the safe place for her to run to. The place where she could lay down her burdens because she knew my shoulders were big and broad enough to carry them.

"Don't worry about it." I said, "Just know that she is."

This time around, I wouldn't give her the opportunity to keep secrets.

This time I was going to make sure I saved Eden from whatever haunted her, even if she didn't want to save herself.

"What's your angle?" I asked the smug man who'd reclined in his chair.

"My angle?"

I had to find a way to get the truth out of Axel. He never did anything on a whim. He never acted or put anything in motion without having every step of his plan already outlined. Which meant only he could explain what was going on in that manipulative mind of his.

"Why show me this? Why give me the heads up?"

"Why not?"

It took a surprising amount of control not to let my frustration show. I'd never been a fan of the mind game bullshit he liked to pull. "I know there's something bigger at play. There always is with you."

His gaze slipped upwards, as he pretended to think before looking at me again. "Just felt like it."

"Why?" Then I added a sarcastic, "She got a connection to you too or something?"

"*I wish.* Because I could use a talent like hers. But no. Unfortunately, I don't give a single fuck about her life." When I tensed at his words, he leaned forward, all pretenses of charm gone as he spoke candidly. "You know the people I actually give a fuck about is extremely small." His gaze didn't sway from mine as he continued. "Lucky for you, your name falls in that very exclusive club."

Axel loved his grandparents and maybe even his younger brother, who he rarely spoke to. And I figured he, at least, *cared* for War because they'd grown up together just like Verse and I had. But I'd never thought in a million years his affection would extend to me.

We'd spent years side by side; I knew where his bodies were buried just like he knew where mine were. But it had always felt like business.

"I know you like to think of our years together as an employee and employer relationship, but we were more than that. We might not be brothers like you and Verse but you're still family. My granddad always looked at you as more than an enforcer and so did I."

Still, my skepticism couldn't be ignored. Despite his words, Axel didn't do *anything* that didn't benefit him.

"So... this out of the kindness of your heart? Simply because I'm in the small circle of people that you'd mourn if they died?"

"Let's not get carried away." That manipulative smirk returned and I crossed my arms, waiting for whatever his angle was. I knew there'd been one. "I'm not *that* damn nice, Keem. Don't insult me."

My lips twitched with the urge to laugh. Despite his many, *many* shortcomings, Axel *had* been there for me. And like he'd said, the time we'd worked together hadn't been *all* bad.

"Am I allowed to know how this will benefit you? Or is that also on a need-to-know basis?"

"Barry's been going off script." He said. "Acting reckless. Fostering deals I didn't approve of. Going behind my back and holding secret meetings with the other leaders. Meetings he thinks I don't know about." His fingers drummed rhythmically on the desktop as he genuinely seemed irritated by his own words. "Meetings he's forcing a *certain* woman to stand in on."

My stomach sank as I pictured her, all five-foot, four inches going head-to-head with a man my size if one of those meetings went south. Women enforcers weren't unheard of but one her size was.

My heart, the muscle that I hadn't even thought existed before meeting her, pounded wildly with the need to protect. To ensure the safety of what's... *mine*.

"So, what are you doing about Barry?"

His lips lifted as he shrugged, keeping his secrets close to the chest. Like always. "You already know how I'll answer, so I'll save us both from having to hear it."

I shrugged. "And that's fine. Keep your secrets. But don't fuck me over because of your obsession with being the puppet master."

His lips parted to argue but I cut him off. "I don't give a fuck about your neutral status. And I don't give a fuck that you don't want to seem like you're picking sides." I didn't envy his position, being the one who kept all the organized crime leaders in line. That shit had to be stressful when stupid, petty arguments could spark the next gang war and fuck up everybody's money.

At the end of the day, it was up to him to prevent things from escalating to that point.

Sometimes that meant fostering deals to satisfy both parties. Other times that meant going in with guns blazing, putting down anyone who disagreed with his ruling or tried to buck the system.

It was a fine line he had to tiptoe and being seen as anything other than a neutral party would unbalance the whole thing. Declaring me as protected all those years ago had already put him on

Barry's bad side and we both knew that intervening again could be seen as an act of war.

"I'll try my best." He finally said.

I was shaking my head before he even finished his sentence. "That's not good enough."

His eyes flicked to War, as if waiting for him to back him up. But, like always, War remained quiet, arms folded and lips pressed together. The only deviation from his normally blank expression was the curiosity lifting his brows, as if itching to see how this would play out.

"I won't show favoritism to you." He pointed out.

Again, I shrugged. "Not asking you to." When he sighed with exasperation, I crossed my arms, widening my stance as I met his glare. "I'm simply asking for a warning. A heads up."

Though he pretended to think about it for a few moments, I already knew that his mind was made up. Axel lived for his role as the puppeteer and even with something as small as this, he couldn't resist flexing the strings a bit.

"I can do that."

Before he could change his mind or request something from me in exchange, I was already heading towards the exit, pulling out my phone as it rang in my pocket. "I'm gonna hold you to it."

Then I left, lifting the phone to my ear as I jogged down the steps.

"Keem?" The low tone on the other end had my brows furrowing.

"Isaiah?"

"Come pick me up, man."

I pulled the phone away, frowning at it. "What?"

"I got into a fight. *Come get me.*"

I didn't know what made him call me of all people but knew it wasn't without good reason. "I'm on my way."

---

"SO you still ain't saying shit?"

Isa pretended not to hear, just like he'd done since I picked him up in front of the convenience store where his clothes had been disheveled and bottom lip busted. Now he sat at my dining table, freshly showered and steadily avoiding my gaze.

The tough teen had been trying to maintain his composure but the watery eyes gave away how upset he was.

"What happened?" Like expected, he avoided my gaze and shrugged again.

I wasn't the person for this shit. A man like me, who loved silence, had no clue how to get him talking. A man like me had no clue how to get another person to express their *emotions*.

"You want to go to your aunt's house?" I offered, expecting a quick yes, especially after our last encounter when he'd admitted to not seeing her in weeks.

But after a moment of hesitation, he shook his head. "Nah... can I... can I stay here?"

I couldn't help the frown that overtook my face. "Your mama know where you're at?"

He sucked his teeth then slouched in the chair. "She's at work and she's *never* home so she won't notice I'm gone."

The familiar despair on his face had my stomach tightening. I'd had similar thoughts about my own mother. But where his worked to support him, mine used all her income to support her habit, leaving me to fend for myself. "My mom was an addict." I said in a gruff tone that betrayed my discomfort.

His head whipped towards me. "My mom's not on *drugs*." The tiny crease between his brows furrowed in a way that was so like his aunt's, it was uncanny. "She just works too much."

I felt my cheeks heat but I kept going, needing to bridge the gap between us. To give him a piece of my pain so he didn't feel so alone. That was all I'd hoped and prayed for as a kid.

Someone I could share my burdens with. A *friend*.

And though my brand of friendship normally meant using my

fists and threats in the background to keep those I cared about safe; I'd try to be different for him.

"I'm not saying your mom is on drugs, Isaiah." I corrected, unable to keep the gruffness out of my tone. But he didn't seem to mind, turning his bruised face towards the dark television as if he wasn't interested. But the set of his shoulders and slight tilt of his head proved I had his attention. "But mine was and she was gone a lot, too. I spent a lot of time alone. I had to grow up too fast and learn how to fend for myself." He turned a bit more to face me. "For a long time, I felt like it was me against the world. I had older brothers who tried to look out for me but we lived separately so our time together was limited." That familiar sense of loss washed over me like it did each time I thought of Nero and Big. Their deaths would never get easier with time. They'd been all I had for so long that nearly two decades later, that pain still felt fresh.

"I don't want you to feel like that. Despite whatever's going on, you still have your aunt." I pretended not to hear his scoff. "And you got me." I fiddled with my hands, unsure what to do with them at that moment as I tried to reach the distant teen. "If you need somebody to tal—"

"I don't want to talk about this, Mr. Keem." He cut me off in a tone so harsh that I frowned, glaring but deciding not to push the kid right now. Not when he looked on the verge of collapsing under the weight of whatever plagued him.

"You hungry?"

He flicked a suspicious glance my way after the abrupt subject change before shaking his head. "No, thank you."

I nodded, getting up and moving towards the television. I felt his gaze on me but didn't acknowledge it. Instead, I switched on the white and black game console before returning to my seat. Without acknowledging the eyes on me, I jumped right into the first-person shooter game where I completed covert missions and rescued hostages. It had been a while since I played, evidenced by the two quick deaths my character experienced in the first few minutes.

It didn't take long for Isaiah to abandon his perch at the dining table and walk over, dropping hard on the sofa next to me. He surprisingly waited patiently until I completed the first mission before he reached for the second controller, pressing the button to pair it with the console.

After going to the settings to turn on multiplayer mode, the two of us dove right back in, playing in silence for nearly half an hour before he spoke. "I saw my dad today." He said without taking his gaze from the screen. "He called me weak. And a nerd because I asked him to help my mom get me a video game."

I waited to see if he would say more but when he didn't, I responded, keeping my gaze on the screen too. "So you went and picked a fight to prove that you're not?" He nodded slowly. "With somebody bigger than you?" Another nod. "Got your ass whooped, huh?" His head whipped around so he could narrow his lids at me. But all I did was chuckle under my breath. "Been there, done that." When he kept his gaze narrowed, I shook my head. "You think I'm weak?"

That bit of anger morphed into confusion. "What?"

"You think I'm weak?" I repeated, pausing the game to give him my full undivided attention.

He scanned my features then my scarred hands and large size before shaking his head. "No."

"I'm playing video games too, right?"

He finally made the connection and shook his head. "But nobody's crazy enough to mess with you. You're *huge*."

"Wasn't always this big." I shot back. "I used to get bullied growing up. I was small for my age then had a crazy growth spurt around ten or eleven. But even before then, I kept reading my comic books." The comic books I'd stolen from the corner store in Uptown but I kept that part to myself. "Regardless of what they called me or thought about me, I kept doing what I liked because their opinion didn't matter."

His shoulders seemed to deflate right in front of me. "But he's my dad."

My fist clenched the handle of the controller before setting it down. I'd be pissed if I broke it. "I can talk to him if you want me to."

This time there was no hesitation on his part. "*No!*" I turned my gaze to him, finding his eyes bucked. "He's uhh... he's in jail and his friends are uhh... *nah.* I'm good."

I fought a smirk, realizing he was trying to keep me from getting involved because of the 400s. If only he knew...

"You can call anytime you need something. Even if it's just a place to crash and lay your head, I got you. A'ight?"

There was a long moment where I wasn't sure he'd respond. But finally, after a long silence, he nodded. "Thank you, Mr. Keem. For having my back."

"Anytime."

# 13

# EDEN

My ankle hurt like a *BITCH*.

And the physical therapist I was seeing three times a week because of it was now my nemesis. But the petite yet tough woman paid me no mind as she pushed the weak limb to its limits.

Sometimes, just stretching made me want to cry from the pain.

Eboni wasn't happy that I'd injured myself, especially with only a few weeks out from my first league contest.

In addition to the injury, my trainer had been on my ass lately. He'd said I resembled a bull set loose in a china shop. All rage and tunnel vision. According to him, I'd lost my finesse and it would cost me in the long run.

Nobody liked being told that they were performing poorly but I'd had to respect what he'd said and buckle down. I *had* gotten lax, letting my fighting in the Pit and shit with the 400s dominate the time I normally spent focusing on my body and career.

But because of my fucked-up confrontation with my family this week, I'd shown up for training with nothing but anger in my heart. So, today, I'd arrived early, hoping to work out my frustration before he arrived. I' d already done a warmup and quick round with the sandbags. Now I was testing the weight of my sore ankle like I'd been instructed to, pushing myself a bit further... a bit harder each time I cycled the exercises and started over.

Pressing the bottom of my injured foot flat on the mat, I focused on the bright blue walls of the room then dropped my gaze to the eggshell-colored floor that was soft and cushioned to absorb the impact of being tossed down.

Deep, even breaths were the only sound in the room as I lifted my uninjured leg slowly, adjusting my weight each time I swayed in either direction.

First, I raised at my knee to a ninety-degree angle, then slowly bent at the waist, stretching that leg in the opposite direction until it pointed straight behind me. After holding that pose for a few seconds, my already sore muscles tensed as a prickling, familiar awareness tingled along the back of my neck.

Heat stirred in the pit of my stomach, swirling in a teasing ball before slowly spreading upwards, warming my entire torso. Then it descended again to that needy part that woke up when I turned and spotted the big, powerful, and *silent* man watching from the corner of the room.

The same corner that had been empty mere moments earlier.

Even with both feet now firmly planted on the floor of the gym, I suddenly felt unsteady.

Like me, he wore black from head to toe. But where mine was athleticwear, his... wasn't.

Dark jeans that I couldn't tell whether they were black or blue from this distance, a fitted black crew neck, and sleek leather jacket. He wore his customary shades and the only jewelry was a simple gold chain the same shade as the zipper on his jacket. His beard was groomed and freshly trimmed and his bald head gleamed.

He looked *good as hell.*

His head was tilted in a predatory way and capable hands rested against his pelvis, one gripping the wrist of the other loosely.

Hakeem's posture was deceptively relaxed because I knew every inch of him was ready to spring into action at a moment's notice.

From the top of his bald head down to the white sneakers that I knew were expensive as hell, everything about him screamed *man.*

From across the room, I spotted a little smirk that made me uncomfortable. *Wary*, even.

But despite him being *my* Hakeem, there were still lies, secrets, and unresolved feelings between us.

Ones big enough that caused him to walk away, leaving behind threats that had devastated me to my core. Ones that had me leaving him alone in the bathroom at the charity event rather than staying like we both wanted.

I didn't know how to feel because I didn't know how he felt about me. Or if he even had *any* residual feelings toward me.

So, I planted my hands on my hips, trying to adopt a confident posture, forcing myself to breathe through the rising nervousness his presence caused.

My gaze kept dropping to his hands, wondering if he were to grab me now, would it be with the gentleness he'd displayed at times during our relationship? Or would it be rough? Cruel and resentful?

At this point, I didn't care. The stubborn part of my brain that refused to shut off all my emotions wanted his touch more than my next breath. The way he grabbed me, whether with adoration or contempt, would be better than the loneliness I experienced.

His powerful body casually pushed off the wall. With each step he took in my direction, my heart pounded wildly from the nervousness I couldn't seem to rid myself of. It wasn't until he was about ten feet away that I noticed what I'd missed from across the room.

A playful glint in his onyx gaze. One that I hadn't expected after the way we left things in the bathroom of the charity event.

That man had been anything *but* playful. He'd been *determined* and full of lust.

"Where's your yellow?" His low rumbling tenor warmed me and I fought the urge to shiver. It wasn't fair the way he affected me.

Never caring about the discomfort he might cause, he walked right up until less than a foot of space separated the tip of my nose from his broad chest. And just like every time he was near, his body was devoid of any cologne. The only scent he emanated was one of complete maleness that was unique to him.

My fingers twitched at my side, aching with the need to touch. This whole situation frustrated me because the man I wanted was right there. Yet he still felt so many miles away.

"You didn't hear me?" He asked.

To my dismay, I jolted before composing myself, replaying his question before shrugging. "Didn't feel like wearing any."

His hum was casual. So instead of allowing him to see just how much he affected me, I dropped my gaze to my watch, frustrated that my trainer still hadn't shown. It wasn't until I pulled out my phone, completely conscious of his overpowering presence, that I saw I'd missed a text. Nearly an hour ago, my trainer had asked if we could reschedule because something came up.

"What's wrong?"

My eyes drifted upwards, cheeks heating with a slow blush from the low lidded look aimed my way. With a sigh, I told him about my trainer and the message I'd missed. The harsh lines in his face eased as he observed me again from head to toe.

"I could spar with you." Before I could stop it, a disbelieving scoff rushed from my lips as I rolled my eyes. "I'm serious." He said with a smirk. "I'm not professional but I've got experience."

Though I doubted what he said, I didn't want to throw the truce he was offering back in his face so I agreed.

I felt his gaze on my ass the entire time we crossed the room before climbing into the elevated cage. I honestly didn't know how he planned to help but he was here and he wasn't angry so I'd take it even if this turned out to be a complete waste of time. I watched as he stripped off his jacket and slipped off his sneakers, placing both in a neat pile on the floor.

Though he said he had experience, I started off light, throwing punches and kicks as slow as possible, giving him plenty of time to avoid them before they could make contact. After my third punch that he blocked easily, he laughed. "You don't have to pull your punches. I can take it, baby."

Pretending not to be affected by the endearment, I got back into my stance. Those slow punches turned into ones of speed and force, making a loud boom each time they connected with the padded gloves he wore.

Hard kicks were tossed, colliding with a powerful forearm that moved just in time to block a shot to the kidney. Within minutes, I started to lose sight of my opponent.

That numbing haze clouded my thoughts, giving me tunnel vision until I started battling him with everything in me. The same way I did each time I stepped into the Pit.

And he let me. He didn't call it off nor did he try to slow me down or bring me back.

While I pushed through the pain in my ankle, he let me attack the pads until I exhausted myself. It wasn't until I aimed a swift kick at his head that his lids narrowed. But I was too far gone.

He nearly lost his balance as he side-stepped, but I followed right behind that with an elbow toss towards his gut, missing by mere centimeters. I was already halfway into the next move when he swiped my feet from underneath, forcing me down while cushioning my fall to the mat.

Freeing myself became my first instinct and I started to thrash.

But when his bulk settled between my thighs and those thick forearms pinned mine down, I froze, snapping back into the present and leaving behind the bloodthirsty version of myself that had taken over.

Sensing that I was calm, he traced the outline of my face, down the slope of my neck and across my shoulders. "If I didn't know better," he mumbled. "I'd think you were *really* trying to hurt me."

I was finally realizing just how much I'd lost control. Not only could I have injured him, but I could have injured *myself* again and jeopardized my chances in the upcoming fight. If he hadn't stopped me, there was no telling how far I would've gone.

Immediately, I parted my lips to apologize but his soft question stopped me. "What's got you all worked up?"

It wasn't the question itself that undid me. It was the genuine care in his tone when he asked. And the way he looked at me right now, as if I was the only thing in the world that mattered, brought to surface all those feelings I'd been fighting. Somewhere inside, I was still angry at how easy I'd been to discard.

But I didn't care if he hated me. I didn't care if he'd be gone when I woke in the morning.

Right now, at this very moment, I *needed* him after the week I'd had. Even if temporarily.

Despite the hurt it would cause, I could handle angry or resentful Hakeem. I could even handle mistrustful, or wary Hakeem.

But what I struggled with was *no* Hakeem.

And I was willing to take him any way that I could tonight. No matter the price I paid for it later.

---

I WAS NERVOUS.

But I also knew that I needed to do this. I needed to *release*.

To put myself at someone else's mercy without the fear of being hurt. Physically, at least. I'd been deprived for *so long*.

Before what happened in the bathroom at the charity event, nearly nine months had passed since the last time hands that weren't mine stroked my body with pleasure. At this point, I was physically conditioned to expect only harshness because there was no softness in my life to balance it out.

But tonight, I hoped he could give me that. I hoped Hakeem could set aside whatever negative feelings still existed between us to give me exactly what I needed.

As I scanned his bedroom, I couldn't help the tiny smile that appeared after realizing that not a single thing had changed in his home.

Even the toiletries resting on the counter in the bathroom were positioned the same. Hakeem was a simple man and clearly liked his things in a very specific way.

From his seated position on the edge of the bed his dark gaze remained on me, silently watching as I rifled through one of his drawers, stopping only after locating the piece of fabric I was searching for.

"What are you doing?"

I ignored his question, dangling one of his ties from my fingers as I padded stark naked towards him. The glass door that led to his balcony was wide open, letting the cool night breeze in to circulate the room. Stopping just in front of him, I held it out, forcing myself to appear confident.

His eyes trailed me slowly, not bothering to hide the lust blazing in his gaze. "What do you want me to do with that?" The husky quality of his tone revealed he knew *exactly* what I wanted but needed me to say it.

"Whatever you want."

His tongue darted out, coating those full lips while he leaned forward. Each move was deliberate as he shifted from his slouched, unbothered position to one that was alert. With elbows planted on his knees and big hands clasped together between his spread thighs, those eyes narrowed slightly, gaze sharpening as he spoke. "Tell me." He demanded in a quiet tone that had my back bowing with submission.

I gave my time, energy, and body to people all the time. But tonight, I knew I could do it without fear of having any part fumbled. Without being disrespected or abused for someone else's pleasure or amusement.

I could completely give myself away, knowing I'd be safe in his hands. In his care.

For once, I could let my guard down.

"Tie me?"

Again, he licked his lips. "You asking? Or telling?" I knew what he wanted. Knew what he was demanding from me.

My unwavering surety.

So I swallowed any apprehension. "Tie me up." This time, my tone was firm and resolute, so he stood, tipping his head with a smirk.

"On the bed. Face down."

I moved to obey, pausing after he caught my arm before I could pass. A gentle touch on my chin lifted my head until we made eye contact. Time seemed to freeze as he searched, penetrating my defenses and seeing right to the heart of me. I couldn't hide from him, not like before. This time, when he looked soul deep, he found everything.

Every hidden, ugly part that I sheltered from the world.

And his eyes softened considerably before his head dipped to press tender kisses against my lips. There was promise in that gentle contact. Reassurances of his ability to take care of me and my pleasure so I pulled back to turn towards the bed, this time moving with unfaked confidence.

Once I was on my stomach, he pushed me to the middle of the mattress, resting a knee between my spread thighs. Calloused palms gripped my hips and lifted, raising me at an angle until my ass was at a point in the air. Without needing to be told, I crossed my wrists at the center of my back, pleased when seconds later, the soft silk looped in intricate patterns until an expert knot secured me in place.

Goosebumps bloomed across my skin as he ran his hand up one thigh, bypassing the liquid heat dripping from my center, before moving down the other. "Are you going to tie my legs, too?" I asked, unashamed by the breathless quality of my tone.

I couldn't hide my want for him. My fierce need for his touch. Many times during our acquaintance, I'd told myself that the way I felt was too much, too soon. But I couldn't help it when it came to this man. I'd been hurt before. Disappointed by men and I'd foolishly gone back each time, expecting a different result.

And sadly, it was no different with Hakeem. He'd hurt me, yet here I was again at his mercy, praying that I meant enough to him not to be cast aside a second time.

"Get out of your head." He said, guiding one hand across my skin until it slipped between my thighs. It created an embarrassing noise as he caressed my wet folds, filling the silence of the room with the slick evidence of my arousal. "I'm leaving your legs free because of your ankle."

My chest warmed at his consideration before I sucked in a low breath when he widened said legs, opening me up to his gaze while his fingers thrust inside. I moaned loud, sinking into an even deeper arch so I could bounce back, fucking myself with his hand. Quickly, my rhythm grew wild and relentless when his digits curled inside me. But right when I felt the approach of the orgasm I chased, he pulled free, leaving me empty and desperate.

"What are you... *oooooh*."

My tirade was cut short when his tongue slurped me from behind. The strength of the tie was being tested as I now rocked against his mouth, desperate to free myself so I could grip his bald head in my hands. But the knot held so I continued to writhe, using only the strength in my legs to hump his face.

"You taste so good." His normal silence was replaced by low, sexy grunts and groans that rivaled my own. That partnered with the expert movement of his tongue was too much and I knew I wouldn't be able to last much longer. His velvety tongue coupled with the wiry hairs on his face were a whirlpool of sensations on my hypersensitive flesh. He stroked along the length of my pussy before teasing my clit. Circling it slowly before slurping it fully between his lips.

He savored me, emitting a sexy groan as he sucked on my folds then inhaled deeply.

The pleasure was exquisite. So intense that it bordered on discomfort and I loved that sweet spot only he could get me to.

I could barely handle my affection for him. It swelled in my chest, blooming bigger and bigger until it burst and that explosion made me tremble. Making me grow wetter with want for him. With *need* for him. And that thought ignited the spark of my orgasm. "Keem... I'm... I'm bout to..."

"Not yet." Suddenly his lips and fingers detached, leaving me on edge. I squeaked out a protest but he ignored me, standing to his full height and moving into my line of sight, heavy-lidded eyes locked on mine. "You're waiting for me, baby."

# 14

# HAKEEM

Her irritation was adorable.

She still kneeled; ass pointed in the air as I stood next to the bed. Reaching down, I swiped my thumb across one of her diamond-hard nipples, loving the little gasp of pleasure she emitted. "What do you need from me right now?"

Her eyes narrowed to slits. "What?"

"I can be gentle."

"But that's not what you're in the mood for, is it?" She asked as I shook my head, hoping she was on the same page as me. I enjoyed the soft shit but she was right, I needed to feed the beast tonight. With her offering herself up to me the way she had and looking so fucking sexy restrained in my bed, that thing that lived inside me felt insatiable and only a long, hard fuck would quench his thirst tonight.

"You have my permission to do whatever you want to me. *However* you want."

My fingers flexed at my side. There was no way she'd just uttered those words. No way she realized the implication of saying something like that to a man like me.

"I'm giving you another chance." I offered, barely restraining myself. "I can be gentle, if that's what you need."

Again, she shook her head. "What I need is for you to give me what *you* need."

She'd barely completed her thought before my hands yanked at the ties around her wrist and ankles. There was a slight indent in her skin from where the fabric had been tied and I made a mental note to take care of it later.

But right now, all I could focus on was gripping her the back of her neck, yanking her up towards me, and slamming my mouth against hers. I lapped eagerly at her lips, loving that her tongue immediately darted forward to dance with mine.

My hands slid across smooth, silky skin until I slipped into the thick ropes of her fresh braids. My fingers clenched in the strands, pulling her even closer and enjoying her little squeak of surprise.

"On your back." My command was low and gravel-filled, slicing from between gritted teeth.

The beast in me puffed out his chest with pride when she eagerly followed my order, spreading her muscled thighs wide for me to see her drenched center.

Gotdamn, she was made just for me.

The temptation to bury my head between them again nearly took over but I held back, needing to be lodged deep inside. Once I fucked her to our satisfaction, then I would go down and taste again, getting my fill of her essence.

Pure need pumped through my veins as I kneeled on the edge of the bed and yanked her to me, propping an ankle on each shoulder. She gasped from the sudden intrusion of me sliding deep. The wetness practically dripped from her, making it an effortless glide between her walls. The warm slickness had me closing my eyes, fighting not to bust on entry.

I was a man who always remained in control and was always aware of my surroundings. But at this moment, I was completely defenseless and vulnerable. Nothing besides her sweet moans of pleasure and wet muscles constricting around me mattered as I hammered into her. If anyone ever wanted to get the drop on me, the perfect opportunity would be when I was mindlessly lost in her oasis.

The big bed beneath us shook with each of my strokes, creating a concerning creak from my bedframe. I don't think I'd ever fucked her this hard. Not even that first night when she'd propositioned me at the bar.

With my arms locked around each of her legs, I yanked her to me, unable to look away from her full breasts bouncing wildly each time I connected.

"Oh my God, *Hakeem*." She cried out, arching into my thrusts. Her hands gripped my wrist, then slid to my forearms, my stomach, chest and then repeating the motion all over again as if she couldn't decide on what part to touch. I loved that she enjoyed my roughness just as much as she enjoyed the times when our union was slow and sweet.

Within minutes, the familiar swell in my balls urged me to thrust harder.

"Play with your clit."

She was already so damn close to the edge but so was I. And the last thing I wanted was to lose complete control before she got hers. No matter how good it felt, her pleasure would always come before mine.

One of her indecisive hands slipped right to the apex of her thighs, caressing, rubbing, and circling the plump pleasure button I'd licked to orgasm earlier.

Her walls clamped down harder and it didn't take long for both of us to topple over the edge into a descent of mind-numbing pleasure. My normally sturdy legs trembled from the force of my orgasm as I continued to pump into her. She pulsed around me in a distractingly sexy rhythm that was damn near in sync with the pleasurable throb in my dick.

Once her tightness drained every drop from my shaft, I met her gaze, releasing a breathless chuckle at the ecstasy and fulfillment on her face. Her eyes were glazed over and all she could do was give me a sleepy, sweet smile in return.

"You good?" I asked.

This time, she released a breathless chuckle, caressing the side of my face. She seemed so serene now, completely relaxed and at ease as she finally responded making me burst into laughter.

"Oh, I'm *perfect.*"

# 15

# EDEN

THE JARRING SOUND of my phone's ringtone woke me.

At first, I struggled to place my surroundings, squinting at the furniture that wasn't mine as it slowly came into focus. It didn't take long to realize I was in Hakeem's bedroom. Sensing that I was alone, I started to get up when the phone started ringing again, reminding me that it had woken me in the first place. A quick glance at the clock revealed the time... just after four am.

Who the hell was calling this early?

My stomach took a swan dive and I scrambled to answer after spotting Mona's name.

"What's wrong?" I answered, trying to stamp down the mounting panic. There was only one reason she'd be calling this late. Well, early.

*Isaiah.*

"*Oh my God*, Eden."

The shakiness in her tone did nothing to settle my nerves. I was already swinging my legs off the edge of the bed, prepared to do... *something*. "What is it? Where's Isa?"

"*I don't know*!" The fear and panic in her voice was obvious.

Immediately, I took a few deep breaths to settle my nerves. Getting riled up wouldn't get me any answers.

"Mona... What happened?"

"We had an argument and he went to a friend's house on Tuesday but was supposed to be home last night. He wasn't, so I just assumed he was running late. I went to work around eight last night and I just got home but he's still not here! And he won't answer his phone."

Her tone grew shriller with each word.

"When was the last time you actually spoke to him?" I placed the phone on speaker and reached for the overnight bag I'd packed, slipping into a matching yellow tank and black drawstring shorts set. The outfit had been picked with the intent of lounging around, not searching the streets for my nephew in the middle of the night but it would have to do.

"Yesterday morning." She said through a sniffle as I tied the strings on my sneakers. "But when I called his friend's mom, she said he left hours ago, before the sun went down." A heartbroken sob came through the receiver. "I know you probably think I'm a terrible mom but it's been rough, Eden. I'm working so many hours that we're rarely in the house at the same time. Benji's not sending as much money as he used to since I broke up with him. Rome and Barry..." Finally, her words trailed as if she didn't want to admit what I already knew.

"They told you not to let me see him, right?"

She sighed. "*Yes*! But they're not helping at all. My mom is sick, so Ms. Lou and you are the only relief I have. I just can't do it by myself anymore."

I understood and sympathized. But I couldn't ignore how she'd lied and blew me off each time I tried to reach out over the last few months. I was all out of comforting words. For everyone. So an awkward silence ensued as I jogged down the steps to the first floor, searching for Hakeem from one end to the other before realizing that I was alone in the big house.

"I'm sorry, Eden. I know... I could've at least let you talk on the phone to him. I didn't have to completely shut you out."

Another pause before I sighed. "We're good, Mona." Then before she could say anything else, I fired off another question. "You talked to Rome or Barry? They haven't seen him?"

"No." She whined. "I called everybody. Your mom, Madi, Crow, Rome, Barry, my neighbors, his friends' parents... no one has seen him."

*Fuck.* That wasn't good. Though he worked my nerves, I'd prayed that this was just another trick of Rome's trying to get under my skin. But if he hadn't seen him? I had no clue where to start the search.

"You think he ran away?" She asked. I froze, hand on a spare set of Hakeem's keys that I'd apologize for taking later. Though he favored his big, black, decked out truck, there was a Jeep of the same color parked in the garage. "Why would you think he ran away?"

"Because we've been into it so much. He's been disrespectful. And I told him that I was getting tired of his smart mouth." Another muffled sob met my ears. "I told him that if he wanted to be grown so damn bad then he could get out and see what it's *really* like to be grown." When all I could offer was silence, she rushed to quickly explain. "But I didn't mean it. I didn't actually *want* him to leave. I just wanted him to listen and behave. I wanted him to go back to my sweet Isa. Now, he's acting just like...."

"*Benji.*" I finished for her. For years, I'd wondered how my brother and his high-strung girlfriend had managed to create such a mild-mannered child. But lately, he'd been displaying his father's impatience and temperament, something I'd prayed he wouldn't inherit. Though the moniker had been assigned to me, Benji had been the true menace between the two of us. And I'd be damned if my nephew turned out like him.

An asshole who held zero regard for anyone besides himself.

"I'm about to head out, Mona." I said softly, shutting the door behind me as I climbed down the three steps into Hakeem's garage.

As expected, the gleaming Jeep was parked in the center. "I'll call when I find him."

"Please find my baby, Eden."

"I got you."

I climbed into the Jeep, skirting my gaze over the interior before locating the button on the visor to open the garage. The steel door rolled up and I put the car in reverse, making it only about six or seven feet before Hakeem's truck pulled up the driveway, blocking me in.

"Where you going?" He asked after we both hopped out.

"I gotta go, Keem." I gestured towards his truck. "Can you move, please? I promise to bring it back unharmed."

His forehead crinkled. "I don't give a fuck about you driving it but where are you going right now? *This* late?"

Though this felt like a waste of time, I owed him an explanation. "Mona called and said Isa is missing. She hasn't heard from him since yesterday. I need to go look—" I stopped when the passenger door of his SUV swung open and the exact person I was prepared to do an entire manhunt for hopped out as if me and his mom hadn't been on the verge of a panic attack.

"Isa?" His eyes swung to mine, bucking slightly. "Where the *hell* have you been?"

The wild thunder in my heart slowed only a bit when my nephew merely hefted his bookbag higher on his shoulder and nodded. "Hey Tee." My anger threatened to boil over at his casual tone. "Can I go to my room, Mr. Keem?"

"*Your* room?"

Isa flicked a nervous glance at me before returning it to Hakeem who nodded. My nephew didn't spare me another glance before he ran inside, closing the door quietly behind him.

Immediately, I switched my angry glare to the man who was already watching me.

"What the *fuck* is going on?"

---

MY ENTIRE BODY thrummed with bottled up irritation as I paced Hakeem's living room. Instead of answering my question, he'd ushered me inside, instructing me to call Mona and let her know that Isa was fine. It was only after he promised to explain that I obliged. Now, instead of getting the answers I was seeking, I was stuck on the phone.

"Can you keep him for a bit?" I frowned at Mona's request. After telling her he was okay, she hadn't really asked for details. Instead, she'd cried in relief then asked the question that I still hadn't responded to. My silence must've gone on too long because she continued. "It's just... I don't know. I think we need a break from each other. Everything is too much right now."

I bit back a scoff. If anyone knew that everything was *too much*, it was me. But I'd do whatever I could for my nephews, so I'd figure out a way to make it happen like I always did.

"How long?"

"As long as you can keep him." She said quickly. "Him spending more time with the 400s isn't an option because he's turning into one of them and I don't want that. But I need to get myself together. I love him. More than anything. And I'll give you what I can from my paychecks to help support, but right now? I just *can't*."

"Alright." I agreed. "I'll do it. But *you're* telling him. I'm not going to be the bad guy for you. You can let him know when we come to grab some of his things."

"I promise I will. Thank you so much." As I sat on the plush loveseat, I felt conflicted at the sound of the relief in her tone. On one hand, I understood she was struggling and needed a break. But on the other, I would think she'd be more torn up about the decision. Hell, the days and weeks where I was apart from my nephews nearly *destroyed* me.

But I kept my opinion to myself. All that mattered was Isaiah's wellbeing. And if that meant adjusting my entire life to accommodate him, I would.

He and Hakeem chose that very moment to come downstairs, looking way too comfortable for this to have been a coincidental run in.

"How many times have you been over here?" I asked after ending the call.

Isa looked to Hakeem, as if asking for his help. But the big man remained silent. Instead, he dropped his bulk onto the adjacent sofa, watching the two of us without saying a word.

"I don't know." My nephew mumbled. I scooted over, expecting him to sit next to me. But when he stepped over my legs and chose to sit by Hakeem instead, I pretended not to feel the painful clench in my chest. "A few times."

"How? Why?"

"Because..."

I braced on the edge of my seat, waiting for more. But he said nothing.

"Why didn't you call me?" I asked, tossing my arms up helplessly. "If you were upset, angry, or just needed to talk, you know I'll drop everything for you. No matter what time it is, I would've been there."

"Would you?"

"*What?*"

"Would you really have shown up for me if I called? Hakeem was there when I needed him. I can't say the same for you."

My back met the cushion of the sofa as I reared back, sucking in a low breath to mask my hurt once again. "Isa..."

"I don't want to talk about this." He snapped in a sharp tone that even had Hakeem's brows furrowing. He'd *never* spoken to me like that.

But instead of matching his energy and telling him to watch his mouth, my patience won out and I scooted to the edge of my seat. "Well, we're going to. Right now."

"Why? It ain't like you're going to do anything about it! You let them keep us apart! You let them take us away from you! Why should I trust you to do anything for me when the decision isn't yours?" He jumped to his feet, veins popping in his slender neck as he yelled. "They *own* you. You do whatever they tell you to do, even if it hurts me and Jayce. So I don't want to hear you say shit about putting us first because it isn't true!"

I could only stare wide-eyed. I couldn't form a word because my heart was breaking. I was breaking and shattering into millions of little pieces. He'd wrecked me with his words yet all I could do was sit there rather than defend myself, explain, or apologize.

When he saw my stunned expression and speechlessness, he laughed in a low tone that sounded uncomfortably like his father's. "See, even you know it's true!"

I needed a moment. I needed to walk away. My brain was unable to process his words nor could my heart make sense of the crushing it had just experienced. So I stood, fighting back tears. Before I could fully round the sofa, a firm grip on my wrist stopped me.

"Sit your ass back down." Hakeem snapped, tugging me towards him.

Confusion contorted my features at the angry demand and I found myself complying without argument, lowering into the space Isa had just vacated.

"Who do you think you're talking to?" Hakeem asked in a low tone, still not releasing my wrist as his hard gaze zeroed in on my nephew who seemed to shrink right in front of us.

"*Keem.*"

A warning glare had my lips slamming closed.

"Who the fuck has been filling your head with that bullshit?" I wanted to tell *him* to watch his language but knew he wouldn't listen to a damn thing I had to say. Not right now. "Your aunt takes care of you. Better than anyone else. That's what you said, right? That she always sacrifices herself for everyone, especially you and Jayce, right?" Isaiah gave a small nod. "So treat her like she does. I don't care what anyone else has said about her or *to* her, you show her the respect she deserves, am I clear?"

My nephew's gaze flicked to mine before lowering in shame. "Yes, sir."

"*Apologize.*" This time, he couldn't meet my eye as a low apology fell from his lips. The intensity of Hakeem's glare had the both of us squirming before he finally sucked his teeth. "Don't let me hear you talking to her like that again. Now take your little disrespectful ass back upstairs."

I bristled at his tone but said nothing. Maybe he needed that toughness. Though it bothered me to see him being scolded so harshly, I prayed it had the intended effect.

Once he left, the room remained silent. I could feel his eyes on me yet mine remained focused on the space Isa had just occupied. It wasn't until a big hand came into view, gently swiping away the tears that I hadn't noticed falling before I swung my gaze to him.

Still, I didn't say a word, afraid the emotional dam I was scrambling to hold together would burst. If it did, I'd break down completely, releasing every pent-up emotion until I was a weak mess on the floor. I avoided crying for this very reason. Because I didn't know how to cry rationally. When I got to the point of tears, everything came rushing to the surface and there was nothing I could do to stop it.

That girl who felt everything... that girl I'd muted long ago clawed her way free of the confines I'd placed her in until she was once again in control.

"You don't have to be tough with me."

I chuckled humorlessly, still spilling tears at an alarming rate. "I have to be tough with *everyone*."

"Not with me." He repeated. The hand that had swiped at my tears cupped my chin, holding my head still so he could keep his gaze on mine. "*Never* with me." Then before I could process his words, he stood, towering over me. "You want to take a bath?"

This time, humor laced my watery laugh. "What?"

He didn't bother repeating himself. Instead, he scooped me from the sofa bridal-style, carrying me across the first floor and up the staircase until we reached my favorite room.

He sat me on the counter as he moved towards the jetted, massive tub that I thought about way too often. As the water rushed from the spout to fill the tub, he moved back in my direction. The closer he got, the higher my gaze lifted, never breaking the intense eye contact we were locked in.

A shiver went through me when he gripped the hem of my shirt. But instead of taking it off, he waited, lifting a brow, not moving until I nodded. It amused me that he'd had me tied up in his bed less than eight hours ago yet he wouldn't undress me without permission. I wondered if I'd ever solve the puzzle that was Hakeem.

Once undressed, he lowered me into the hot, yet perfect water. A low, satisfied moan escaped before I could stop it.

His hands lingered a moment longer, brushing gently across my hips then the soft skin of my belly before he moved away. There was a low creak then thump as he opened and closed a cabinet before returning to my side.

Peeking one eye open, I was so distracted by the sheer maleness of him that I nearly missed what he had in his hands.

The familiar logo had me once again fighting back the sting of tears. He passed me the pear scented body wash and shower oil. The exact brand that I kept stocked at my place.

My first thought was that I'd left these here all those months ago when we were still a thing. But both bottles were full and had a plastic seal across the lid. "Why do you have these?"

"Why do you think?" Then he gave me a weighted look. One I was too emotionally wrung out to decipher. So I nodded, mumbling a quiet thanks.

He must've sensed my exhaustion because he didn't push. Instead, he shoved his hands in his pockets, unashamedly scanning my nakedness underneath the water before moving towards the door. "Take as long as you want. We'll talk after."

---

AFTER FORCING myself out of the tub once the water grew cold, I found Hakeem was already stretched across his massive bed with a thick comforter pulled up to his waist. His tattooed upper torso was bare, causing my mouth to water as he unknowingly put on a show, casually lifting his arms to cross them behind his head.

"You checked on Isaiah?" I asked, unable to get over the anger and pain on his face earlier. Despite the shit the 400s had put me through, somehow, I'd successfully managed to keep him and Jayce separate from it. But like he'd said, I was no longer in control. They owned me and I was at their mercy for the foreseeable future. And because of Madi's stupid decision and my martyrdom, the two of them were suffering more than anyone.

"He's already asleep."

I squirmed in the subsequent awkward silence. I didn't know how to handle it because I was mentally exhausted and way past tired, but I doubted Hakeem would let me off that easily. I still had questions about how much time he and Isaiah had been spending together and we *still* hadn't had a conversation about whatever the hell we were doing at the moment.

But I couldn't seem to make my brain work the way it should. Right now, all it signaled was that I needed a minimum of eight hours of sleep while snuggled between the arms of the man currently eyeing me. "Clearly things are... *weird* right now. But the past few weeks have felt like a shit-on-Eden fest." He merely tilted his head, patiently waiting for the question I was tiptoeing around. "And even though every-damn-body seems to be joining the hate train..."

His answering eye roll was out-of-character and so damn dramatic that a startled laugh shot out, interrupting what I'd been about to say. He continued watching through it all, still not jumping in to save me from this awkward moment after my laughter ceased. "Anyway, I'm kind of in limbo on what to do right now. If I'm being honest, I just want to... not feel like the biggest piece of shit. I want to be comforted. I want to not be so strong, even if only for a few hours. I know we still need to talk. I know there's a lot of unresolved shit between us but, if you don't mind, can we just table it for now? I promise to address it later, but right now, I just need this break."

The pressing sting of tears appeared midway through my speech, threatening to fall by the time my words trailed.

"But only if it's okay with you." I added. "If not, then we can go ahead and talk if that's what you prefer."

I couldn't read his expression but relief flooded me when he hefted his chin in agreement. Quickly, before he could change his mind, I closed the distance and climbed next to him in bed, ignoring the way his oversized shirt rose up my hips, leaving my bare ass against soft sheets. The second I was tucked under the blankets, he tugged my back flush against his front.

The tickle of his beard was my only warning before his lips pressed right behind my ear. I was prepared to feel his hands traveling under the fabric to grab my breasts. Or for his fingers to ease down to tease between my clenched thighs. But he did neither.

He just squeezed me, giving exactly what I requested by being my safe place.

After realizing that he truly had no intention of bringing up any difficult topics or physically taking it further, I started to drift off.

Right when I was about to give up the fight to sleep, he grumbled something in my ear that had another tiny fissure in my heart repairing itself.

"There's nothing you could ever say or do to make me hate you. *Nothing*." Another squeeze. "And don't ever be scared to say you want comfort. Demand that shit. I've already told you to say what you want or need and I'll make it happen. Just like I've told you that you don't have to be strong all the time. Share your burdens with me. I can handle them, I promise."

# 16

# HAKEEM

I DIDN'T GIVE a damn about her past.

With her stretched beside me, face relaxed in peaceful sleep, I realized that none of that shit mattered. The deeds she'd done, the choices she'd made, the people she'd associated with... all of that had brought her to this point and made her exactly who she was.

The woman that was perfect for me, flaws and all.

I still had amends to make before she was fully mine again but for now, I'd take this.

A low groan accompanied a cute frown as she shifted, rolling to the opposite side, giving an up-close view of her smooth, muscled back and round, firm ass. The body that was tiny compared to mine housed so much power and strength that I couldn't help but admire her discipline and tenacity.

Aggressive knocks at my door had me frowning, wondering who the fuck had come all the way out here. A peek at the doorbell camera on my phone revealed a pursed lipped Gia, glaring directly at the screen. "Open the door."

I quickly realized that I was dressed in only boxer briefs but Gia's incessant knocks would likely wake Eden or Isaiah so I skipped getting dressed and moved to open the door.

"Oh *hell nah*." Was what left her lips the moment she laid eyes on me.

"Damn, Uncle Keem, you swole as a bi—" Gia's hand colliding with the back of her son's head halted what he'd been about to say.

Instead of greeting the uninvited duo, I lifted a brow. But being Gia, she only sucked her teeth. "*Move, nigga*." She pushed me aside, barging in with grocery bags in tow. Junior followed right behind his mom, playfully flexing my way before flinching when I bucked back. "We're hanging out here today."

"Why?"

"None of your business."

My face contorted but Junior jumped in before I could respond. "Because she's avoiding dad. As if our location sharing isn't on."

Her lids narrowed in warning and he immediately turned, already stripping off his shirt as he slipped through the patio door towards the pool.

Turning back to my unsolicited guest, I could only shake my head, refusing to touch that subject. Gia and her ex-husband's relationship confused the hell out of me and everyone else who knew them. "Because I want to. It's just me and Junior. I promise you won't die from the social interaction."

She pretended not to see my glare, focusing instead on the food she unpacked on the countertop. More than once, I flicked my gaze towards the staircase, expecting Eden or Isaiah to come down and investigate the noise at any moment.

"Who's here?" Gia asked, drawing my gaze back to her. Her tone was filled with suspicion as she kept flicking her gaze in the same direction mine had. "You finally stopped moping over Eden and brought somebody home?" Realizing my lips would remain sealed, she sucked her teeth, pausing what she was doing to observe me. "Honestly, this was supposed to be an intervention because we're all worried about you. But if you're fucking...somebody else..."

Eden's footsteps halted after noticing the other woman. For some reason, the first thing that came to mind was pride at the sight of my oversized shirt covering her frame. It stopped right above her knees and she damn near drowned in the fabric in a way that was adorable.

If Gia and Junior weren't present, or if I didn't fear being discovered by Isa, I'd place her on the counter and yank it up to her waist so I could feast on a much more pleasing meal than the one I'd planned to fix on the stove. Shyly, she waved at Gia before turning to me, missing the curious gape aimed at her back.

"Can you give me a ride back to my place? I'm supposed to pick up Jayce from my mom's."

I wasn't ready for my time with her to end. Wasn't ready for her to withdraw back into her space. I wasn't ready to be *alone* again. "Bring him back with you. Y'all can spend the day here."

I could see the refusal on the tip of her tongue and braced myself for rejection but Gia spoke before she could. "That's a great idea. Junior's here too, so I'm sure he and Isa would love to spend time together." Though she was helping my case, I didn't like the twinkle in her eye that let me know she was up to something. But if it meant having more time with Eden, I'd allow it. For *now*. Eden's hesitation proved she was wary of Gia's motives too but she agreed anyway with a reluctant nod. "Do you mind if I ride with you?" Gia asked, already reaching for her purse. "I need to make a quick stop at the store."

Not a single person in this room believed she only wanted a ride to the damn store but didn't call her on it. Instead, Eden sliced one of those guarded looks my way. "Sure, let me check on Isa, get changed, then we can leave."

After she'd jogged up the stairs, I turned to Gia. "Stop playing."

"No, *you* stop playing, nigga." She whisper-shouted back. "The hell y'all got going on? We're thinking you depressed and shit and y'all are playing house again. Why you ain't tell me?" I remained silent but she wasn't going for it. "Don't you pull that shit with me, Hakeem." She licked her lips, face contorting as she crossed her arms. "How are you feeling right now? Are you okay? *Really*? Because that's all I care about. If you're good mentally and emotionally, then I'll leave it alone."

I shrugged. "I'm straight."

She sucked her teeth. "Have y'all even talked about what happened? Cleared up the confusion from the first time?" I shook my head, earning another eye roll. "What the *fuck*?"

"How's your communication with Israel?" I shot back, pressing my hands flat on the cool marble countertop. "Have you cleared up what happened between y'all?"

Her lids dropped to thin slits as she pointed. "I *will* fight you."

I snorted. "Exactly. Let me handle my shit and you handle yours, yeah?"

"Umm hmm. Yeah, *whatever*."

# 17

# EDEN

THE SILENCE in the car was beyond awkward.

I could tell she wanted to say something but for whatever reason, held back. Gia hadn't said much outside of telling me which store she wanted to stop at it. Once she'd gone in and returned with two small bags, I pulled off, hoping she'd let the music be the only noise between us for the rest of the ride to and from my parents' home.

"So..." she began not even a second later. "You and Hakeem are... back together."

It was voiced like a statement, but I could hear the question in her tone.

"We're..." I hesitated, searching for the word to describe the current limbo he and I were in. "Reconnecting."

From the corner of my eye, I spotted her gaze shooting from the road to me. "So, like I said... *y'all back together.*"

I couldn't help the chuckle that slipped free. I loved Gia's bluntness. It was refreshing albeit intimidating at times. She was self-assured and knew exactly who she was. Every word that left her lips was coated with a layer of confidence that I couldn't help but admire.

"Something like that, I guess."

*"Hmm."*

I was grateful when my parent's neighborhood came into sight. I knew she wasn't done with her questions but at least for now, they'd be postponed.

"'You can wait in the car if you want. I won't be long." I offered, after parking behind my dad's truck. *Please wait in the car.* The last thing I wanted was someone from a strong familial unit witnessing the blatant distance and dysfunction of mine.

"No, I'll come in. Take your time, I'm in no rush."

Then she opened the car door, easing those long, model legs outside onto the driveway. Each move she made was elegant and graceful as she raked her nails through her shoulder-length bob before meeting me near the hood.

I opened my mouth to warn her, but hesitated, unsure how to even prepare someone for the embarrassing dynamic they'd witness. So, I closed my mouth and prayed that today was peaceful.

I knocked then stepped back, unprepared for my mother to answer so quickly. "You're late."

I stiffened at her tone, glancing at my phone. "*Actually*, I'm early. I wasn't supposed to come until twelve, it's just now ten thirty." When I returned my gaze to her face, I noticed her red-rimmed eyes and puffy lids. "What's wrong?" I asked, stepping inside, briefly forgetting that Gia was behind me as I scanned the always-neat living room. "What's going on?"

She cut her eyes to the hallway, right as my father stepped into it. His normally unpleasant expression had soured even more, twisted up with his own irritation at whatever had gone down.

"He had a bitch in my house while I was at work last night."

*Again?* I bit my lip just in time to catch my question before it slipped free.

"Don't bring her into our business, Lou. This is between me and you." His tone was commanding and bold, which normally caused her to immediately bow to his demands.

But this time, she whirled, approaching with a finger pointed. "You mean between me, you, and Sherry?"

My eyes bucked. Sherry had been one of my teachers in middle school and an old high school friend of my mom's. They'd grown apart over the years but still kept in touch. Again, I bit my lip to keep from jumping in. I'd spent too many years defending her, only for them to tag team me. So right now, all I cared about was removing myself from the familiar argument. I wasn't getting involved in whatever was going on. Not this time.

"Where's Jaycce?" I interrupted before my father could respond.

Both whipped around to face me. "Do you even care, Eden?" My mom scoffed. "Or are our problems beneath you now that you've finally made it to your little fighting league?"

Movement at my back had me tensing before I relaxed, remembering Gia. My mom seemed to notice at the same time, causing her to flash a polite smile. "Hey, baby. I'm Lou, Eden's mom. This is her dad."

I didn't miss how she'd intentionally left his name out of the introduction, just like I didn't miss the way my father's eyes scanned the beauty with interest as she moved to shake my mother's hand.

"Hi, I'm a friend of Eden's, Gia."

My mom returned the handshake, alternating between smiling at her and glaring at me. "Nice to meet you, I'm sorry you had to see that. Eden should've told us she was bringing a guest with her. She knows better."

I let the accusation roll off my shoulders. I was so used to them at this point, that I barely felt the sting anymore.

"I actually kind of forced myself into her car." Gia defended with a slight laugh. "She didn't know I was going to tag along."

"Oh, well..." My mom's surprise was evident as she struggled to find something to say. "She could've called on the drive over, at least. But that's just how my child is, inconsiderate of others."

That insult did *not* roll off my shoulders. Because she could say a lot of things about me, but inconsiderate was the farthest from the truth. If anything, I've been *too* considerate at the sacrifice of my *own* wellbeing.

"Lou, can you fix me a plate, the game's about to start."

"Are you serious?" My mom snapped, hands resting on her ample hips.

He sighed, then looked at me. "Eden, fix me a plate and bring it to the den."

"I'm not your wife. Fix your own fucking plate." I snapped, unable to believe he was demanding things right after being caught cheating. Then had the nerve to tell *me*. I might've been forced to do that bullshit growing up but I'd be damned if I did it now. "It's the least you can do since you contribute nothing else around here." I was too angry to be embarrassed at the wide-eyed look Gia swung between the three of us.

"Don't forget. I'm still your father."

"Are you?" I shot back. "Because you haven't done anything fatherly, or husbandly, in a *very* long time. At this point, she might as well file you on her taxes as a dependent because you've contributed nothing over the last two decades. All you've been is a cheating, lying bum that refuses to get off his ass and go to work."

My mom whirled, hand raised as if to slap my face. I could've easily evaded it, but I remained still, not flinching even after her palm stopped inches from my cheek.

I tilted my head, holding her stare as she pulled back. "Nah... go ahead. Take it out on me like you always do."

Her eyes grew sad and she reached out again, this time with a trembling hand before stopping right before contact. I could physically see her rebuilding walls before her chin lifted. "Stop being dramatic, Eden. Nobody takes anything out on you."

None of this shit would ever change. And I'd already allowed myself to get more involved than I wanted, so I nodded towards Jayce's overnight bag. "Is he in our old room or yours?"

Her mouth balled up, as if preparing to spew more venom my

way, but she remembered our guest before gesturing down the hall. "Your old room."

I nodded, brushing past my father while returning his glare. Jayce was flat on his stomach, flipping the pages of a book. His legs alternated between scissoring open and closed on the bed and bouncing off the mattress. He even hummed a little tune to himself that brought a smile to my face.

"You ready, baby?"

His head shot up and he jumped from the bed in a daring leap that caused my heart to stutter. I caught him midair. "Don't do that."

He laughed, squeezing his arms around my neck. "It's been four years since I seen you!"

I cracked up. This child had absolutely no concept of time. "It's only been like three days."

"Nope, years!"

"Well you get to stay with me *all* week. And guess who you get to see today?"

He mushed my cheeks with his hands, causing my lips to poke out. I bucked my eyes and made a funny face that made him burst into giggles. "Who?"

"Isaiah and Mr. Keem. You can swim in his pool, too."

Yet again, he nearly gave me a heart attack when he leapt out of my arms, landing on his knees. Before I could ask if he was okay, he moved quickly around the room, grabbing everything he'd brought with him and stuffing it into his monster truck book bag. Once it was full, he faced me with a beaming smile. "Ready!"

"Grandma Lou is going to miss you." My mom said from the doorway, causing my spine to stiffen. I didn't face her. Instead, I kept my gaze on Jayce as he grinned, hugging her legs before gasping when he peeked down the hall.

"*Ms. Gia?*"

My mom's face contorted when he ran past her.

"Oh, you're a handsome young man, but I'm looking for Jayce."

Gia teased when he made it to her. "He was a little baby. You're way too big to be him."

"It's me!" He cried and I smiled, stepping into the hall to see him jumping up and down in front of her. "*I'm* Jayce. I'm big and strong now. See?" He flexed his muscles, causing her to burst into laughter.

She bent at the waist, grabbing him before swinging him high in the air. He remained in Gia's arms as we left, catching her up on the excitement in his little life all the way to the car.

My mom's footsteps trailed us onto the front porch but it wasn't until she closed the door that she spoke. "You're determined to keep your family at arm's length, huh?"

Gia's hands paused as she helped Jayce snap in, flicking her eyes up to us, before resuming her task.

I snorted, determined to walk away but something inside stopped me. "I asked Benji this question before, but he could never come up with an answer that made sense. And I was too scared to ask you myself." She lifted a brow as if shocked I'd admit to fearing anything. "Why did you and dad dislike me so much?"

"Why did... *what*?"

"I understand that y'all don't like me now, and that's fine. I'm an adult so it's whatever. But when I was a kid? Explain to me what I did to make you feel that way about me back then?" Her lips parted but before she could answer, I cut her off. "Don't try to pretend like you don't understand. Don't try to act like you never treated me any differently. For once, I'm asking you to give me the truth. It's not going to change anything between us now but I would like to know."

I could tell the moment she decided to do exactly as I'd said. Her relaxed posture turned defensive, already preparing to justify whatever bullshit she was about to spew. She took one last glance towards the car where Gia and Jayce both waited before she spoke. "You were *arrogant*." Her eyes rolled upwards as she scoffed. "Even as a child, you had too much confidence. You needed to be *humbled* and I did it the best way I knew how."

"What does that even mean?" I questioned, lifting my arms in confusion. "Why did you feel the need to destroy my confidence and humble me as a *child*?"

She laughed, folding her arms across her ample chest. "You couldn't walk around like the world owed you something. That's not how it works. You adapt to the world. It doesn't adapt to you. But that's how you moved." She punctuated that statement with a dismissive flick of her wrist. "It was so irritating being called up to the school all the damn time. If you thought the teacher was wrong, you argued until they sent you to the office. If someone smaller was being picked on, you had to get involved. You just didn't know how to shut up and play your role. So, I made sure you learned. And I don't regret it because you wouldn't be where you are without it."

I paused a moment to take it in. To wrap my mind around her fucked-up mindset. There was no way she was delusional enough to believe what she said. Then again, she'd been knowingly cheated on for over two decades and refused to leave her husband because she didn't believe in divorce. She believed a man had the right to do as he pleased, as long as he came home to her when he was finished.

"You know what... I'm not even going to argue with you about how wrong that is. But I do have another question... why I did I need that treatment but not Benji and Madi? You needed to humble *me* but you let them act like complete assholes without reprimand. What lessons were you teaching *them* by allowing that?"

"What I did with them is none of your business."

I sucked my teeth. "So, I had to be humbled because I spoke up for myself and defended others. But Benji didn't need to be humbled when he was a bully. And you're okay with that?"

"Weren't you right there with him? I'm sick of you thinking you're better or *different* than your siblings. You were right in the middle of the shit, too."

"I got in trouble with Benji sometimes, yes. But I never bullied anybody. I defended myself in fights. I defended other kids who were picked on. But I never went and purposely hurt those who didn't want to fight or those who were smaller than me. Not like him."

She waved her hand, speaking in a sarcastic tone. "There you go again. *Eden is so much better than everybody else.*"

"What about Madi?" I asked rather than entertaining her taunt. "When she did things to me, instead of correcting or *humbling* her, you told me to be the bigger person. You put it in her head that it was okay to hurt or disrespect me because I could take it. You're okay with the piece of shit, selfish person that she is? Because your inability to *humble* her helped create it."

"Eden, I'm not going to stand here and let you turn this into a hate-your-siblings session. This is about you. Leave them out of it." She stepped closer, finger jabbing inches from my nose as she spoke. "You were tough." She snapped at my silence. "You could handle it. You didn't need anybody to fight your battles. You were always independent. I didn't need to coddle you."

"That's *bullshit.* Regardless of how strong, tough, or arrogant you thought I was... I was still your child and deserved protection, just like them." When her expression didn't change, my shoulders deflated. I'd done it to myself again. Got all worked up over something that would never change. "It is what it is at this point." I said with a sigh. "I honestly didn't want to turn this into an argument."

"But you did anyway. Just like you always do."

More finger pointing that I refused to stand here and take, so I changed the subject. "I have a fight coming up so I'll need Jayce to stay here. I'll text you to let you know the details." I'd made it all the way to the car where I'd forgotten the windows were down, so Gia had heard every word.

Right when I reached for the handle, my mom couldn't resist throwing one last jab from the front porch. "You're sacrificing a lot of time with the boys for this career of yours." My grip tightened to the point of pain. "I hope you think it's worth it. Because it looks like they've been pushed to the bottom of your priority list. Don't do that to them, Eden. They deserve better than scraps of your time."

*Fuck.*

How do I keep letting her get to me?

A watery laugh broke free as I faced her. "As much as I love those boys, as much as I do for them... at the end of the day, they're not mine, mama. Trust me, when their parents get angry for whatever reason, they make sure to remind me of that fact by keeping them away." I shook my head, wondering if she too had been part of the reason for Isaiah's recent distance. "Mona recently asked for a *break* from her child, Benji's in jail, Rome is a shit-parent, and I wouldn't trust Madi to raise a rock... I am the *only* stability in those boys' lives. So fuck you or anybody else who says otherwise."

Her eyes bucked. "I know you've lost your mind talking to me like th—"

I climbed in the car and slammed the door, cutting off whatever she'd been about to say. I didn't have to take that shit. *Especially* from her.

And I meant exactly what I said. Fuck every last one of them.

---

"JAYCE, can you run inside? Junior, Keem, and Isaiah are by the pool. I want to talk to your aunt for a second."

He swiftly unbuckled, climbing from the backseat and taking off into the house without a backward glance.

I frowned at Gia, who lifted her phone. "I already texted Keem that he was coming in." Then she unbuckled her own seatbelt, turning sideways to face me. "Eden..."

"I don't want to talk about what you saw or overheard today, okay? Just forget it."

She fell silent for a moment, observing the side of my face since I was avoiding her gaze. "You know, I asked to ride with you because I was ready to call you all kinds of bitches."

My head jerked over, finding her expression completely serious which made me laugh. "You'll have to get in line." Then I shrugged. "I'm sure my family will let you join in. Ganging up on me has always been their favorite bonding exercise."

Her gentle hand rested on mine and I startled, cringing at the emotion in her gaze. *Pity*.

God, I hated that.

I'd hated it when teachers realized my mom always showed up to parent-teacher conferences with the words *'what did she do now'* falling from her lips before knowing what was going on. I'd hated it in Luke's gaze as a teenager when I stayed at the gym well past closing rather than going home.

"Does Hakeem know?"

I laughed. "Does he know how pathetically lonely most of my life has been? Does he know that I'm an outcast with my own family?" I shrugged. "Somewhat."

"But not the full extent."

"It doesn't matter, Gia." I snapped, tossing up my hands. "None of what you saw matters because it's never going to change. It's a nasty cycle I've learned to live with. So just... pretend you didn't see it and don't tell Hakeem. If I want him to know, I'll decide when to tell him."

She held my gaze before climbing from the car. I watched with shock as she came to my side and pulled my door open. "Get out."

I bristled at her tone but did it, unsure about what the hell was about to happen.

I tried to prepare myself for every reaction. Yelling, a finger in my face, a slap... I didn't know what to expect but the one thing I hadn't prepared for was the tight hug she engulfed me in.

I went as stiff as a board but she only tightened her arms. "I judged you prematurely in St. Leesburg. And even though I did warm up to you, I still had my good eye on you in case you fucked up." I snorted. "Then y'all broke up and he started retreating into himself. I loved how animated he'd become during your relationship and I blamed you for when he reverted to the quiet, withdrawn Hakeem." She pulled back enough to make eye contact. "I made some *threats* against you, girl, do you hear me?"

I laughed again, not surprised one bit.

"I only cared about your effect on him. I never once considered *your* feelings. Or your past. None of that mattered to me. I only saw you as the woman who made Hakeem happy, then I judged you as the woman who broke his heart. Even if I never got the chance to express those feelings to you, I still want to apologize. It wasn't fair and I promise to mind my nosy ass business when it comes to your relationship with Hakeem." She released me from the hug, smoothing a motherly hand down my braids before adding, "Now that doesn't mean I'll turn away if you *offer* up the details because I *love* to gossip."

This interaction had not gone the way I'd expected but I was happy it happened. A little bit of the pressure and nerves I'd felt after spotting her in the kitchen faded.

But before I could grab my phone and Jayce's bags, she stopped me again. "Seriously, if you want to talk, I'm willing to listen. And if you need something, help with the boys, help with anything... let us know. You don't have to depend on family that treats you like that. Make your own. *We'll* be your family if that's what you want."

Those words sounded eerily familiar. "Your brother told me something similar not too long ago."

Her smile was huge as it stretched her lips. It was hard not to be in awe of this woman's beauty. "Where do you think he gets it from?" She shrugged. "He wants to be so much like me that it's actually kind of embarrassing." Then she pulled on her shades and turned to the house, walking off with that runway worthy strut while I cracked up behind her.

## 18

## HAKEEM

I'd been worried about how Eden and Gia would get along but something must've happened during that drive because they spent most of the day laughing and talking like old friends.

Though I was glad that she seemed to be enjoying herself, we needed to wrap things up. *Soon.* Our guests needed to leave and Jayce and Isaiah needed to go to bed because I had *plans* for her.

Though we hadn't exchanged many words since Gia occupied most of her time, my gaze never strayed far. And because of it, I'd spent most of the day hiding the huge bulge tenting the front of my swim trunks because Eden was strutting around in a sexy ass two-piece.

Each time she bounced Jayce in the air or ran from Isa or Junior during a playful game of tag, those bountiful breasts of hers jiggled in the barely-there bikini top. More than once, she'd surfaced, water cascading over her skin, accidentally flashing side peeks of her deep, brown areola before adjusting the fabric before the boys could see.

And that yellow bikini bottom kept slipping between those plump cheeks that had just enough jiggle to keep me rock hard all day.

On cue, she climbed from the water, giggling at the boys wrestling in the pool. I'd tolerated being social long enough. It was time for me and her to be alone.

Water dripped from her skin as she passed, flashing a coy grin as she grabbed her towel and entered the house.

My dick jumped beneath my trunks and I moved to follow, sending Gia a look that had her grinning. She knew exactly what I wanted—watch the boys because I was about to go fuck the shit out of their aunt.

"*Mr. Keem*!"

I froze with one foot inside, looking back over my shoulder at a grinning Jayce.

"Did you see me?"

I debated lying, just so I could go inside faster but I frowned, moving back to the pool's edge. I squatted, ruffling the top of his head, unable to resist a smile at his contagious grin. "Nah. Show me."

"Okay. Look."

Then he pinched his nose, closed his eyes, and dipped under the water. He stayed there for about three seconds then popped back up, frantically wiping his face.

That was it. *That' was all he did.*

"You saw me?"

I laughed and nodded. "I did. Keep practicing and you'll be able to stay under longer than me."

His eyes bucked wide before he pinched his nose again and sank. Another laugh rumbled up as I stood and continued towards the house.

Today, with Eden and the boys, I'd felt... *normal*. My friends had never been able to give me fulfillment like this. Neither had hookups with random women over the years.

What I felt could *only* be created by them and their presence.

After heading upstairs, I found her in the master bath, standing under the spray of the shower, still wearing that sexy ass swimsuit.

For a moment, I just watched from the doorway as she rinsed the chlorine from her face and out of her braids.

Finally, she caught a glimpse of me and flashed one of her rare, sweet smiles over her shoulder. I took that as an invitation, quickly stepping in behind her.

Once I slid the glass door closed, she tilted her head back and I couldn't resist dropping a kiss on those full lips. Her damp skin was soft and supple under my touch and I made a trail across her stomach, down to the area she kept completely devoid of hair because of her sport.

I honestly didn't care whether she kept it bald, trimmed, or bushy... I wanted that pussy in my mouth as often as she'd allow.

With my left hand, I held her neck, keeping it tilted back as my right slipped through those slick folds to caress the plump, hidden treasure beneath. I craved her reactions. Fed off the moans she offered up as I circled it with my index and middle finger.

Her choked gasps encouraged me to go faster. And she held onto each of my wrists, propping a foot on the towel handle, spreading herself wide. I took advantage of the offer, easing my swim trunks down just enough to free my dick so I could dip my knees and slip into her from behind.

"*Please.*"

"Please what, baby?" I asked, still holding her throat and teasing her clit while roughly pounding into her. Loud claps filled the air each time I collided with her thick, round ass. Her tight walls hugged me on each thrust forward, not wanting to let go as I retreated then slammed back home.

"I don't know." She whined, face contorting as if in pain. "Just... please."

I loved when she got like this. Loved that I *made* her like this. Almost incoherent and unable to complete a thought because of how good I made her feel.

"What do you need?" I asked in a strained tone.

"You. I just need you."

A breathless chuckle rushed out. "You already have me, baby." I shook my head. "I don't even think you realize how much you do." Then I shoved myself deep and lightly pinched her clit.

She shrieked, bucking in my hands, spasming around me as the orgasm ripped through her. She came violently, losing every ounce of control. And I fucked her through it, holding back my own release long enough for her to stop thrashing. Once I was sure I wouldn't collapse on my shaky legs, I switched off the water and scooped her trembling frame in my arms. She seemed half comatose as I dried her with a towel and dressed her in another of my t-shirts.

Then she sat on the edge of the bed, eyeing me as I changed out of my own damp clothes. "Bout to check on the boys."

Her smile was sleepy and she waved a tired hand in the air. I chuckled, kissed her forehead again then closed the door quietly behind me.

When I got downstairs, Gia was washing dishes while Jayce stood shirtless on a chair next to her, drying and stacking them neatly on the counter.

"Where Tee?" Jayce asked before falling into a fit of giggles when I swiped him from the chair, holding him high above my head.

"Taking a nap."

"I damn bet." Gia mumbled. I cut my eyes at her and she laughed. "Junior and Isa are in the shower. This little man is the only one who offered to help clean up so he's going to take his bath after." With the last dish washed, she turned to me, drying her hands. "Once Junior finishes, we're going to head out."

"Y'all can stay in one of the spare rooms." I grunted, fighting to hold onto Jayce's wriggling form as he situated himself on my shoulders. He had to have grown a *few* inches over the last few months because the last time we'd done this, his legs definitely hadn't stretched past my damn armpits.

"No, I have to stop by Birdie's. Might crash there if it gets too late."

My brows lifted. "You really running from Israel right now,

huh?" Another of her infamous glares sliced me but before she could say a word, I headed back towards the stairs. "Ready for your bath?"

His aggressive nod shook his whole body and I once again had to keep him from toppling off my shoulders. "Yes, sir. But don't forget my bubbles. My Tee always puts bubbles for me."

I laughed, savoring that warmth in my chest. "I got you, little man."

---

NOISES on the stairs had my lids popping open.

Eden still rested peacefully next to me. Instinct had me reaching for a gun before the distinct sound of light feet crossing the floor and my refrigerator being opened calmed my racing heart.

Silently, I climbed from the bed, making my way down the stairs. The gleam from the refrigerator light beamed across the floor, highlighting Jayce bent at the waist, rooting around in the bottom freezer drawer.

Instead of interrupting, I frowned, waiting to see if he would find what he was looking for.

Finally, a triumphant smile spread his cheeks as he found the bright orange box of popsicles. He was wrist deep before he stiffened, noticing my presence in the doorway. His expressive eyes grew wide with fear. Then his shoulders sank, adorable face immediately tugging at my heartstrings when it dropped with almost a dramatic level of sadness.

Fighting a smile, I pushed off the wall. "You're good. Just get me a blue one."

Immediately his entire expression transformed. Once again, he beamed, dropping the red he'd had in his hand and replacing it with two blues.

We ate our popsicles in silence, me leaning against the counter while he sat on top of it, swinging his legs happily. Somehow, he finished before I did. And the questions started.

"How old are?"

"39."

"Wow. That's old."

"*I guess.*"

"Where are you from?"

"Uptown."

"I don't know where that is. What's your favorite color?"

"Uh... black."

"What's your favorite game?"

"I don't have one. I like a lot of them."

"Where do you live?"

I paused after that question, wondering if he was being serious. A bright, blue-stained smile had me chuckling under my breath.

"I don't remember you talking this much."

"Because I'm *big* now. You missed my birthday."

Though he'd said it with no malice, I still felt the sting of his words because they were true. During the eight months Eden and I were apart, I'd missed his birthday and Isaiah's. I felt guilty about that and realized I owed more than Eden an apology.

"I'm sorry about that, little man."

He shrugged. "It's ok. Madi and Rome forgot, too." I frowned, realizing he called both his parents by their first names. "But my Tee didn't. She took me to *Fun World* and bought my class cupcakes."

That woman was literally a superhero and deserved better from all of us.

"I'm glad you had a good birthday. And I promise not to miss anymore."

"Can you get me a dog?"

I snorted. "You'll have to ask your aunt about that, okay?"

He gave the funniest eyeroll that morphed into giggles when I playfully pinched his side. "What were you doing up so late?"

He frowned, dropping his gaze to his knees. "I have nightmares sometimes when I'm not with my Tee. I think I forgot she was here because it's not her house so I had a scary dream."

"About what?"

He shrugged. "Scary stuff. Like being in the house by myself and it's dark."

I tilted my head. "Have you ever been left in the house by yourself when it's dark, Jay?"

He lifted his gaze to mine, searching for something before his tone dropped. "Not at night. Madi leaves me at Rome's house. It's really big and scary. I just sit in my bed until he gets there."

Fuck.

These kids had more toughness in them than some adults I knew. Just like their aunt, they'd been dealt a shitty hand but didn't let it completely destroy their happiness. They still managed to find joy in the little things and each other.

"I'm sleepy again." He suddenly declared, then looked at me expectantly. With a laugh, I lifted him on my shoulders, carrying him back upstairs and placing him in bed. He made me promise to stay with him until I fell asleep. It didn't take long, maybe five minutes at the most, before I was able to pull the covers up to his chin and return to my room.

I could tell she was awake the moment I opened the door.

Instead of rounding to my side, I walked right up to hers, meeting her gaze in the dark.

She didn't say a word as I pulled the cover back slowly. She even remained silent when I gripped the bottom of the shirt she wore and slipped it up and over her head.

Then I stripped down, too, slipping between her thighs but not inside. Instead, I slid my length through her folds, feeling her wetness coating me on each glide forward.

"Jayce?" she asked through a low moan. I nodded, pressing kisses up and down the side of her neck. "Another nightmare?" I hesitated then nodded again. She sighed, sounding so damn sad that I cupped her cheek, kissing the tip of her nose. "I'm failing them."

I stiffened, halting my movement. "No, you're not."

She swiped her hand up and down the length of my back. "I am. This... *all of this* is my fault."

The defeat in her tone felt like a punch to the chest. "It's not your fucking fault. None of this is. From what I could tell, you're the *only* good in those boys' life."

When she released a choked sob, I moved to get up so I could hold her but she stopped me, reaching between us to guide my length into her tight heat.

Though I'd just been inside her a few hours ago, it still felt like heaven on that initial stroke. She fit me like the perfect glove and I couldn't resist the groan that rushed from my lips. Nor could I resist lightly rocking in and out of her.

"*Please.*" She begged, matching my gentle motion.

"You using me to feel better?" When she said nothing, I increased the force of my thrusts, loving the helpless mewls she emitted. Her nails raked downwards, digging into my skin as she fucked me back. "What about tomorrow?"

"Tomorrow?"

"What about tomorrow?" I repeated, ignoring the hitch in my own tone. "You gonna pretend this shit ain't happening between us? Am I going to wake up to an empty house? Are you going to go ghost on me until I chase you down again? Because I will. You *know* I will."

She sighed. "What do you want, Hakeem?"

"That ain't what I'm asking. What do *you* want? From this situation? From me? Just tell me." I already knew the answer. Could see it in every fiber of her being despite her pride fighting to win out. She was at war with herself and in denial about what she really wanted. And this wouldn't fix all the problems that currently existed between us but at least it would be a step in the right direction.

"I don't know."

I stopped moving, refusing to break her stare. "What do you want, Eden? Right now. Stop thinking so damn hard and just *tell* me."

"I want *you.*" She snapped. Her eyes welled with tears and her fists clenched the seat. "There's a hundred other things I could ask for. *Should* ask for. But right now, I just want you. I *need* you."

I couldn't describe the feeling that overcame me at the admission. I knew it wasn't easy for her to ask for anything. And I promised to never take advantage of that vulnerability she'd exposed.

"And you got me. You'll always have me as long as you want to. *Anytime* the three of you need me, I'll be there." I pressed a kiss against her lips, resuming the slow, teasing rhythm between her thighs. "You hear me?" At her slow nod, I cupped her chin, maintaining eye contact. "I know you're still working for Barry. Fighting in the Pit." Her eyes ballooned and she tried to squirm free but I held on. "That shit's gotta stop, Eden. You're putting yourself in something you don't want to be part of, trust me." Her discomfort was apparent, and I figured she had enough to deal with without me heaping more shit on. So I decided to let it go. "We'll talk about it eventually, but it doesn't have to be today. Just know that I'm *here*. I'll always be here."

# 19

# EDEN

"Can we talk?"

Isa's spoon froze halfway to his lips. Hakeem and Jayce were playfighting in bed upstairs, so I took the opportunity to speak to my oldest nephew alone.

The fun we'd had with Gia, Junior, and Hakeem yesterday had been a fun distraction but the reality of what went down between us still remained undiscussed.

"Isa?"

He frowned at his bowl before sighing. "Yes, ma'am."

When I suggested we go outside to the patio, he followed silently, still not making eye contact.

I knew this conversation would be like pulling teeth so I didn't hesitate to jump right in. "Let's start with this." I leaned over, brushing the backs of my fingers across the faint bruising on his face. I expected him to recoil but he remained still, keeping his gaze on the fingers he drummed on the tabletop.

"Got into a fight." He muttered.

"With who?"

"Some boys from D-Block." I frowned at the familiar side of

White Grove that he'd had no business even being on. I'd done my share of dirt on that side of town. Kicking in doors and making threats against the lower leveled gang members who'd tried to get one over on Barry on Rome.

"Why, Isaiah?" He parted his lips to respond but I held up my hand, stopping what he'd been about to say. "Save us both the time of me having to ask for every single detail. Just tell me the whole story."

Finally his gaze met mine and my heart stuttered. I'd expected to see traces of Mona and Benji in his gaze, so it surprised me when I'd caught a glimpse of a young Eden in his mature eyes. He looked exactly like I did as a teenager. Lost. Confused. In need of guidance but too afraid to ask for it. He looked exactly like me when I'd struggled to figure out who the hell I was. When I realized my parents weren't a safe space for me emotionally, so I'd turned to outside sources and the streets for that love.

"Grandma took me to see dad the other day." He started, dropping his gaze back to the table as if realizing that look had revealed too much. "I asked if he could help my mom get me a game and he started calling me names. Nerd. Weak." He shrugged to prove he didn't care but he couldn't hide the heartbreak all over his face. "It is what it is. He's called me worse." Then he shifted in his seat. "Grandma dropped me at home. Mom was working a double so I was by myself. I didn't want to play video games after what he'd called me, so I left."

"Where?"

"To some of my friend's houses. But when it got late and I had to leave, I just walked because I didn't want to go home yet." *Jesus.* Anything could've happened to him while he'd been out walking the streets. Especially since no one had known where he was. "Went into a gas station in D-Block for some chips. Some older kids were there. One of them started making fun of my shirt because it was anime." His brows collapsed in a frown as if replaying the incident in his mind. "So, I hit that nigga."

I released a shocked gasp then swatted his leg. "Watch your mouth."

Finally, that stoic expression morphed into a sheepish one as he gave me a crooked grin. "Sorry, Tee. But I did." He sat up, leaning forward. "I was holding my own too. *Winning*. But his boys jumped in. They didn't do too much damage because the store clerk broke it up."

"Isaiah."

"This is the second time I got into a fight but this time they stole my bike. So I called Mr. Keem to get me. Just like last time."

*The customized one I'd paid nearly five hundred dollars for?*

I just managed to keep the words from exploding past my lips. I could afford to replace it. The only thing that mattered was that he'd walked away with only a busted lip and a few bruises. I knew firsthand just how fast a fight could go south and have someone wind up in the hospital or in the morgue.

"Are you mad?"

I rubbed my forehead. "About the bike? Not at all. That you were just walking around D-block like it was nothing? *Yes*. But there's nothing we can do about it now. I just hope you learned your lesson and won't take risks like that anymore." At his nod, I kept going. "Now, my question is why did you call Hakeem instead of me? You know I would've dropped whatever I was doing to race to you."

Suddenly, he was quiet again and avoided eye contact.

"Isaiah, I know you're probably mad at the world right now. But I want you to tell me about it. If you hate me for what's going on, you can say that. I promise I won't get upset because you're entitled to feel how you feel. You're entitled to your emotions. But I can't work on making it better if you don't let me in. Let me *fix* it."

"I don't hate you." He grumbled almost immediately. "I don't know why I said that stuff. Maybe because my dad had said we don't fit in your new life."

"What?"

"He said you were going to move away, get rich, famous, and

forget all about us." My stomach tightened with each word he spoke. "Said me and Jayce have been holding you back so you're going to start a life without us and forget about your real family. So when you said you'd come if I called, I got mad and I blamed you for keeping us apart when I know it's not your fault."

Instead of responding right away, I took a moment, resting my elbows on my knees and swiping both palms down my face. Benji was the biggest piece of *shit.* He could insult or hurt me however he wanted. But bringing the boys into it was unacceptable.

"Y'all are my life, Isa. My *whole world.*" I said once I'd found the right words. "You and Jayce could never hold me back because you two keep me going. Whether I live in White Grove, Uptown..." I sucked my teeth at the way his nose scrunched. He'd definitely been around the 400s too long if that was his reaction. "Or if I moved to Hawaii... there's always going to be room for you two. *Always.*"

Unlike the skepticism or mistrust I'd expected, he seemed to accept my answer. Though he didn't immediately launch into my arms like his younger cousin liked to do, I took his slight smile as a positive sign. "I love the two of you more than anything. Everything I do is for you. *Everything.* I don't care what anyone has to say—Benji, Rome, Barry, your mom, your grandma—it doesn't matter. I'm telling you that y'all are my whole world and I'll never turn my back on you. *Never.*" My voice cracked but I paid no mind. I'd be damned if I lost this strong connection with my nephew over some nonsense his dad tried to plant in his head.

Instead of answering, he pushed to his feet so I did the same. For a second, he seemed to debate with himself, shuffling his feet back and forth, almost appearing embarrassed. But for what?

Finally, he walked right up to me, dropping his forehead on my shoulder like my little Isa used to, even though he was less than an inch away from eclipsing my height.

"I believe you, Tee." He grumbled and I squeezed him, fighting back the tears that sprang behind my lids. "*And I love you, too.*"

## 20

## EDEN

My first PFC fight had finally arrived and all I could think about was how much I'd owe Barry after.

Unlike the small league where I was afforded a bit of peace and quiet before each contest, the locker room at the massive arena buzzed with nonstop action. Constant motion and noise from staff and media was making it hard to get in the zone.

People were snapping photos and making demands while others flitted about, accompanying celebrity after celebrity who wanted a photo op before the fight. Any other time, I would've been ecstatic but tonight, each of their faces were a blur because there was too much going on in my mind to even process the interactions.

Finally, fifteen minutes until the start of the fight, the man who'd made so much of tonight possible sauntered in.

"Just dropping in to wish you good luck." Verse greeted with a smile. I didn't return it, merely nodding and switching my gaze between him and the door, buzzing with nervous energy.

His lips curved in a grin. "He's out there."

My eyes ballooned. That heavy tension I'd been experiencing

turned light and airy, transforming my entire mood until I was fighting a smile. Just knowing he was here to support gave me hope.

And I held on to that hope as I slipped in my mouthpiece and stood beside Verse, posing for yet another photo. But unlike those that came before him, he didn't linger, merely wishing me luck once again before leaving.

I held onto that hope as I bounced on the balls of my feet, taking in the screams from the crowd as I was introduced.

The walk-in was unlike anything I'd ever experienced before. The air practically vibrated with energy. The lights were brighter than I was used to but I felt calm and composed as I faced my opponent, Sheena.

We'd battled in the smaller circuits and I'd beaten her twice. But that was almost five years ago and a lot had changed. Since then, she'd shedded the extra weight around her midsection and was ripped beyond belief.

She was quick and sneaky, using maneuvers that lulled opponents into complacency, making them believe she was getting sluggish right before going in for the kill.

Tonight, our battle was a hard fought one and at times, she got the upper hand. But I never lost focus, digging even deeper into my reserves each time I thought I would give out.

Soreness plagued every area of my body while my poor head spun from the hits it'd taken.

Either the competition was getting stiffer or age and fatigue was finally catching up to me. The once-easy battles that I could win in my sleep seemed harder and harder.

The last few sessions with my trainer had been... disappointing to say the least. My ankle still wasn't fully healed and my inability to focus had me knocked on my ass way too many times. So, when I'd arrived at the arena tonight, I'd seen the doubt on everyone's faces.

All the publicity, interviews, photoshops, and social media posts garnered a lot of hype surrounding tonight. Too much hard work had been put in and I couldn't afford to blow it. I couldn't let them down.

But more importantly, I couldn't let *myself* down. I'd sacrificed too much to let it end like this

So, I gave it all I had against the tough woman. And it seemed to be working in my favor until I took an elbow to the temple in the middle of the second round.

Pain unlike anything I'd ever felt shot through my head and my legs turned into noodles as I went down. The crowd's *oohs* barely registered as my opponent wasted no time launching towards me, attacking in a flurry of fists.

I immediately went on defense, protecting my face to prevent further damage. Then she scrambled behind me, attempting a headlock.

Despite increasingly blurred vision, I used pure instinct to guide me as I slipped under her arm then kicked my legs up above my head, locking them on either side of her neck and yanking. Her eyes bucked when she flew over me, landing flat on the mat with a thud.

Not giving her time to recover, I squeezed my thighs, crushing one against her windpipe while the other rested right behind her neck. She fought and scrambled to free herself but I didn't budge, tightening my grip, knowing she was seconds from passing out from lack of air.

Like I guessed, moments later, she tapped my thigh and the ref waved his hands and ran over, yelling to release her.

I immediately did, collapsing against the mat, chest heaving with exhaustion before gingerly standing. The crowd was going crazy and the announcer had climbed in the ring to crown the winner. Strobe lights flashed and people tapped my shoulders, smiling and yelling what I hoped were words of congratulations.

But I felt like I was under water, unable to make out anything they were saying.

Even when my name was called and arm raised in victory, I remained stoic, fighting the urge to flinch every time the cameras flashed in my face and sent a sharp ache through my head.

Finally, I was escorted from the octagon with security on either side. This was definitely a change from the smaller leagues but now that I was running with the big dogs and had gained notoriety, they told me it was necessary.

It still didn't register that I was considered a *celebrity* and had fans.

Once inside the locker room, the throb in my head and neck worsened until I couldn't hide my grimace.

More underwater congratulations met my ears as I climbed on the trainer's table for the medic to check me out.

That also was new.

There were no medics on standby in the smaller leagues. If you suffered any injury, it was up to your team to get you to the emergency room for treatment.

"Turn off that fucking bell." I grumbled, cupping my forehead.

"*Bell?*" I heard a concerned voice utter. "Open your eyes for me, Ms. Foster."

I tensed at the unfamiliar voice then peeked a lid open, flinching from the blinding light.

The medic immediately switched two of them off which dimmed the room considerably. I sighed in gratitude and fully opened both lids for the first time since taking an elbow to the temple.

"Hmm." His tone had me tense with worry. "How are you feeling?"

I thought I'd mumbled that I was fine but the way his brows shot up had me wondering what had actually left my lips.

"And what's today's date?"

Again, I mumbled the answer, frowning when I found it harder to keep myself upright.

"What's your first and last name?"

Okay, he's doing too fuckin' much now. I had a headache but wasn't *stupid.*

This time, with confidence, I mumbled my full government name but again his brows rose and he looked over his shoulder with concern at the people in the room I hadn't noticed until now.

Verse, Rell, Eboni, my new trainer, and about three other people I didn't recognize.

"Can you sit up straight for me, Eden?"

"*I am.*" I muttered before realizing I was pitching forward.

There was a symphony of yelps and gasps before hands gripped me from every direction.

I didn't lose consciousness but didn't feel fully in control of my limbs, either. After getting resituated on the table, the medic whipped out his iPad, putting me through a variety of concussion tests. Before the match, I'd done what they called baseline testing, which consisted of eye control and movements, depth perception, and other minor physical tasks. They were done to have something to compare my post-match results to.

After he input the results into the iPad, he grinned, giving the good news I had sustained a minor head injury but not a concussion.

"It's likely that you won't need to go to the hospital but I do recommend having someone stay with you tonight. That way they can monitor you and get you to the emergency room if your symptoms worsen." While I remained silent, he lifted a brow. "Do you have someone? If not, then I'll call ahead to the hospital and have an observation room prepared. You *can't* be alone tonight."

I nodded, despite not having anyone besides Hakeem to call. I'm sure he'd agree but the problem was that I hated having to ask in the first place. But it seemed as if I had no choice.

"Good." He said then moved on to check out my sore ankle, rattling off more instructions that went in one ear and out the other. All I could focus on was that I had cottonmouth, was battling a persistent ache in my head, and needed a damn shower.

Now that they'd confirmed I wasn't concussed, they could at least let me wash away the remnant of the fight that still clung to my skin.

When his talking didn't seem to have an end in sight, I stood, forcing myself to stand upright and appear strong despite the weakness in my leg. Refusing their offer of crutches, I took two slow, measured steps. Before I could take another, Verse blocked my path.

His expression was pinched as his eyes scanned me with concern. "Take it easy. Whatever you need, somebody can get it for you,"

"What I *need* is to wash my ass. Can you do that for me?"

He briefly looked taken aback at my sarcastic tone before his lips curved with amusement. "I doubt Hakeem or Garryn would like that but at least take the crutches with you. You don't want to make it worse by falling."

He was saved from a snippy, irritated response by the sound of an elevated voice on the other side of the closed door. "*Sir, only people with passes are allowed past this point.*" There was a moment of brief silence before the same voice called out. "*Sir, you can't go back there*!"

This time, there was a familiar tenor that responded, prompting Verse to move towards the commotion. Once the door opened, my eyes bucked at the sight of Hakeem squared off against one of the arena security guards.

They were equal in height and weight but the uniformed man lacked the aura of danger emanating from the one who coolly lifted a brow. "Tell this nigga to let me through, Verse." He growled, all without breaking the guard's stare. "Because I have zero problems fucking his shit up if he thinks I'm not getting..." His eyes swung to me as I approached. "To *her*."

He made a move to step inside but the security blocked him again. Rage blazed in his orbs as he tore his gaze from me and leaned towards the man.

"Relax." Verse urged, smoothly maneuvering between and separating the two. "He's cool, Tony."

The guard's attention switched to Verse, wide-eyed and awestruck. "You know my name?" Verse looked confused before his gaze dropped to the man's chest. The guard followed his line of sight, visibly deflating once he remembered the name badge attached to his shirt. "*Oh*."

Impatient as ever, Hakeem entered the room, aggressively shoulder-checking *Tony* as he passed. I took a cautious step backwards as he approached, caught off guard by that wild look in his eyes.

"You okay?" I nodded slowly and his lids narrowed with suspicion. "Don't lie to me."

"I'm *not*." I attempted to take another step backwards, but he stopped me, bending just enough to scoop me off my feet. "*Keem*!"

His eyes lingered on the wrap around my ankle, brows creasing even further. I squirmed to get down, but despite my effort, he didn't release me. Hell, he didn't even struggle. Instead, he turned to the medic who watched the whole scene with wide eyes. "What's wrong with her?"

He looked mildly uncomfortable as he looked from Keem to me. "Um...I've already given her instructions for treatment and follow-up."

"Did I fucking ask you that?" He snapped, taking threatening steps towards the man.

Yet again, smooth as ever, Verse intervened. "Can we have the room?" Though he'd voiced it as a question, his tone made it obvious that he wasn't asking. The room quickly emptied until the three of us remained. Head tilted, he eyed his friend, observing with that intense scrutiny that made me want to squirm. "You good?"

I lifted my head to observe Hakeem's response, finding that his eyes had calmed a bit. "Just worried about her."

"Tell him you're fine, Eden." Verse's demand caught me off guard, especially since he never broke eye contact with Hakeem. There was something deeper going on. Some hidden meaning that only made sense to the two friends.

"I'm fine." I whispered, switching my focus between them, trying to make sense of what the hell was going on. "I have a sprained ankle and head injury." His entire frame stiffened and the loose grip holding me in place tightened. "A minor one." I rushed to add, hoping to calm him. "I don't have a concussion. The doctor just wants someone to monitor me tonight while I sleep. As a *precaution*. That's it."

Finally, whatever had been happening between him and Verse broke. Still, I experienced a nervous clench in my gut when his gaze dropped to mine. "You're staying with me." Then, as if that settled everything, he turned to leave.

"*Wait.*" He froze after my request. "I have to meet with Eboni. I need to speak to the press. I need to *shower*."

"Eboni can wait until tomorrow. *Fuck* the press. And you can shower at my place."

Verse snorted, earning a harsh glare from me. "I can't just say fuck the press. This is my job, Keem. I can't just abandon my responsibilities because I got hurt."

Though I wanted to let him whisk me away, I couldn't. Tonight was my first league contest and there were certain obligations I needed to fulfill.

Keem seemed to debate over what to do. And I thought I'd have to fight or argue my case more but he reluctantly lowered me to my feet with a frown.

"*Fine.*"

# 21

# HAKEEM

I'd conceded to staying at the arena but that didn't mean I wouldn't be watching her every move.

Eden pretended to be annoyed but the coy looks she shot my way while showering proved otherwise. After Verse provided an all-access badge, he left, promising to keep everyone at bay long enough for her to get changed. My plan was to help her but two hair-raising glares had ensured that I remained only a spectator.

Done with her shower, she stood in the dressing room, attempting to slip on underwear. She bent at the waist but paused midway with a grimace, as if contemplating whether wearing any at all was worth it. Though every instinct urged me to snatch them out of her hand and squat to help, I didn't want to bruise her pride.

It was obvious she was in pain. But her head remained high and though her movements were slow and hindered, she's turned down crutches and anyone's assistance. But I'd seen the bruises staining her smooth skin before she'd stepped in the shower.

The woman was the epitome of tough and I admired the hell out of her, even if she frustrated the fuck out of me by refusing help.

The initial panic I'd felt after watching her go down in the octagon had eased. I'd been watching from the skybox, pacing in front of the window, unable to sit down from the moment I'd arrived. From the beginning of the fight, I could tell it would be a tough one but had seen her beat adversity enough times to not panic. Eden had a second gear that cranked up when the pressure was at its peak. Which normally put any fears or worries I had to bed.

But this time, even though she'd upped her intensity, I'd gotten the sense that something was off. She hadn't looked *right* after she'd taken that hit. She'd fought through the pain and even stood there after her victory but the squint in her eye and body language let me know that something was wrong.

The skybox had been a great place to watch the fight but it had taken way too long to get to her from there. My unease had mounted until I'd stood outside the locker room, ready to go to war with the arena security for not letting me pass. I understood it was his job but rationale was absent the longer she'd been out of view.

Panic wasn't an emotion I was familiar with. Nor was it one I felt equipped to handle. Which was why I'd nearly lost control. Verse had sensed it, quickly diffusing the situation before it could turn into a shitshow.

"*Dammit.*" She attempted to bend again, nearly toppling over. But I held her upright. I'd been content with letting her be stubborn and prideful, but not at the price of injuring herself further.

I respected the hell out of her and the career she chose. And I wanted her to succeed more than anything I'd ever wanted for myself. But I'd never be okay with her being hurt. I'd never be okay watching her body being battered and bruised for others entertainment. But I could deal with it because it was what *she* loved. And because of that single reason, I'd be at every fight, offering my support any way that I could. And once it was over, I'd be waiting in the locker room, ready to help her begin the recovery process.

Even if her stubborn ass refused it.

When she tried for a third time, I finally snatched the underwear and kneeled. "*You don't have to treat me like an infant.*" She complained but I ignored her, grinning despite the glare on her face. Stubbornly, she refused to lift a leg but I merely held the plain, high-waist black underwear open, refusing to budge.

"Come on, put your granny panties on."

"Granny—" Her offended squeak and slack-jawed look was worth the smack against my chest. "*They're compression underwear.*"

When I snorted in amusement, she rolled her eyes and stubbornly lifted her leg, placing her hands on my shoulders for balance.

Immediately, my gaze shot between her thighs. Normally, the temptation to glide my tongue between would take over. But not now. Despite the delicious nudity on display, all I cared about was taking *care* of her.

Once they were securely on her hips, I stood, stopping her before she could turn away. "You don't have to do everything alone." I reminded, cupping her cheek and her eyelids fluttered but she remained still, watching almost nervously as I lowered my forehead to hers. "It's okay to ask for help. Especially from people who won't punish you for needing it."

If I wasn't so close, I might've missed the flinch. My baby didn't know how to be taken care of. But I'd fix that. I just needed the time to prove she was deserving of having her every need catered to simply because seeing her whole and happy pleased me.

When she didn't respond, I stepped back, allowing her to continue her ginger walk across the room where she stopped in front of her bag. Instead of reaching inside, she just stared at it, remaining still for so long that I became concerned, wondering if this was a lingering effect from her head injury.

"Can you help with the rest of my clothes?" The question was barely audible but it still stopped me in my tracks. If I hadn't started across the room, I might've missed it altogether because of the soft, unsure tone. "It's a little... uncomfortable when I bend over."

I swiftly closed the distance between us, jumping in before she could change her mind. She steadily avoided my gaze as I helped her dress and I knew it would take time. This wouldn't be an overnight process. But I was learning to be patient. Teaching myself *how* to be patient, so I could be what she needed.

A lot of our encounters the first time around had been at my pace. We mostly got together whenever it was convenient for me. And being who she was, she just went with the flow. But that hadn't been fair to her. Her time was just as precious as mine, and it deserved to be respected. I never wanted to be another person who took advantage of her giving nature.

So I vowed to let her dictate our pace. Even though I was more than ready to jump in headfirst and resume where we left off, I could tell she was a bit more skittish. She was holding back and I didn't blame her. We had gotten involved and fell hard and fast. All without fully revealing who we were behind the mask that both of us had perfected wearing out of self-preservation.

"Thank you." Yet again, her words emerged in an unsure tone.

The contrasts inside this woman would always amaze me. Less than an hour ago, she was blood spattered and fighting like a mad woman for victory. Now, she was soft and sweet, vulnerable in a way that balanced out the other side perfectly.

"You're welcome." I whispered back, loving that the corner of her lips kicked up in a slight grin.

Swiftly, I leaned down and placed a kiss against the fullness before pulling back. "You ready?"

Her nod was resigned but she marched towards the door anyway. Her agent, a woman she introduced as Eboni, barely spared me a glance as she talked a mile a minute, prepping Eden for what was to come. She'd done interviews before but based on what the two of them were saying, this would be her first live interaction with the media.

"Oh, you can wait back here" Eboni finally acknowledged my presence, holding out a hand as if to stop me.

I eyed her for a moment, then slowly rolled my gaze over to Eden who huffed and rolled her eyes. "That meant that he's not *staying* anywhere."

I barely restrained my smile, pleased that she had become proficient in what Krystal called *Hakeem speak*. Though she was the only one who had a name for it, only those closest to me were skilled in deciphering what I was thinking without having to say a word.

With a satisfied nod, I returned my gaze back to the agent, waiting to see if she would give pushback or just accept the fact that I was coming along. Her eyes bounced between the two of us before finally settling on Eden. "You got new security that I don't know about?"

Eden laughed. "Something like that."

That shrewd gaze of Eboni's returned to me. This time, sizing me up before she hummed and kept going.

She was a powerhouse in heels and I liked her.

More than once, she'd recognized that she'd been walking too fast and adjusted her speed to accommodate Eden's injury. And though she talked a mile per minute and could come off as pushy, it was obvious there was mutual respect between them.

"Okay..." Eboni stopped again and turned to me. "You really can't go further than this." Before I could even react, she kept going. "From this point, only athletes are allowed through. We'll walk around to the other side where we can have a clear view of her from the back of the room while she does her interview. Once it's over, we can circle back around to meet her. I promise no one is going to attack her in the few minutes that we're separated." Then she flashed a grin. "But if they do? I think our girl is more than capable of defending herself, don't you?"

I didn't know whether to be elated that someone recognized her as my girl. Or jealous that someone had the nerve to refer to her as *our girl*. Even if platonically.

So I did what I did best and said nothing.

She stared for a few seconds, waiting for me to speak. But when I didn't, she tossed up her hands and turned to Eden. "Okay, what did *that* mean?"

Eden's lips twitched as she shrugged. "That means Hakeem is

going to do what he wants, but I believe he's okay with what you said."

The woman was getting ready to open her mouth yet again but I frankly was tired of the conversation even though I hadn't said a word. So I stepped up to Eden, gently cupping the back of her head to draw her close. We held eye contact and I poured every ounce of confidence I had in her into the look, hoping it would dispel the nervousness I spotted in her gaze. "Good luck."

"Oh, so he *can* speak?" Eboni commented from behind us, causing both our shoulders to bounce with laughter.

"Make sure they know who you are." I said to the woman in front of me once our humor subsided.

She reached up to cup the hand that cradled her head. "Who *am* I?"

There were layers to that question. Layers that I knew we'd unpeel one day, just not tonight. "You're Eden fuckin' Foster." A soft tuft of air rushed past as she sighed. "You're an inspiration. You're the face of *Her-letics* clothing line. You're the only woman to maintain an undefeated record in the minor circuit. You just won your first PFC contest. You're the first woman to sign with VP Sports." Her eyelids fluttered closed as she basked in my praise. "You're the *baddest* muthafucker I know. And you're fine as hell, too. So make sure they know I'll sweep through that room like a tornado if any of them try you."

She laughed under her breath as the nervousness that had obviously bothered her seemed to fade. Stepping closer, she practically melted against me and dropped her forehead against my chest, wrapping her arms around my waist. She didn't respond, but I could feel gratitude in the hug.

Then she stepped back, squared her shoulders, and walked away. Eboni tried to usher me away but I took a second longer, admiring *my* tough-as-nails woman as she approached the podium without a hint of the limp she'd had since the fight ended.

Only then did I follow Eboni, rushing to the back of the media room to watch *my* baby breeze through the post-fight interview. She was confident, self-assured, and likable. She answered truthfully while still being evasive enough to avoid trap questions—like her opinions on other fighters and any possible injuries she might have.

The media couldn't get enough of her. And for nearly half an hour, we watched her transform into the star she was capable of being. Then, once the signal was given, she thanked the media for their time and with her head held high and limp-free, she strolled off with even more confidence than what she'd approached the podium with.

Just like the fucking warrior she was.

# 22

# EDEN

My neck felt stiff. And sore.

But I already felt miles better than I had before falling asleep.

Flashes of the night before played through my mind. Hakeem being so gentle and caring at the arena. The way he'd stood guard during my press conference.

The silent ride to his place and a second embarrassing, supervised shower before I pulled on one of his shirts.

The soft touches and conversation we shared before finally dozing off.

Without turning, I stretched out a hand, gliding it across the bed, feeling the cool sheets next to me. He obviously hadn't slept in the bed and I wondered where he was.

Judging by the lack of light peeking through the curtains, it was still early which meant he was probably asleep in one of the guest rooms. I started to relax again, hoping for a few more hours myself when a light snore had me shooting to a sitting position, scanning the room. Near the foot of the bed, Hakeem slept in a chair, one elbow resting on the arm, supporting the fist that propped up his chin. From his rumpled appearance and yesterday's clothes, he'd obviously been there all night.

While he slept, I observed him. His healthy beard with strands of gray sprinkled throughout. Full lips pursed in a small pout. Long, enviable lashes that fanned out over the hills of his cheeks. The not-quite-smooth head that had sprouted enough hair to give his normally bald scalp a dark tint.

Even in sleep, Hakeem didn't appear soft or tender. He was too intimidating for that, even with his eyes closed. But he was most relaxed like this and I enjoyed the view.

Wanting a closer look, I uncurled my legs to crawl towards him. Halfway across the plush mattress, I froze in place when he went from relaxed to stiff in a split second. The snores ceased and in their place were his normal, even breaths. It was obvious he was now awake but kept his lids closed, pretending not to be as he listened for more movement.

Rather than announcing that I knew he was awake, I didn't move either, wondering how long it would take for him to open his eyes.

Minutes passed and I was just on the verge of giving up when he mumbled, "How long we gonna play this game?" Finally, his lids peeked and a slight smile softened his lips.

Immediately, mine curved. "You look worse than I do." I commented, moving to sit on the edge of the bed, legs dangling between his that were spread.

His smile grew as he cupped my thigh, squeezing gently. Then he lifted his opposite wrist, glancing at his watch. "Damn. It's already seven?" He grumbled, sitting up from his slouched position, leaning forward to press a kiss against my forehead. "Didn't fall asleep until like five."

"Why?"

He stood with an exaggerated grunt and I chuckled under my breath, watching him move across the room to rifle through his drawers. "Keeping an eye on you. Didn't want something to happen while I was sleeping but, I couldn't fight it anymore."

His normally deep tone rumbled out in an exhausted rasp. He looked so damn tired and out of sorts that I honestly felt bad. He didn't have to volunteer to stay with me last night and now he was suffering for it. Climbing from the bed, I walked over, smiling at how adorable he looked when he rubbed his eyes. Then he glanced over his shoulder with alarm, eyeing my slight limp with concern before relaxing when I wrapped my arms around him from behind.

This morning, the normal intensity between us had eased off, leaving behind only affection and comfort.

I didn't know if this was another level of our weird connection that we'd unlocked but I enjoyed it. I'd fully embrace it for as long as it lasted.

"You have your schedule and shit saved on your phone's calendar?"

Not wanting to release him just yet, I stayed put, nodding against his broad back.

"A'ight. I'll need it in a minute."

"Why?" At my muffled response, his big frame bounced against my face with his snickers.

"So I can sync it to mine."

"Okay...." I really didn't understand what he was saying. Nor did I really want to. Not when I was this comfortable.

He must've sensed that I was half listening because he sucked his teeth, lightly tapping the hands curled around his front. "You got a security team yet? Somebody guarding you when you're at all these events and shit? Cause I damn sure didn't see any last night."

Again, I offered a muffled, "No."

"Well, until then, I'll be it."

"I don't *need* security." I said with a laugh that he didn't join in. "But if I did, I couldn't afford it anyway. Not right now and especially one with *your* price tag. So thanks but I'm good."

Before I could react, he'd turned in my arms, returning my hug while having the nerve to look offended. "You think I'd charge you?"

"Uh... why wouldn't you? That's your business. I'm not asking you to do anything pro bono." I shrugged helplessly when he just continued staring. "Besides, me and you, we aren't..."

"We aren't *what*?" He asked harshly. That easy vibe I'd just been basking in disappeared and that familiar intensity that seemed to be a part of his natural personality filled the air.

"We're not... what we were anymore." I squirmed under his glare then forced myself to stop, hating that I let him affect me this way. "You don't have to do this because of whatever misguided feelings you're having about me and the boys. If you want to see and spend time with them, I'm fine with it. They love you and you're good with them. They could use that, especially in my absence. And if you want to spend time with me, I'm cool with that, too. But you don't have to..."

"You done." He interrupted. I opened my mouth to tell him that I wasn't but he kept going. "No, that wasn't a question. That was me telling you that you *were* done." My neck jerked backwards and I immediately regretted it at the twinge of pain I felt in my head. He scowled when I grimaced, reaching up to gently massage the back of my neck and head before easing those fingers around my hairline, up to my ear. "Ain't shit misguided over here." He tugged the lobe and for some stupid reason, it made me blush. "Especially when it comes to you. Everything I do is with intent. And looking out for you *pro bono* is what I want to do. You can try to stop me but I'll just assign someone else. *Then* I'll be paying out of pocket for their services. At least with me, your guilt can be eased since I won't be losing any money. So which would you prefer?"

Then the arrogant fucker had the nerve to raise a brow, as if my answer was already a foregone conclusion. When I only offered an eye roll in response, he smiled, smacking the curve of my ass. "That's what I thought." Then he grabbed his clothes, walking towards the door of his bedroom. "Bout to shower in the other room if you want to use that one." He nodded towards the master bath then his night-stand. "My phone's over there. Go ahead and sync our calendars so I can let my secretary know to work my schedule around yours."

I sucked my teeth, reluctantly pulling myself away from him.

"I got some shit to handle this weekend at HB," he said, stopping in the doorway. "After that I'm yours."

I watched his retreating back, reaching for his phone. Before I could grab his, mine buzzed with a text.

**Rome: Saturday at 7.**

A second message came through with an address just on the outskirts of White Grove. Then a third, with a warning of *don't fuck up*.

Of all times for him to reach out. I'd honestly forgotten about the so-called meeting I had to attend with Crow in exchange for the extra time I'd gotten with Jayce and a few weeks off from fighting in the Pit. At times, I wondered if they purposely made me wait like this to lull me into a sense of complacency before they sprang their demands on me at the worst time.

If I told the man down the hall about the meeting, he'd surely step in. But did I truly want him to? I'd never forgive myself if he got hurt because of me. Because of his need to protect me.

Besides, it was only a meeting. One that probably would be over in less than hour. Compared to some of the other shit they'd made me do, this would be a walk in a park.

"You good?"

I jumped, nearly dropping my phone. He was too damn big to be so light on his feet. "Uh..." I stammered, knowing I looked suspicious as hell. I hated that the cool, composed version of myself always chose to play hide-and-seek when he was around. "Yeah. I'm good." Then before he could question that statement, I kept talking. "Do you have a code on your phone?" I asked, now holding both in my hand. I knew he didn't. He'd told me before that he didn't give enough fucks to bother creating one.

"You sure you're good?" He asked instead and familiar guilt plagued me. This was the exact thing that had caused division between us the first time. And I found myself falling right back into the habit of keeping secrets.

"Yeah. Yeah. I'm good."

Though he obviously didn't buy it, he didn't push for more. Instead, he opened one of his drawers, pulling out a pair of black socks before looking my way again. "You'd tell me if something was up, right?"

Shit. Why couldn't he just leave it alone? I promise, after this one last meeting, I'd be done going on jobs for the 400s. If we couldn't return to our monetary only arrangement, then they could kiss my ass.

"Go shower." I said instead, avoiding the question.

"Do you need help? Getting ready, I mean."

I was briefly confused by the subject change before shaking my head. "Nah. I actually feel fine. I mean... I'm sore of course but my head feels fine."

"Hmm." He leaned over, kissing my forehead once. Then he did it again. "Don't try to be a badass. Call me if you need me. And *sit the fuck down* if you feel dizzy or light-headed.."

I snorted at his harsh, yet caring instructions. "*Yes, sir.*"

He playfully thumped my nose. "Yeah, a'ight." Then he walked out, closing the door gently behind him.

---

HAKEEM WAS bad for my health.

Since the man had appointed himself as my bodyguard, we'd spent damn near every moment of the last four days together.

As instructed by the medic after the fight, I'd gone to see my primary care physician and was cleared to resume physical activity. Of course, like he'd suspected, I didn't have a concussion but was banged up enough to limit my activity to stretching and keeping my muscles loose and fluid for whenever I resumed contact training.

But Hakeem's incessant need to be where I was and follow me around wasn't why he was bad for my health.

No, it was because the man had been feeding me some of the most delicious and unhealthy foods that I could spoon between my lips. After only a week, I wouldn't be surprised if I'd packed on five pounds because of the terrible diet and sedentary lifestyle. An active person like me who was used to always being on the go meant that I rarely had downtime. But the imposed rest I was now getting wasn't as bad as I thought it would be.

Maybe, with time, I'd become bored, but at the moment, I was enjoying every minute. Just like I enjoyed every minute spent with the man catering to my every need.

"You feeling up to this?" I glanced at the man in question before shrugging.

Even if I wasn't ready, there was nothing I could do about it now because we were literally walking into the building for the podcast interview.

Something had come up with Eboni's daughter so she'd had to back out at the last minute. Just like the part-time assistant that I was testing out. Managing everything had become too much for me and Eboni, who also had other clients that needed her attention.

So after a round of interviews, we agreed on a part-time assistant named Nate. He was good at his job, touting an ability to get stuff done with what seemed like a snap of his fingers, even if he was a bit high-strung at times.

But I still gave him the benefit of the doubt because he was so damn efficient. If he did a good enough job, I'd consider turning his temporary position into one more permanent.

"Yeah, I guess." I finally answered once we stopped in front of the elevator.

I'd convinced Eboni that I was fine going alone. Besides, it wouldn't look good to reschedule so close to the date and I was actually excited to meet with the host of the popular podcast.

I could handle whatever questions were thrown my way, especially since we'd already pre-screened the list of topics that would be discussed. People *wanted* to know more about who Eden Foster was and this was a great opportunity to give them a chance to do so.

"*Hi, Eden.*"

Both of us froze once the door of the elevator opened, unprepared for the woman waiting there with a smile.

"Hi." I said cautiously.

My interview was with the Lady Sports Talk podcast but Eboni had done most of the scheduling, so I actually didn't know who I was supposed to meet. I was assuming that she was an employee but I'd rather be safe than sorry. So, my cautiousness remained high just like the man who stepped forward, halfway blocking me with his body.

The lady flicked a nervous glance in his direction before she jutted out her hand. "I'm Nala, Lady Bee's outreach manager, I saw the two of you approaching on camera so I just wanted to come out and greet you before we record."

I shook her hand, flashing the smile that no longer felt so uncomfortable when I was forced to show it. "Thank you. I'm honored to be here." Then I placed a hand on Hakeem's arm, fighting my smile when instead of sticking out his hand, he merely nodded at the woman.

"Oh, okay. Um, there's a refreshment area down the hall if you want to wait while she's recording. It has snacks, drinks, a television... anything you might like is probably in there and if it's not, we'll find it for you." Then her focus switched back to me. "The episodes are typically between an hour to an hour and a half. But recording normally takes between three to five hours so I hope you're prepared to be here for a while."

That had been explained to me prior to agreeing so I merely smiled and nodded.

"Is there another spot where I can wait that's still within view of her?" I think both of us were shocked when Hakeem spoke up.

"Uh, yes." She said after a moment of hesitation, gesturing for us to follow into a spacious area where three or four people tinkered with laptops and camera equipment. On the opposite wall was a two-way glass that had a clear view of the recording studio. "You can sit in here. There's a chair over in the corner if you won't mind the noise."

He thanked her then turned to me. I could see that the urge to show some sort of affection had hit him strongly but he was trying to resist.

I was a pseudo-celebrity now and the last thing I wanted was for the public to start speculating about my love life, especially when I didn't even have clarification myself. Keeping my name away from the gossip blog, *The Rumor Mill*, was priority number one.

Thankfully, he seemed to have the same thought process because he gave me a short nod, whispered good luck then stepped inside.

I followed Nala to the recording room, trying to ignore the flutter of nerves in my stomach. Lady Bee was a trailblazer in the sports podcast industry. She hadn't been an athlete herself but an avid fan for most of her life and was knowledgeable in every single sport, based on the previous episodes I'd seen. I was a huge fan and had been following her for years.

It felt surreal that I was now one of her guests, which was why I gave an uncharacteristically shy wave when I stepped inside and laid eyes on her sitting at the iconic hot pink table while fiddling with the recording equipment.

Her gaze jerked up at our movement and she stood. "Hi!" She greeted enthusiastically, giving a warm hug that I hadn't expected." I'm so glad to have you on the show. Thank you for agreeing."

"No, thank *you*." I gushed back. "For even considering me, Lady Bee. I'm excited to be here."

"Oh, please just call me Bee."

"Ready, ladies?" I jumped at the unexpectedly deep voice coming from behind me.

Turning, I found a stern-faced, yet extremely handsome man with a cap twisted backwards on his head and a bulky pair of head-phones hanging from around his neck. His dark-eyed gaze swung between the three of us before finally settling on Bee. If I wasn't mistaken, there was a bit of heat behind that gaze. And the woman who'd displayed nothing but confidence while presenting an award at last year's ESPYS blushed prettily.

"Yeah," she said softly. "We're ready." Then she turned to me. "This is Saint, my audio and video engineer." Then her smile turned teasing. "I'm the boss but somehow I find myself answering to him."

"You *love* answering to me."

Nala and I exchanged glances, confirming without saying a word that we both felt the sexual tension.

Bee cleared her throat and gestured towards the open seat adjacent to hers. "Okay, let's get started."

It took a few minutes for everyone to get in place and I took several sips of the bottled water that Nala had offered, constantly flicking glances towards the dark room on the other side of the two-way glass where I could only make out the shapes of the occupants inside.

"What's good, my loves? Welcome back to another episode of the Lady Sports Talk podcast. I'm your host Lady Bee and we have a very, *very* special guest today. A woman who popped up on Verse Presley's Snapshot page almost a year ago and now we can't get enough of her. A woman who snatched our edges with one of the *sickest* photo shoots to ever bless our eyes. Y'all remember that dress and those *legs*." I giggled into the mic after she flashed a wink. "A badass woman who just won her first PFC contest last week. A woman who, despite all the shit I said doesn't really need an introduction, because she is a legend in the making. Ladies and gentleman, *Ms. Eden Foster*."

"Wow." I said with a laugh when the crew in this room and the next applauded along with the sound bite. "That was a hell of an introduction, thank you so much."

"Okay, before we start, can I just say that you are fine as shit, Ms. Eden?" A surprised laugh shot out again as I blushed. That was a huge compliment coming from a woman who was *nineties fine*, like

Nia Long and Regina King. The short pixie cut that framed her dark-brown face accentuated her almond-shaped eyes and full, cupid's bow lips.

"You're going to boost my head with all these compliments."

"You deserve every bit of it." The tension I felt eased a bit more. "So I'm going to dive right in because I've been waiting to get my hands on you for weeks..." She paused long enough for both of our laughs to subside. "Tell me... what made Eden Foster who she is today?"

I sighed, taking a moment to think. "A lot of things, really. My environment, upbringing, friends, family..." She didn't need to know that their influence helped by pushing me to be the exact opposite of them. "And a shit ton of hard work. I didn't just stumble on this talent and career as an adult. It was something I intentionally went after at a young age and pursued with everything I had." I licked my lips, coaching myself to remember that footage would be uploaded to her channel as well so I had to be cognizant of my facial expressions. "My brother was a fan of boxing. And I would watch it just to bond with him. But with time, I learned to love it on my own."

"Were there any challenges?" Then she scoffed. "Let me rephrase that. You're a woman in a male-dominated space—something I can definitely relate to—so what were the challenges I'm sure you faced?"

"There were plenty." I agreed. "I heard a lot of no's. I was told by *way* too many people that I couldn't do it. Because I was a woman. Because I was a *black* woman. Because I was too short. Because I was too thick. Because I wasn't tough enough."

"They said *you* weren't tough enough?" She scoffed. "Not from what I've seen."

I chuckled. "That woman you see in the octagon took time to develop, too. I was a sensitive little girl so they thought that would translate into my matches. They thought I'd be too passive and would get bullied in the ring. And I made it my mission to prove them wrong. I'm not ashamed to say that the naysayers were the fuel behind my obsession with going so hard early on. Now, I fight for myself and the love of it, but back then, I enjoyed the look on their faces when I not only did what they said I couldn't... but I *dominated.*"

She blinked then switched her gaze to the camera. "Okay, so Eden is now officially a permanent guest on my show. She'll be coming back weekly because I love having boss bitches around me." We laughed again. "But seriously, there's space for everyone in *all* industries. Let me and this gorgeous, talented woman sitting right here be an example of what's possible after receiving a bunch of no's. Fight for what you want and don't let anybody stop you."

Then her attention returned to me. Her energy was contagious and within minutes the interview felt more like a conversation between old friends. And before I knew it, one hour turned into two. Before coming, we'd been told that they often took breaks if the conversation wasn't flowing as organically as it should have. But, neither of us wanted to call for a break so the cameras kept rolling.

"Okay." She said abruptly, "Now that you're officially my good, good girlfriend, let me ask you a question."

"Oh hell." I said with an eye roll that sent her into a fit of giggles.

"I'm nosy by nature, so I gotta ask... is there a special someone in your life at the moment?"

Maybe she *had* gotten too comfortable because that question was *not* on the list that had been sent over. But I'd expected it, so my plan had been to play it off or crack a joke to change the subject. But my gaze flicked to the two-way mirror before a sheepish smile gently lifted my lips. "There's *someone.*"

"Ooh, y'all see that?" Bee chuckled. "Got her blushing just from thinking about him."

"Don't do that." I giggled, covering my face.

"Alright, I'm not gonna do you like that. My curiosity has been satisfied for now."

"Thank God."

Her gorgeous eyes were lit with amusement as she changed the subject. "So, what do you think is the biggest change you've experienced since becoming the first woman to join the PFC? And how has your life changed? Or..." She paused as she thought out the question she wanted to ask. "What's something you're still getting used to?"

"Honestly? People *recognize* me. People want to meet *me*. And having actual fans?" I shook my head with a laugh. "Never in a million years did I believe that I'd be someone who got stopped on the street and asked for a photo simply because of who I was. Getting into the PFC was a goal of mine but the fame and notoriety that came along with it never factored into my decision. And now that it's here? It's *crazy*."

She immediately jumped into a monologue about her experiences when she first started. And how uncomfortable she felt when people started approaching her in public, asking if she was *the* Lady K. "I lied the first couple times and said I wasn't because I ain't know them people and I didn't know what the hell they wanted."

After our laughter died down, she glanced briefly at her notes before smiling. "Now, I've heard rumors about you possibly being in talks for having a shot at the featherweight title. Which I believe you fully deserve it, by the way." I nodded in thanks, feeling pride surge in my chest. "But, of course, with the good comes the bad. How do you feel about those who think your name being mentioned is premature?"

Normally, it took years, or at the very least, several fights to get an opportunity like that. Though nothing was official, the hype around me and the buzz my name was causing had the higherups wanting to capitalize off it.

I merely shrugged. "I can understand why they feel that way if they don't know anything about me or my career. To them, this unknown woman pops up almost a year ago, gets signed to VP Sports, gets all of this publicity out of nowhere, wins one fight, and now sports analyst are mentioning my name with those who've been in the PFC almost a decade. I can get why they think it's unjustified."

Then I leaned into the mic, speaking with the utmost confidence.

"But I've been at this for more than a decade, too. I've never lost a single contest. I've never even had a draw. And despite all the strikes against me... despite my newness in the league doesn't erase the fact that I've put in the time. I've put in the work. Even if I don't get the title shot, I want to make it clear to any naysayers that I'm not undeserving of anything. If I do get the shot and people still choose not to believe in me, they can just wait and see. I love proving people wrong."

"*Holy shit.*" She whispered, staring at me awestruck. "If her highlights and that speech wasn't enough to convince you, I don't know what will. This woman is for real and I can't wait until I get the chance to see you fight in person for the first time."

Her gaze flicked to Saint who was giving her a signal behind the camera that she responded to with a subtle nod. "I could honestly spend the rest of today talking to this woman because her spirit is so beautiful. Just like she is." I smiled, placing a hand against my heart before linking it with hers when she reached out. "Everybody knows I like to end my show with a fun game, but we can do that the next time since you'll definitely be back." Then she looked towards Nala. "Set that up *immediately*."

Laughter struck out across the room again.

"But we're going to do something a bit different. I'm normally a stickler for routine but when my spirit tells me to do something, I listen." The cameras, microphones, and lights seemed to fade into the background as she faced me. From the corner of my eye, I spotted Saint, adjusting the tripod to account for the new position but I couldn't look away from the sudden intensity radiating from this normally easy-going woman.

"You are special, Ms. Eden Foster. You are... a breath of fresh air in this crazy, cutthroat world that sometimes makes me forget why I do this. This world that sometimes makes me wonder why I ever thought quitting my corporate job to pursue this dream was a good idea." Her smile wobbled a bit as she patted my hand. "Today, you reminded me of my *why*. And I want to thank you. For being you."

She paused, closing her eyes and tilting her head with a gentle smile as if someone was whispering sweet nothings in her ear. "The blessings are about to come at you so *fast.* God, your entire life is about to change and I can't think of a more deserving person."

With my free hand, I reached for the box of tissues at the center of the table, dabbing at the corner of my eyes to catch the tears before they fell.

"Do you know how many little brown girls and boys are going to see this episode... see *you* and say wow, I can do that. Somebody told them that they couldn't but now, they know it's possible because Eden Foster did it first. You're a trailblazer and you don't even realize it. Your impact is going to be amazing. And I know at the moment, it feels like you are in the first step of living your dream, but you're also impacting lives while yours is being changed. You are a fascinating human being. *Fascinating* with a beautiful soul and I'm so excited to see what's next for you."

Again, her head tilted while the air filled with silence that surprisingly wasn't uncomfortable.

"I just feel like you need to hear this... and I know we just met, but I love you, girl. *We* love you." She gestured to her team around the room who stood just as transfixed as I was while she spoke. "And before it's all said and done, the *world* is going to love you. The name Eden Foster is going to go down in history. Mark my words."

I gave up on stopping the tears from leaking. Now, I just mopped them as they streaked over my cheeks. She was right. I *did* need to hear that. Those words had the exact impact she'd intended and I'd never forget them.

"And on that note," she turned back to the camera with a serene smile, "Thank you for tuning in for another amazing episode. This is definitely one of my favorites." She squeezed my hand that was still clasped between both of hers. "And a special thanks goes out to today's guest. I'm so glad that I got to meet you at the beginning of your journey so that when you're too big and famous to acknowledge my little podcast, I can remind your ass that I'm your good, good girlfriend, okay?" Thank God for her humor because if she'd kept going with what she'd been saying minutes earlier, I'd be a blubbering mess.

"Alright, my loves. Don't forget to stay cute, stay true, and most importantly, stay you. Lady Bee signing off. See you next week."

# 23

# EDEN

I HAD no business being out here.

No *business* sitting in this dark, secluded building with Crow, waiting to meet up with someone named War. Rome hadn't let me in on what the meeting was about but told me to accompany Crow and watch his back.

I'd put a bullet in the asshole myself if I thought it was worth the blowback.

"When he gets here, don't say shit..." I folded my arms across my chest, not saying a word. At my silence, Crow's lids narrowed and he stalked towards me. I braced but didn't retreat. "I don't know why the fuck he sent you anyway." Before another insult could fly from his lips, we both tensed at the disturbance in the air that warned we were no longer alone.

Flicking my gaze to the entrance, I tensed when two men walked in, both radiating an aura of danger. One that felt eerily like the first time I laid eyes on Hakeem.

The one in front was dark, tall, broad-shouldered, and gorgeous. Sharp, masculine features and long locs stretched well past his shoulders as he walked in as if he owned the place.

Behind him was another beautiful man with just as much height. But he was broader, stockier. He sported a bored, indifferent look, as if he'd rather be anywhere but here. Definitely the muscle of the two.

I couldn't get a read on the one who'd walked in first. His expression was calm and easygoing, but I got the sense that it was just a mask. A front for whatever lurked just below the surface.

The indifferent one waited near the door while the guy with locs closed the distance between us and flashed a smile.

"What's your name, gorgeous?"

From beside me, Crow bristled at being ignored. And before I could part my lips, he spoke. "Pretend she's not here. I'm Cr—"

"I know who you are." His tone was cutting as he interrupted. "You can wait for her outside. She's the only person I'm interested in speaking with."

"But Barry said—"

"I really don't give a fuck about what Barry says or thinks. I'm here for her, that's it. Now you can leave and wait outside or War can make you. Your choice."

We both flicked a glance towards the man who managed to look both bored and dangerous at the same time. Alert yet relaxed as he glared in our direction.

Crow was a dumbass but he knew when not to argue. So, after flashing a warning glare my way, he strolled out, slamming the door like a childish teen behind him. Once Crow was gone, the man with the locs smirked, tilting his head and observing me from head to toe as if he had every right.

"I definitely get the hype." When I didn't respond, his tongue swiped across his bottom lip. "You're not going to give me your name?" I frowned at the charm that oozed from him, still not saying a word as I tilted my head, attempting to see past the facade, down to what I knew was a sinister energy that lurked below. His attractive smile didn't fade as he slipped both hands in his pockets. "I only asked as a courtesy. I already know who you are, Eden. Or do you prefer Menace?" After a few seconds of my silence, he hummed. "I guess we'll go with Eden."

From the corner of my eye, I spotted the other guy surveying the room, lingering a few seconds on each of the exits before coming back to us.

"What do you want from me?"

That agreeable smile faded, replaced by one that was beautiful and terrifying at the same time, making me realize that I was in the presence of a very dangerous man.

"Nothing at all, Eden. I'm merely here to satisfy my curiosity."

Again, I tilted my head. "Regarding?"

"I just wanted to meet the modern-day Helen of Troy." My brows lifted, not understanding the reference. "Her beauty was supposedly so otherworldly that men were willing to go to war for it. *The face that launched a thousand ships*." He licked his lips, probably realizing but not caring that I was failing to see the correlation. "Had to see for myself the woman who could bring the untouchable Hakeem to his knees."

I flinched then immediately stiffened, hoping he didn't see it. Of course, he did, if that little smirk that lifted his lips was anything to go by.

"Who are you?"

That smile turned sinister. "You know exactly who I am."

I'd had an inkling but his smug tone confirmed it. "Axel Knight."

Like me, he neither confirmed nor denied.

"Does Hakeem know you're meeting with shady men in abandoned warehouses?" That smile grew. "Does Mr. Presley know his star athlete is still doing shakedowns for the 400s?" He tsked. "It'd be a shame if they found out."

I took a step towards him, pretending not to see how the man at the door suddenly snapped to attention, drifting his hand over to grip the gun at his waist. "You threatening me?"

"I don't know. Am I?"

"What I do or don't do is none of your fuckin' business."

He chuckled in a way that grated over my nerves. "You're part of the 400s. Doing work on their behalf. You might think Barry is your boss but that nigga answers to *me*. So that means every-fucking-thing about you is my business, beautiful. Including those two little boys you don't get to see as often as you'd like." My entire frame stiffened and momentarily, he dropped the smile as sincerity flashed across his face. "Now that *wasn't* a threat. Merely an observation. Don't get all worked up."

I had no choice but to get worked up. Especially after finding out my babies were on this man's radar. Barry and Rome were cruel and vindictive and even they feared the man standing before me. If I hadn't heard of his deeds for so long, I might've thought it was all exaggerated because of the calmness of his demeanor.

But because I had, I realized that charm was his greatest weapon. A tool used to disarm you and make you complacent until he had you right where he wanted you.

He moved around me, foolishly giving me his back. Then again, the guard dog standing by the door probably would put two hot ones in me before I even had a chance to make a move. Finally, Axel turned, giving me a smile that proved he knew the exact train of my thoughts.

"How long are you going to do this?"

I frowned. "Do what?"

"This shit for the 400s. I told you… I see all, hear all, and know all, Ms. Foster. That contract you signed with VP Sports is going to set you up nicely now that you've started competing. Those winnings are ten times more than the pennies you're being paid by Barry in the Pit."

My gaze flew to his but I remained composed, narrowing my lids at his smile.

"Did you and the rest of them really think I don't know about the little fight club they opened without my permission?" He hummed as if disappointed, twirling the lone ring he wore in circles around his thick finger. "Everybody assumes I sit in an ivory tower, unaware of all the shit they *think* I don't know about." He stopped toying with the jewelry as a thoughtful expression smoothed his handsome features. "People must think I'm getting *soft*. Can you believe that?" His tone was conversational, as if we'd known each other for years.

I kept my mouth closed, choosing not to engage with the dangerously deceptive man.

"Nothing goes on without my notice. Sometimes, I let it slide because it amuses me to see the lengths people will go to hide shit that doesn't really matter." Again, his tone shifted into one that had the hairs on my arm raising. "And sometimes, I wait it out, allowing them to feel empowered. I let them tighten that noose around their neck bit by bit. And then, just when they think they've won... just when they think they've gotten one up on me, I send my *friends* in to put every single one of them down before they see it coming. Friends like that guy over there..." He paused to hike his chin at the brooding man before stepping closer. "Friends like your boyfriend. And just between the two of us, Hakeem was the best at it." An amused snort came from the direction of the door but I was too focused on Axel as he took another step closer, leaning down to whisper in my ear. "War can get a bit... jealous sometimes. He doesn't like when I play favorites."

What the fuck was going on?

"Why are you telling me all this?" I asked after finally finding my voice.

He shrugged, taking enough steps back to give me room to breathe. "Because that noose just got a bit tighter. And I'm this close..." His thumb and index finger parted about an inch. "This close to sending my friends in. I'd hate for you to be a casualty of war so consider this a warning. Keep your ass out of territory that doesn't belong to you. Keep your ass out of business that doesn't concern you. You're swimming with sharks now, Eden. And the only reason you haven't been bitten is because I haven't allowed it. You can thank my fondness for Hakeem for that."

That creepy, unblinking stare remained on mine until I almost squirmed from the pressure of it. Then as if he hadn't just made veiled threats, he smiled, dipped his head in farewell, then turned to leave.

"What are you getting out of it?" I asked, causing him to face me again. "Why are you helping me?"

He snorted as if my statement was completely ridiculous. "I'm not helping you. I'm helping *myself*. If anything happens to you, that man of yours will stir up so much shit it'll take me years to clean it all up. I'm not sure if you're aware but he's a bit of a loose cannon when someone he cares about is threatened."

Axel checked his watch, brows furrowing before the charming mask slipped back in place.

"Seems like I've reached my time limit, love. Being such a busy man and all." His hands shoved deep into his pockets. "Please take heed to what I've said. For your sake, Hakeem's sake, and mine. Keep your nose out of shit it doesn't belong in and everything will be fine."

"And how exactly am I supposed to do that? Since you know so much about me and what I do, then you know I'm acting under orders. I owe a *debt*."

"I'm sure you'll figure it out." He said with a wink. "It's nice to *officially* meet you, Eden. I'm sure we'll be seeing more of each other."

# 24

# HAKEEM

Humor bloomed in my chest, almost making me smile at the sight of Eden's brother hesitating in the doorway of the visitation room.

He frowned at the sight of me then strode over, trying to play tough and pretend like I hadn't just seen his nervousness. By the time he made it over, the unsurety was gone, replaced by a smug smile that was out of place on his heavily bruised face. "What the hell did I do to deserve a visit from the infamous Reaper?" I merely stared while he flashed a pain-filled smirk, morphing into the asshole I'd heard he could be. "My bad, you're like my sister, huh? Y'all go by government names now and shit. Trying to live on the straight and narrow?"

I briefly entertained the thought of swapping insults but decided not to waste my time. The less time I spent here, the better. "I didn't come here to spar with you."

"Then what did you come for?"

"To talk about your sister."

His jaw slackened before he grimaced. "The fuck did she do now?"

That nearly got my temper started. His automatic accusation was bullshit and probably something she'd dealt with her whole life. "She didn't do anything." I squinted.

"Then what's the reason for all this?" He asked, gesturing towards his face. "I'm not stupid enough to believe your visit is a coincidence. It hasn't even been three days since I got jumped in the yard."

I tilted my head. "Maybe you ought to watch how you talk to and treat your son, then."

Our deadlocked glare was intense enough to cause the air to crackle between us. Finally, after several long, silent minutes, he sniffed. "Ain't this some shit. My sister's nigga is pressing me over how I treat *my* son." Then he laughed again. "So if you're not here to rub it in, then why are you here?"

"I'm aware of the power you still possess from here so I'm telling you to use it on your sister's behalf. Make your people fall back."

He smiled as if I hadn't said a word. "My loyalty lies with the 400s, why the fuck would I step in?"

"Because as her older brother, your loyalty should be with *her*." His smile melted but I kept going, pulling out the threats. "You make sure they leave her alone... and I can make your stay here a lot more pleasant." I paused, making sure his gaze didn't stray from mine before I continued. "Twenty-five to life is a long time for a nigga with a target on his back." I leaned forward, grinning a bit. "I'm already prepared to put a few niggas in the dirt behind her, your nephew, and son. The only reason you ain't on the list is because you're her brother. But don't push me. I'm sure I can get her to forgive me for it later." I tilted my head. "If you know what's good for you, you'll find a way to make it happen. Because if you don't..." I paused to smile. "You already know how I get down. There won't be a nigga left breathing with a chain-link tattooed on 'em."

"You're really sitting here threatening me? Because you can't let go of shit that happened damn near twenty years ago?" He leaned forward. 'That's why you're fucking with my sister? On some revenge shit?"

Irritation flooded me because the murder of my brothers was being referred to as *some shit that happened twenty years ago* and because he thought my involvement with Eden was tied to that.

"She's under my protection and I'm giving you a chance to spread the word because if something happens to her, Jayce, or Isaiah, I'll lay every one of y'all down. Including you. Even the untouchable can be touched."

Benji smiled but he knew I was serious.

"It's fucked up that I gotta threaten a nigga to look out for his sister." I snorted. "Guess that family shit y'all like to preach is bullshit."

His smug smile fell again. "Don't be mistaken, nigga. Just because we don't see eye to eye don't mean shit. My family is still protected."

"Does she feel the same way?"

He sucked his teeth. "You don't know shit. You don't understand our relationship. That's my *sister* and that shit ain't gone change. She's mad right now but she'll be right back where you're sitting when she gets out of her feelings."

I kept my shrug casual. "That may be true. But if she does decide to give your ass another chance, I promise she won't be alone when she comes back." Then I stood. "But remember what I said. You know about me so you know that idle threats aren't what I do. Handle that and your remaining time here could be a breeze."

His lids hung low, narrowed as he thought over his response before he sniffed, nodding his head and slouching in his seat. "A'ight, nigga."

# 25

# EDEN

Things were too quiet.

And I didn't just mean because the man stretched across the bed next to me hadn't said two words since getting home. I'd skipped out on three fights in the Pit over the last month. And instead of the normal threats I'd expected, there'd been... nothing. Not a harassing phone call, visit, or promise to keep the boys away from me.

If anything, with Isa officially moved out of Mona's and Jayce coming over multiple times per week, I had more access to them than I'd had in months. It was suspicious but I couldn't give the 400s and their bullshit any more of my mental space because I had another match scheduled.

After discussing it with my team, they felt that another contest where I could show off my skill and dominance might increase my chances for a title fight.

Like I'd told Lady Bee, I knew that I was deserving of the shot and was fully confident that I'd pull out the win if given the chance. So, if another fight within two months of my first put me in the position to do so, I'd take it.

"What's on your mind?"

Hakeem's question startled me and I glanced over, not realizing that he'd switched his gaze from the television. He'd been unnaturally quiet all day, especially considering how easy things had been between us lately. We'd somehow found a happy medium. A tentative one, but happy nonetheless.

I could count on one hand the amount of times I'd spent the night in my condo since we'd officially reconnected. Nowadays, I only went there to grab fresh clothes which were quickly filling up a section of his closet that once stood empty.

"Nothing." I said automatically. Then I sighed, recognizing that was a habit I'd have to break. "Just thinking about the fight." When he didn't say anything, I turned to face him, scanning his pinched expression. "What about you? Are *you* good?"

"Yeah." Everything about that gruff tone proved that he was *not* good and I wasn't going to let it go.

"*Keem.*"

He looked back to the television, resting an arm against the pillow behind his head. "Just thinking about some shit." His eyes touched mine. "About us."

If this was a few months ago, or even a few weeks ago, I might've avoided the topic. But right now, I was ready for whatever conversation he wanted to have. I was over the tension and unease that picked the worst times to appear between us.

"Like?"

His gaze dropped to my hand that trailed over the scars and tattoos scattered across his chest. "I don't know if I've actually said the words, but I'm sorry." My brows almost met in the middle. "For that shit I pulled at your place after I found out about your connection to the 400s. I reacted terribly. And I never should've come at you like that. I shouldn't have had that gun. Loaded or unloaded, it was fucked up."

For a moment, I was speechless. I figured he'd regretted his actions but never once thought an apology would be offered. I couldn't remember the last time I'd gotten a genuine apology from anyone. Lord knows I'd deserved quite a few but had little hope of ever receiving them.

But since he was humbling himself to admit his wrongs, then it was only fair that I did the same.

"I'm sorry too. For not telling you sooner. For... keeping that from you, especially after learning about your brothers. It was selfish of me."

"You don't have anything to apologize for." He soothed as he twirled my braid around his finger. "You were just trying to protect yourself and I get it. We were building something real and you wanted to keep me to yourself because you weren't used to having that."

I jolted with the reality of his words but kept quiet.

"What we have between us is different from what you're used to. It's not one-sided. It's a mutual exchange and I can understand why you wouldn't want to let that go. Especially after what you've experienced before."

He was being extra free with his words tonight, speaking truths that I'd never said aloud to anyone else.

But it was obvious how much of a people pleaser I was. Always in desperate need of affection or approval. Everything I'd done, all the things that I'd involved myself in, every move I've made in my life—outside of MMA—had been for others.

Growing up, our home hadn't been filled with outward expressions of love, so I found myself either acting out or doing wild shit to earn my mom's attention. She was always working and my dad was never there. So the only time she snapped out of her monotonous routine was when I did something wrong.

Benji had recognized it too, so he'd stepped in but even that was manipulative since he'd aligned all my interests with his. I'd been so desperate for his approval that I never protested, even when he got me involved in things that I didn't like or wasn't comfortable with. I just wanted to be around him and with him, so I kept quiet.

Then I met Rome. And he helped Benji get initiated into the 400s so it only seemed like the next logical step for me to do it too. I had already been known as a scrappy kid and was suspended so many times for fighting that I'd lost count. So I'd been eager to show them what I was capable of.

And over time, my participation in the underground fights had gained Barry's interest. I hadn't wanted to work for him but again, I knew it would please Rome, so I'd done it.

Then I'd become involved in the seedy side of things, doing collections and cash pickups from businesses who owed them a debt.

Most days it was easy because everybody knew what the deal was and paid with no problem.

But the times where someone didn't want to, I was the one who showed up, making threats to loved ones and hurting the people in their lives to ensure it.

It had stained my soul but Barry convinced me that we were family and they'd always look out for me. He'd said all the right words to keep me going because even he sensed my desperate need for approval.

It wasn't until Isaiah's birth and the unconditional love I felt with him, even at such a young age, that I realized so many relationships in my life had been one sided. I gave and gave and gave only to receive nothing in return. And instead of snapping out of it, I just continued to give with the hopes that one day they'd see my worth.

But it never happened.

So Hakeem was right that secrecy was my way of being selfish and keeping him close because he'd shown me that same unconditional feeling that Isaiah and Jayce had.

I hadn't felt like I had to sacrifice myself to keep him around. He liked me for me. And that might have been the first time that's ever happened in my life.

And I'd been terrified to lose it.

"I was afraid that this was only real for me. Scared of being in another unbalanced relationship." I admitted, practically melting into his arms when he pulled me close. "That's part of the reason I held back. Not just because of the 400s. I didn't like to show it, but it hurt when I give so much of myself and got nothing in return. I feared that my need to be validated would only transfer from my family to you." I buried my face in his chest. "But I don't care anymore. Being without you is worse than any fears I might've had."

I didn't get a response nor had I expected one. Hakeem knew when I was expecting reassurances versus just getting something off my chest. I knew how much he hated the one-sided relationships I'd been in for too long. Just like I knew he'd never treat me the way they had. We might argue, we might disagree but one thing I never had to worry about was being alone in a relationship with him or being used. His silent, steady presence was more comforting than any empty words Rome, or anyone else that I'd dated, had tried to manipulate me with.

"So where does this leave us?" I asked, meeting his gaze and trying not to squirm from the gentle brushes of his fingertips against my side. "What are we doing?

He shrugged so casually that I couldn't resist a slight smile. "Completely up to you." He gently pushed me to my back, slipping between my thighs so he could hover over me. "But I want to make sure we're on the same page. I let you do that mysterious shit and get away with it before. I let you keep secrets and protect yourself last time, which was fine. But we can't have shit like that between us anymore. I'm not going in with sixty percent of you, love. It's all or nothing. Am I clear?"

I didn't immediately give him an answer because if that was how things were going to be, I had a few more confessions to make.

"Sometimes I go to meet-ups as backup. And last month, I went with Crow to see Axel but–"

"With *who*?"

I hadn't expected the interruption, so it took a second before my words started flowing again. "Axel Knight. He didn't really want anything. Just warning me to stay out of shit that didn't concern me." Then I sighed. "I did a job a few months ago. In the Red District. Apparently, he found out and wanted to warn me. Barry sent me there to collect something that he claimed had been stolen from him."

Still, he didn't say a word, which only fueled the motor in my mouth. What was supposed to be me simply clearing the air about who I was turned into a full-blown confession. Without meaning to, I told him everything. From the job I'd done to the threats I'd lived under. I even told him about Rome's offer of coming back *home* in exchange for unlimited access to Jayce.

The longer his silence stretched, the more I spoke. And with every secret I revealed, the lighter I felt. Hell, I didn't even realize how much had been pent up until it all came spilling free.

And he just listened, tensing occasionally but he let me purge. He let me unburden myself, being that place of comfort that allowed me to let my walls down.

But then, when I spoke about what happened in my apartment not long after our breakup, every inch of him went stone still.

"But I don't want to get you involved," I hastily added, remembering what he was capable of. "I just didn't want any more secrets between us. I didn't tell you that so you could retaliate or anything." I didn't need him trying to fix this shit. I wanted to keep this, what we had, right where it was and not ruin it so soon after finding it again. Which would surely happen if we allowed the 400s to taint our connection. "They haven't called me to do any jobs or fights lately, so maybe I'm off the hook." I didn't believe a damn word I said and based on his incredulous expression, neither did he. "If they do, I'll just cut a deal where I continue paying them instead of fighting. I can't keep risk my body like that."

Finally, he moved, leaning close to my face, lids narrowed with a hidden emotion in their depths. An emotion that looked like the one in his eyes after my head injury. That wild, uncaged one that proved the predator beneath had crept close to the surface and was at risk of bursting free. "You're not stepping foot in that underground ring again. You're not going on anymore jobs for them. And you're not paying them a *fuckin'* dime."

I parted my lips to argue but he rolled out of bed and padded barefoot across the floor into the bathroom, not giving me time to argue. I pursed my lips with annoyance but remained quiet, knowing that he'd said what he said and assumed that was the end of the argument. But moments later, he emerged with that frown still creasing the skin between his brows.

"Who all was there that night?" I tilted my head, prepared to ask for clarification on which night. But he gave it before I could. "At your apartment. When they hurt you and threatened the boys."

"Why does that matt–"

"*Who?*" My lips slammed closed at the harsh demand. But he waited me out, staring me down until I finally gave in and answered. Then he simply nodded. "*Bet.*"

"Wh-what does that mean?" When he didn't answer, I scrambled from the bed. "Keem, what are you going to do?"

"What do you want from me?" He asked instead. "Because I know you're not asking me to sit back and do nothing knowing what the woman I love went through."

My mouth parted.

All I could do was stare while he merely lifted a brow, as if daring me to challenge what he'd said. But my reaction wasn't a challenge to his words. I was in shock. And needed him to confirm that what he'd just said wasn't in the heat of the moment. I needed him to tell me that he really meant it.

"Hakeem, you just said... you...."

"Love the fuck out of you?" He shrugged. "I do."

"But what..."

"Did you think I didn't? I know I'm not the best with using my words but... I thought it was obvious."

I felt lightheaded, which had to be the explanation behind the current hallucination I was trapped in. Because having this complex man who preferred his silence openly confessing that he loved me had to be a dream.

"I didn't know what to call it." He continued, holding my gaze hostage. The depth of emotion swirling in his left me speechless. This was, without a doubt, the most open, honest, and vulnerable that I'd seen this man. And I was not going to ruin it. "I think the first time I realized I felt something deeper for you was in St. Leesburg. I saw you playing on the beach with Jayce. Of course, he was being his normal silly self and you were laughing at him." I smiled, instantly remembering that day. St. Leesburg had been an experience unlike any other. One I'd forever cherish. "But beneath that humor, you were... happy. Relaxed and at peace. And seeing you like that instantly brightened my day."

He laughed and gave a little headshake, slipping his hands into the pocket of his sweats, appearing almost embarrassed by his confession. I flashed him a smile of encouragement that must've eased his nerves because he kept going.

"Knowing that the people I care about are safe and protected has always given me a sense of pride. But I've never had my own happiness directly tied to someone else's. When you're happy, I can feel a physical difference in my own body. Just like I feel it when you're discouraged, upset, or mad. So that day, I knew what I felt for you was *different*. And it's only gotten stronger. Even during those months we weren't together, it kept growing and I couldn't do anything to stop it." This time, a wistful smile softened his lips. "*Shit*. I didn't want to stop it because that was the only connection I had to you at the time." His thumb brushed away a rogue tear as if slid down my cheek. "You mean so much to me that I don't even think you realize it. But that's fine. It's my job to show you and prove it to you. And I can't start until this is taken care of."

Love. That elusive emotion that had made a fool out of me so many times. That had made me do out-of-character things in search of it. That turned me into a person I'd never wanted to be.

The only kind of love I've known– outside of Jayce and Isa–was unhealthy and toxic. The kind that was full of manipulation, blackmail, guilt-trips, and deceit. The kind that was weaponized and withheld until I did what I was told. And despite knowing that Hakeem would never do that, my mind was struggling to get on board.

"I'm... scared." I confessed. This time, I was the one fidgeting and unable to hold eye contact as I spoke words that rarely fell from my lips. Fear was frowned upon in the world I'd been born into.

"What are you scared of, love?"

I jolted at that endearment, still unused to the feeling it created, knowing that the emotion backed it up. "Of how I feel. Of *losing* you because it feels like I just found you all over again. I'm terrified that I can't trust myself. Because my heart believes you, but my mind is so used to love being weaponized that I can't help wondering why you're telling me this. And why now?"

"Because I've already waited too fuckin' long. Because I can't walk around another day without letting you know how I feel. How I *truly* feel."

It's still going to take time for me to completely move past my hangups. It had taken thirty-plus years for life to teach me those hard lessons so overcoming them wouldn't be an overnight fix. But the genuine glint in his gaze and passion in his tone was enough for me to believe him. To believe that he truly loved me.

Hakeem fucking loves *me*. I'd probably spend the next month repeating that statement over and over in my mind until it settled in.

"I love you," He repeated, this time with a shift in his tone that caused my breath to hitch.

"Don't say it like it's *goodbye*." I expressed hastily. Especially if he was still intent on following through on what he'd said.

"I'm not." He laughed, cupping my cheek while closing the distance between us. "I just want to make sure you never forget it." He kissed one of my eyelids. "I know you're used to taking care of yourself. I know you always feel like you have to fight alone." He leaned down, resting his forehead against mine. "I'm going to take care of you and the boys because it's past time that someone does. Your pride might try to interfere but don't let it. You deserve to have someone in your corner. And whether you want it or not, I'm there. So don't ask me to stop because I *can't*."

# 26

# HAKEEM

I USED to think falling in love made you weak.

But now? Now I know better because falling for Eden hadn't suddenly drained me of my strength. It hadn't taken away the darkness that lived inside me nor the violence that I liked to let creep to the surface every now and then. If anything, falling in love with her had made me more dangerous. In fact, that feeling only amplified that there was no limit to what I'd do to protect her.

And the entire time she'd spoken and confessed just how deep she'd been entrenched in the world of the 400s, it had taken every ounce of my control not to react.

I hadn't wanted to make her clam up. So while she spoke, I remained quiet, stewing in my anger and already planning how much blood would be spilled.

It wouldn't be the first time I left a trail of it in my wake as a tool of revenge. And it damn sure wouldn't be the last time if people thought fucking with her would go unanswered.

I couldn't believe some of the shit she'd confessed. Couldn't believe what they'd put her through, much of which had occurred right under my nose. All of it had been fucked up, but what really pissed me off was the shit that had occurred only days after I'd foolishly threatened her in her apartment in White Grove.

They'd broken in. Attacked her. Pistol whipped her and threatened the boys.

That's what Isaiah had meant when he said they'd hurt her.

That's why he'd felt the need to get a gun. To protect her because I'd left them defenseless. I was a fucking idiot and I'd punish myself for those mistakes for the rest of my life. But I'd make it right.

I'd finally found someone I looked forward to seeing at the end of the day. Someone who enjoyed my presence, no matter how silent it could be. And I'd destroy any-damn-thing that tried to take that away from me. That tried to take *her* away.

A watery laugh rushed from her lips and I glanced down, "It's crazy how I've damn near begged someone to care about me… to *notice me* for so long." She shook her head. "I did so much stupid shit in the name of love and never received it. But you're right here, offering it and I didn't even ask for it. You're offering exactly what I want and I have no clue how to accept it." Her hand lifted to rest against my chest. "How fucked up is that?"

"Not at all. You're cautious because affection has been dangled in front of you as bait. It came with strings and demands. It's not your fault that you feel that way. And however long it takes for you to get comfortable with what I'm offering, just know I'm not going anywhere. I'm here to stay and if you push me away or refuse it ninety-nine times, I'll come back a hundred, just to show you what it feels like to have someone love you as deeply as I do."

Her eyes bucked, staring as if waiting for me to take back the words I'd sincerely spoken. Just like she'd done after I first said them. But I wouldn't. I didn't care if she didn't say it back. I didn't care if it would take time to get there. I didn't regret a single thing I'd said to her tonight.

When she realized I'd meant them, her face crumpled before she burst into tears. Her nose buried in the center of my chest and I smirked, lifting her in my arms, rolling her until she was on top of me.

Once she'd settled, I placed soothing kisses against her forehead which only made her cry harder.

If only she knew how much love and affection I had to offer. Love and affection that had built up over time because I'd never had anyone to give it to. But this beautifully shattered woman in my arms was the most deserving of it. She needed it. She needed to see that she deserved it. To see that the only thing I wanted from her in return was reciprocity. And even that could happen in her own time.

She wrapped around me like a child, arms squeezing my neck while her thighs pressed against my hips. Our size difference was never more apparent than in that moment but her heart more than made up for what she lacked in height.

"I uh... I love you, too." She muttered, almost shyly.

Though she couldn't see it, a huge smile broke free at the same time my chest expanded, puffing up with pride at having this woman's love. At *earning* it. While she clutched me like I was her lifeline, I silently made promises.

To take care of her heart and guard it with my life.

To make sure her path going forward in life was as easy as possible. She'd seen enough hardship, and it was past time for peace and quiet.

To care for those two boys she loved and covered like a mama bear.

To be what they needed and their protector as well.

And even though she would probably be irritated, I was still going to handle the situation with the 400s. I'd underestimated them once and I wouldn't make that mistake again.

Every single person who'd hurt her that night would feel me.

I promise that.

So, I held her, mumbling reassurances and repeating my love until she drifted off. I waited another half hour, making sure she wouldn't wake before easing from under her and pulling the covers up to her chin.

I kissed the side of her forearm, brushing back her braids from her forehead before I walked to the very back of my closet, squatting and pressing a particular spot that caused the small, hidden door to swing open. Behind it rested a safe. One that I put the combination into before reaching inside to pull out the contents. I stared at the black duffel, fighting off the memories of all the times I'd done this exact thing.

But unlike then where it'd been a job, this time was personal. As fuckin' personal as it could get. And I wouldn't rest until it was done.

Whatever plans Axel had been cooking up behind the scenes mattered very little now. I was ending this shit tonight.

So I pulled out the bag, rifling through it to see what I had. After the quick inventory, I moved throughout the house to the other hidden safe, grabbing the necessary items before changing into black from head toe. The final touch was my all-black beanie that I tugged down until the tops of my ears were covered.

After checking on Eden once more as she slept, I locked up the house and climbed in my rarely used Jeep, tossing the duffel into the passenger seat.

It was time to go hunting.

---

THE SILENCE in the open space was heavy and stifling from all the testosterone floating around it.

Barry and his nephew Rome stood opposite me in the open space of the Pit, looking way too smug for men that would meet their maker by the end of the night. The ring I'd watched Eden compete in too many times before stood empty behind them, as was the rest of the building which was customary for a Wednesday night.

"You've been a busy man tonight." Barry said with a grin. His nephew, on the other hand, remained unmoved, glaring at me like he couldn't wait to get his hands on me.

Like Barry said, from the second I'd left Eden sleeping, I'd gone to the familiar spots owned by the 400s that I'd watched over the last few months. Building after building, I'd combed for the men I was looking for. The three who'd actually been involved in her beating had been pretty easy to find. Two had been at a bar frequented by members of the 400s. My face was one that would've brought too much attention because of my reputation so I'd stayed inside long enough to confirm that they were there before returning to the place where I was most comfortable.

The shadows.

In the dark parking lot, I'd scanned the vehicles, narrowing down their potential ride to three of the flashy sports cars. Not knowing how much time I'd have, I'd placed a cut in all three fuel lines, mumbling an apology to the other two who'd surely be pissed when they came outside.

Mere minutes after I'd climbed back into my Jeep and they'd emerged. Loud, rowdy, and thankfully climbing into one of the cars I'd messed with.

I'd followed at a good distance, waiting for the right moment.

It came about a mile down the road when the leak had seeped enough fuel for their car to sputter to a stop. While they'd both been looking at the dash, trying to figure out the problem, I'd pulled up next to the open window.

Two muffled shots emerged from my silencer and I was gone before either had slumped over.

The third man had been just as easy to find since he was home. Breaking and entering was child's play to me, especially at a complex with such little security.

I'd spent a little more time with him since he'd been the one to hit her with the pistol and I made sure to return the favor. After a little... convincing, he'd easily given up Barry and Rome's whereabouts. With a new destination in mind, I'd ended him the same way I'd done his friends before leaving.

Bold as can be, I'd strode in through the front door, already knowing that I was outnumbered. Barry was always too guarded to get the drop on him. My only chance was making him feel at ease by walking in under the guise of settling Eden's debt.

"So... you're here to beg us on her behalf, huh?"

I snorted, unable to hide my amusement. I didn't beg for *shit*.

"No, I'm here to tell you that her debt is forgiven and you'll leave her the fuck alone going forward."

This time he laughed. "Forgiven? Just because you said so?"

I nodded. "Yep."

He looked at his angry-faced nephew then Crow and the other men behind him before he smiled. "You've got balls. I'll give you that."

"Bullets, too." His smile dropped as fast as it'd appeared. "I'm giving you an out, Barry. The deal of a lifetime. One that I won't offer twice."

Again, he merely laughed. "Giving *me* an out? You can't touch me. Not without Axel's permission which I'm sure you don't have. He'll never give you the green light to knock me off, Reaper. I make him way too much fuckin' money." He shifted in his chair, eyes flicking over to his nephew smugly. "Now I'm giving *you* an out. Get the fuck out my building while you still can."

Midway through his rant, I started smiling. A huge one that stretched across my face.

I reveled in the obvious discomfort that spread throughout the room at the sight of it. They could play tough all they wanted but they weren't immune to its effect.

"Just to be clear, you're turning my offer down?" I craned my neck in either direction, never breaking our eye contact. I pushed the Hakeem of the present to the back of my mind, letting the Reaper from my past resurface.

Despite his long stretches of inactivity, that dormant part snapped to attention as if he'd been biding his time for a moment like this. A moment to flex his skills in defense of someone he loved.

Barry scoffed. "She's my highest earning fighter and you expect me to just let her go with no compensation?"

"Your life is compensation enough. And the fact that I won't tell Axel about all the little underground operations you have going on. The Pit, right?" I nodded. "What about those trucks coming and going out of that building on 45th? I'm *sure* he knows about that, right? The guns you're running right under his nose?"

Everyone in this room knew what would happen if Axel caught wind of what had been going on. What I'd done to them all those years ago would be mild in comparison. Barry seemed to recognize it too because the smugness faded from his expression. "Let's say I... *release* her from the fighting obligation. What about the debt she owes?"

"You mean the debt her sister owes?" I shrugged. "Better put her ass in the ring if you want it because Eden's not giving you another fucking dime."

Barry laughed. "So you came to make demands with nothing to offer in return?" He scoffed. "I'm insulted you thought coming in here on this bullshit was acceptable in the first place." His hand waved dismissively in the air towards the exit. "Now get the fuck out before I sic him on you." He paused then nodded towards Rome who'd alternated between clenching his fists and gripping his gun.

Since my arrival, his anger and dislike had been palpable, tainting the air surrounding us with the full force of it. He could barely contain himself. And the corner of my lips twitched. Because even though I had no respect for him, I could understand his anger.

Foolishly, he'd let Eden slip through his fingers. And rather than accepting whatever he'd offered her, she'd taken the harder path rather than letting him back in her life.

Not to mention, she'd moved on despite him holding debt over her head. Now, he was feeling stupid for letting her go but his loss was my gain. And at this very moment, I was willing to fight to the death to preserve what I'd found with her.

Under their watchful gaze, my movements were slow and deceptively calm as I pushed off the wall. The second I'd straightened to my full height, each man in the room reached for their gun, eyeing me with a mix of hatred, fear, and uncertainty.

All of which the beast inside of me feasted on.

I liked keeping them guessing. I liked knowing that I made them nervous. Because it would make what came next even better. More enjoyable for me.

"Your first mistake was thinking you owned her." I drawled, taking slow measured steps. Stopping in the center of the room, I glanced over my shoulder, pleased at the way Barry's brows furrowed. "Your second was not putting a bullet in me the second I walked in." I kept my gaze unwavering and directly on his despite the shadow I saw slowly moving near the rear of the room. A familiar-shaped shadow that I'd been unsure of whether they would actually show up.

It was no secret that War and I weren't friends, so my calling on him for backup because I knew I'd be outnumbered had been a shot in the dark. The man had neither confirmed nor denied whether he would be there, so I'd continued with my plans, hoping the very thin threads of a relationship that existed between us was enough.

Thankfully, the military-trained man's entrance was stealthy and silent enough not to capture anyone's attention. I didn't know whether he'd eliminated or simply avoided the group of men standing guard outside, but my only focus at the moment was keeping the men in this room focused on me as he moved to a better vantage point.

Barry's smugness had long since faded into uncertainty and discomfort.

But he was too scared to move on me. Not without Axel's go-ahead. Too bad for him, I didn't give a fuck if Axel gave his blessing or not. I'd deal with the consequences of whatever happened later.

"Your third mistake..." I paused for dramatic effect just for the hell of it. "Was threatening her. Harming and blackmailing her. Disrespecting her and not treating her like she deserves." Then my head tilted slightly to the left in the way that Gia had always said looked animalistic or predatory.

"What the fuck are you talking about?" Barry finally snapped, which caused the men posted around the room to straighten their postures.

"What I'm saying is..." I swung my gaze between him and his nephew and swiped my hand across my beard, giving War the signal. "Now, it's your turn."

The breaker box in the corner of the room exploded from the round War had fired into it, immediately submerging us into darkness.

And I managed to duck behind one of the shipping crates right as the explosion of gunfire started.

*Now the fun can really begin.*

# 27

# EDEN

DEEP, even breaths rushed from me, barely disturbing the night air.

The strings on my boots were tight, supporting my feet as I skirted along the outside of the building quietly, keeping my eyes and ears open for movement.

Hakeem had me fucked up if he thought I would stay behind while he went after them alone. Though I knew enough about the man to know he could hold his own, I also knew the two assholes he were after didn't fight fair. They didn't play by the rules. They lived for deceit and manipulation. And I didn't want him caught up in it. Especially if there was no one there to watch his back.

Being under Barry's thumb had made me privy to his schedule which was why I knew he'd be at the Pit on Wednesday.

Creeping near the front door, my eyes fell on two unfamiliar bodies hidden in the brush along the side of the building.

My brow lifted as I paused, watching for the rise and fall of their chests. After a few moments when nothing happened, I kept going, moving closer until I could barely make out the sound of voices rumbling through the cracked front door.

*"...threatening her. Harming and blackmailing her. Disrespecting her and not treating her like she deserves..."*

Hakeem's familiar tenor was easily distinguishable as I crept inside, palming my gun, aiming it as I moved closer.

Barry's response was too muffled to understand but Hakeem's calm retort had me tensing.

Seconds later, there was a loud pop, the lights went out, and all hell broke loose.

I went from squatting to diving behind the bar when the rhythmic claps of gunfire sounded off in the room. Bottles on the shelves above me exploded and glass rained down. Thankfully the shards weren't big or sharp enough to cause damage so I remained relatively unscathed as I scooted across the floor, trying to get into a better position.

My heart pounded wildly and I barely resisted the urge to rush to Hakeem's aid. I needed to know that he was alright but also knew I'd be no good to him dead. I had to reign in my emotions and lock in. I had to let Menace take over. I had to let her free because where I reigned supreme in the octagon, she specialized in situations like these.

"You're not getting out of here, nigga." Rome taunted. "You and whoever the fuck is helping you."

Random bursts of gunfire disturbed the quiet, but I couldn't pinpoint where anyone was from my position.

"I don't think you're supposed to be here..." The shadows next to me whispered.

I startled and the gun I held was turned in that direction, finger depressing the trigger without a second thoughy.

The familiar man shoved my arm aside just in time, barely avoiding the bullet. "Careful with that."

War, the quiet man who'd trailed behind Axel Knight, squatted beside me with a nonchalant expression in place. In each hand, he held a gun, looking unphased as I followed the movement of his head with the barrel of mine, keeping it aimed in the center of his forehead.

"Friend or foe?"

My eyes slowly adjusted to the lack of light and I spotted a gleam of white teeth as he whispered back. "*Neither*. I'm just a man following orders."

"*Get those fucking lights on, Rome.*" Barry seethed from somewhere in the darkness.

"Whose orders?" I asked, switching my gaze between him and the shadows moving in the dark but unable to locate the one familiar one that would ease my nerves.

"One who told me to make sure your man doesn't get himself killed." Then a smile built on his handsome face. "Which I guess means I have to make sure you don't die too. Lucky you."

The lights flicked back on and I flinched at the sudden brightness.

"C'mon out." Barry taunted, sounding out of breath. "If you want him to live..."

My gaze flicked over to my partner for the moment who merely lifted a brow. "It's on you."

Rolling my eyes, I stood, leaving our hiding spot and moving towards the center of the room with my arms raised where Keem, Rome, Barry, Crow, and one other guy stood with guns aimed at each another. One man lay at their feet, eyes blank with death.

Despite being outnumbered, Hakeem showed no fear.

But that familiar annoyance contorted his features the second he laid eyes on me. One brow lifted slowly and I could practically hear his annoyed grunt of *what the fuck are you doing here*?

Ignoring the question in his gaze, I surveyed him, eyeing the blood seeping through the sleeve of his hoodie. But he didn't acknowledge his injury nor did Barry who had a hand cradled against the side of his neck.

"You're outnumbered, babe." Rome taunted. "Outnumbered and outgunned."

I frowned as if concerned then pulled the trigger twice before he could react.

By the time he had, my gun was aimed back at him and Crow along with the other man were splayed on the ground, dead from the two on-target bullets I'd fired.

"Now we're even."

From the corner of my eye, I spotted Keem's smirk briefly before his expression cleared. Only he'd find the humor in a situation like this.

"*You stupid bitch.*" Barry's arm swung to me but before he could squeeze the trigger, Hakeem fired off a shot, hitting his hand and causing him to drop his gun.

"Goddammit!" He snapped, cradling his hand. "You've got balls. I'll give you that. But you're *stupid*. You don't just come for the head of the snake. You weaken the body first, Hakeem. Killing my men is an inconvenience more than anything. But if you were more than muscle, you might've realized that."

Midway through his rant, Hakeem smiled. A huge one that stretched across his face. "I love that just because I've played a role as the muscle, people start to believe that's all there is to me. As if Axel and Verse forced me there." A wild look flared in his gaze and a chill raced down my spine. The man who'd just spoken sweet declarations of love to me earlier had flipped the switch and morphed into this terrifying version. "Nigga, I chose to stay behind the scenes because the last time I took *myself* off the leash, I painted half of White Grove red with members of *your* organization. Don't mistake my silence for passiveness. I'm a whole nut ass nigga who don't play about mine."

"*Ah-ah*." I warned Rome as he started then stopped advancing towards Hakeem. "I wouldn't do that."

"Did you forget about this shit?" He gestured towards his chain-link tattoo, glaring my way as if I was someone he'd never seen before. "You'll shoot me for him?"

I tilted my head like I'd seen Hakeem do plenty of times and his low chuckle rumbled from next to me. "Shoot you?" I scoffed. "I'll *kill* you for him."

There was a pause before Rome's maniacal laugh rang out, echoing across the massive space. "What's that crazy shit niggas always say before killing their bitch?" That grin turned vicious as he scratched the side of his head with the barrel of his gun. "If I can't have you, then nobody can, right?"

His gun dropped in my direction but I was shoved aside before the bullet reached me.

Hakeem grunted at the same time I adjusted my aim.

One shot went off. Then another.

The bullet from my gun entered his throat at the same moment War's entered Barry's forehead. Once they were down, I moved to Hakeem, yanking up his shirt to inspect the bullet that he'd foolishly taken for me.

"Where did it hit you?"

"I'm fine." He grumbled in that pissy tone I've grown to love.

"Keem, let me see." I ordered, scanning his torso for injury.

I'd started following a trail of blood to find its origin but again I was shoved aside. This time, his big arm curled around my waist, pushing me behind him at the same time Loc walked in.

There was suspicion on Hakeem's face as he leveled his gun at the man, watching with the careful stillness that fascinated me.

Loc scanned him before flicking his gaze to me. "Looks like I'm too late, huh?"

My brows shot up, not expecting that to come from his lips. "What?"

"Talked to your brother a few days ago." He made a show of holding his gun up, barrel facing down before slowly tucking it in the back of his pants. "Told me to make sure you stayed out of trouble. To make sure you didn't fuck anything up for Barry." He paused to look around at the death surrounding us, ignoring the sour expression I'd adopted at hearing how *caring* my brother was. "I was coming by for my normal drop when I heard shit popping off." Then he shrugged. "Guess I won't be doing that drop after all."

I was still stumped by his casual demeanor. "*What?*"

Loc met my gaze briefly before returning his to Hakeem who still hadn't lowered his gun. "Heard about what they did to you. To the boys." He shook his head. "I don't stand for shit like that, E." Then suddenly, he tensed, flicking his gaze behind us. Hakeem and I turned at the same moment, guns aimed at the door. With everything else that had happened tonight, I wasn't surprised in the slightest to see Axel strolling in with the confidence of a man who'd just won the lottery.

"Well... this turned out better than I expected." He mumbled before frowning. "Who are you?"

"*Loc.*" War answered. "With the 400s."

"Hmm." Axel muttered thoughtfully. "Not really fond of loose ends." His gun was out and aimed before any of us could blink.

"*Wait!*" Loc and I called at the same time.

Axel merely tilted his head, ignoring the man whose life he held in his hands and stared right at me with that soul-piercing gaze. "I'm listening."

"You need him. You need someone with the 400s to corroborate whatever story you're going to come up with about what happened here. Loc joined even before I did. He's been around long enough for them to trust his word."

Axel's lips curved as he nodded. "True." Then he fired twice, hitting Loc in the shoulder and thigh. "But if he's going to say he was in this chaos, he can't leave unscathed. It would be suspicious if he didn't have *any* injuries, right?"

A pained grunt had me glancing over my shoulder, finding Loc on the ground. His expression was contorted with pain, but he still didn't say a word. He knew the man in front of us held his life in his hands and if taking non-fatal bullets was the price he had to pay to keep it, then he would.

"He and I can have a little chat about the story of what happened here tonight, right?" War suggested casually, looking unbothered despite the carnage surrounding us.

Loc sucked his teeth, clutching his thigh but he nodded, seeming to recognize War was not a man to be tested. I didn't know anything about him. But Loc's quiet acceptance and Hakeem putting away his weapon told me we had nothing to worry about.

At least I hoped we didn't.

What had gone down tonight was a massacre. One of epic proportions that would have the entire 400s gunning for us in retaliation if they learned the truth.

I'd never been the type to put my fate in anyone else's hands, but I was trusting Hakeem, War, Axel, and Loc to ensure that none of this came back to touch me or my boys.

I was trusting them to make all this go away so I could finally start living life peacefully.

War hovered over Loc, gaze swinging around the building, inspecting it as if seeing something we were missing.

"Might want to disappear before anyone can place y'all at the scene." He said distractedly. "I have some rearranging to do."

My first instinct was to ask questions but I refrained.

I was tired, exhausted, and didn't want to waste anymore energy in this place.

I wanted to walk away and leave the men who'd made my life miserable behind.

Axel's deceptively charming smile stretched his full lips and he focused on the man still cupping my waist protectively. "You owe me again, Keem."

There was an unspoken conversation going on between the two. And after several seconds of uncomfortable silence, they finally seemed to come to an agreement. Keem grunted, nodding towards him and War before linking his fingers with mine.

It wasn't like the movies where the hero and protagonist stood in the middle of the carnage and kissed despite the blood and very-present danger surrounding them.

We weren't like the movies. And though I could feel the love between us practically bursting from the seams as if it couldn't be contained, we still got the hell out of there.

As he pulled me towards the exit, I spared one last glance at Loc, who flashed a shaky smile before I turned and followed the man I loved outside, leaving the past that had haunted me for nearly a decade bleeding out on the warehouse floor.

# 28

# HAKEEM

I FELT NO REGRET.

Not an ounce of guilt plagued me because of how things went down tonight.

Like with Christian, the man who'd hurt Remedy, I felt nothing but relief that it was over.

But despite my lack of remorse, I kept my gaze on Eden. She was quiet, suspiciously so since we'd burned our clothes near the rear of my property, showered and climbed in bed.

By this point, the adrenaline had worn off and whatever her real emotions were about the situation would surely present themselves soon.

Right now, she was curled into a tiny ball, tucked right up against my side.

Having someone this close, being this intimate with her, still felt like a privilege I didn't deserve sometimes.

"You mind not staring at me?" Her grumpy, sleep-laden voice met my ears as she scooted closer. "Leave that creep shit in parking lots." Humor was a good sign. "How's your arm?"

I lifted my eyes from her round ass cheeks to meet her gaze, finding her concerned expression directed towards my bandaged arm. I rotated it slowly, feeling the tight pull from another set of her makeshift stitches. Thankfully Rome's aim had been off and instead of a direct hit, his bullet grazed me, leaving a cut in its wake.

"It's fine." Which it was, even with the slight pain. I'd lived through worse. This was minor compared to some of the shit I'd patched up while working under Axel.

Her pursed lips revealed she didn't believe me and before I could stop her, she was tossing a leg over my hips, straddling me to lean down and peek under the bandage. I remained still, letting her have her way. Besides, her spread legs gave me an unobstructed view of her pussy so she could stay up there as long as she wanted.

When she seemed satisfied with her inspection, her gaze lifted back to mine suddenly somber in a way that had my stomach tightening. "What is it?" I asked.

"If any of this shit comes back on us?" She said, licking her full lips. "I'll take the fall. I'll take the blame since it's my mess that you got involved in."

I cupped her chin, holding it tight and making sure her eyes wouldn't stray from mine before I spoke. "How many ways do I have to show you that I don't need your sacrifice for me to love you?" Her eyes watered and she tilted her head as I slid my hand from her chin to hold the side of her face. "You don't have to take the blame for anything. You got two boys to look out for. If shit goes south and Axel can't get us out of it, I'm taking the blame. You hear me?

"But it's my fault that you got involved." She said softly. "It's not fair for you to take the blame for something that should have never touched you in the first place." She was showing that heart again. That heart that had easily won me over and latched onto mine, refusing to let go before I even recognized it for what it was.

"The second you became mine, any problems from your past did too. My job is to protect you. To look out for you and make sure you and those boys are safe at all times. There's no separation of our problems once we're together. Anything that comes at us, we'll confront together. Just like we did tonight." Then I smirked, grinning at the curious glint in her gaze at the rare expression. "But, based on what I saw, you really don't need a nigga for real, do you?"

She burst into laughter, forehead dropping to rest against my neck and I inhaled, savoring that sweet pear scent she favored. I couldn't get enough of it.

"I didn't like what I had to do tonight." She admitted quietly. "I never really cared for that type of violence. Fighting in the ring is one thing, but taking a life? I never could quite stomach it, whether I pulled the trigger or not. That shit always made me throw up everything I ate that day." Her eyes flicked away from mine before returning somberly. "But tonight, I don't feel any of that. No regret. No nausea. No panic. Just...relief that it's over. Relief that I don't have to worry about them anymore."

I hauled her closer. "Tonight didn't go quite the way I'd planned." I admitted. "Shit, if it was up to me, you would've never lifted a gun tonight. You would have never had to fire a single bullet if I could help it. But you did and I'm sorry for that. But going forward, I'm making it my personal mission to make sure you never have to again. I'm making it my personal mission to make sure you don't ever have to resort to the type of violence that makes you sick to your stomach. You're finally free of them. Free of the shit they were holding over your head. Free of everything they were putting you through."

When her lids filled with tears, I gently cupped her cheek and drew her closer until our lips touched, speaking directly against her mouth. "Now it's time for you to start *living* like you're free. You deserve it."

# 29

# HAKEEM

"You love a good corner, don't you?"

My smile was already stretching my lips before I glanced over at Garryn. The champagne-colored dress she wore flattered her figure, though it did nothing to hide the slight bump protruding at her midsection.

"Getting out there, aren't you?" I teased back, earning an eyeroll and swat to the arm.

"I actually came over to be nice to you. But if you want me to be a bitch, just say that." Then she smirked. "Want to walk with me to the food table? I've already been twice and I don't want to look greedy."

I laughed and extended an elbow, which she took, allowing me to escort her across the room of yet *another* industry party the two of us despised but were forced to attend because of our significant others. While we waited for the small crowd around it to disperse, I scanned the room. Like a magnet, I couldn't keep my gaze away from Eden for too long.

While Garryn finally stepped up to the table and filled her third plate of the night. I looked at the woman who was the center of attention.

The woman whose smile was wide and bright as she moved with unfaked confidence. She mingled with the crowd and charmed every person she spoke with.

"You can't keep your eyes off of her, can you?"

"*Nope.*" I admitted unashamedly. I'd never be embarrassed about my love for that woman. It had changed me for the better. Made me better by pulling me out of a desolate existence that I'd given up hope of ever escaping.

"How long before you put her in this position?" I glanced back to see her gesturing towards her belly as she stuffed a crab roll between her lips.

"Whenever she's ready." Which was the truth. I wasn't trying to postpone becoming a father. Nor was I rushing her into parenthood. We already had two boys at home that felt like mine and if they were the only ones we'd get to raise, then I was fine with that, too.

Besides Eden's focus was currently on her career and I respected that. We were on *her* timeline for the foreseeable future.

I didn't mind being the supporting cast to her starring role when it came to her fame and notoriety. Because when it was just the two of us, when we were alone in the confines of our home, we were on equal footing.

We balanced each other out. Always being exactly who or what the other needed. Sometimes, I gave more to the relationship on her bad days. And sometimes she gave more when I had them too.

But that's what made us perfect. We were both willing to pick up the slack when the other was struggling to carry their load. That's what having a true partner meant. And for the rest of my life, I'd thank the man above for sending her my way.

After wrapping up her conversation, she excused herself only to be stopped mere feet away by someone else. Everybody wanted a piece of Eden Foster. Especially after her dominating performance in her second PFC match. She'd fought with a sense of freeness that I'd never seen before. Eden had knocked her opponent—a former featherweight champion—out in the first round which solidified her as a contender for the title at the beginning of next year.

Though only a few weeks had passed since her victory, training had already begun. She complained about her body sometimes. Somehow, believing that she was losing her touch. But I've yet to see *any* indication of aging when it mattered. Eden was in her prime and likely had several more years of it left.

Her dedication to her career and her body was admirable. At the moment, everyone in the house was practicing clean eating. Which really meant she and I were practicing clean eating while the boys hoarded unhealthy snacks in hiding spots around the house and ate them when her back was turned.

I was determined to support her in any way I could and refused to give in or cheat. Even though my mouth watered for a bite of the roll currently disappearing between Garryn's lips at an alarming rate.

"What are you eating?"

She jumped as if caught, facing her husband with a guilty expression. His hand immediately settled on her belly, smiling down at her.

I shook my head. We were a far cry from those two boys who'd raised hell in Uptown. Now look at us. *Simps* for women who didn't even come up to our shoulders.

"You good, baby?" He asked, brushing away the crumbs that had clung to her lipstick.

"Yes." She said, looking around the crowded room. "Just thirsty."

The last syllable hadn't even passed her lips before he was off, fetching her a drink. When he returned, I thought about teasing him but figured I'd better keep my mouth shut. Eden had me wrapped around her damn finger too and I didn't want him calling me out when I rushed around to fulfill her needs.

Like now, from across the room. she lifted her head and caught my eye, flashing a quick wink. Without her saying a word, I was walking away from the couple who cracked up behind me. I didn't care what they thought.

I wasn't sure is that wink had been a signal to come over or just her acknowledging the eye contact we'd made. But whatever the reason, I'd spent too much time apart from her tonight and it time to fix that.

"Hey, love," she greeted softly, wrapping her arm around my waist upon my approach. With her other hand, she fiddled with the tie on my chest that matched the of her dress before she beamed at the women standing in front of us.

"Hakeem, this is Natasha and Vickie, they're the owners of *Her-letics*."

I tilted my head, sending her a look that earned a slow eyeroll. She already knew what I wanted. "Ladies, this is Hakeem. The love of my life."

Only then did I greet them, reaching out to shake their hands.

"You two look *good* together." One of the women complimented.

While Eden thanked them, I said nothing because I already knew we did. But even if we didn't, I really didn't give a fuck because we *felt* good together and that was all that mattered.

"Ladies, if you'll excuse me, I see someone over there that I need to introduce Hakeem to."

Internally, I rolled my eyes at being forced to sit through another introduction. But for her I would.

So I nodded at the two women and linked my fingers with hers, following her lead. It didn't take long to realize that we were bypassing the crowds of people mingling in the room. Several times during our walk, people tried to stop or get her attention, but her legs never stopped moving. She merely waved and smiled, pulling me along with her.

"Where are we going?" I asked under my breath, after we'd exited through a glass, patio door that overlooked a huge garden maze.

When her gaze lifted to mine, I realized that her irises were alit with excitement and my heart started to pound, already knowing where her thoughts were going. But like always, I wanted her to voice them.

"Want to have a quickie the maze?" She asked with a little grin that made me laugh. I'd discovered that my baby had a little kink. She wanted nothing to do with allowing people to watch us have sex, but she did enjoy fucking in public places. I think the thrill of possibly getting caught was what did it for her, rather than actually being caught. And if it did it for her, then it did for me, too.

So, without another word, I took her hand and pulled, keeping track of every turn we took in the maze until we got to a spot that was just out of view of the cameras overlooking the property. There were less lights on this end and we pressed deeper into our little private alcove to engage in my favorite pastime.

"Don't mess up my hair." She warned but I didn't bother to respond, too focused on hiking her legs around my hips and slipping her panties to the side.

Without delay, I slid home. She released a sharp cry that I quickly muffled with my mouth. My hips retreated, slipping just enough for the tip to remain inside before sinking into her again. She wasn't as wet as she'd normally be if we'd had time for foreplay, so I kept my strokes slow but steady, giving her body time to create that slick essence that made my motion easier.

When I started slipping in and out of her with ease, I picked up the pace, slamming my hips against her roughly while nibbling her lips. Sucking on her tongue. Kissing her nose. Biting the side of her neck.

My mouth didn't know where to linger. I just knew that I couldn't get enough of the taste of her, no matter which part of her body it was.

"Oh, fuck!" She cried, digging her nails into my back, eyes rolling into the back of her head. "I'm about to cum already."

"Then what are you waiting for?"

Her lower half jerked against me in a wild rhythm. One that made me nearly lose my grip on her bucking hips until she reached her peak. Then she went stiff, mouth hanging suspended, face contorted as if in pain as I fucked her at pace that had me emptying my load in her not long after.

"Oh.' She muttered as her tight walls pulsated around my shaft. I could honestly go another round but we'd already pushed our luck.

If we tried for a second round, it would last longer than the first and increase the risk of getting caught. Sometimes I still had to remind myself that Eden was a f sometimes I had to remind myself that eating was a full-blown celebrity now. A famous figure that was one mistake away from scandal. So, I had to be extra cautious with her, making sure nothing would taint her or her reputation.

And though the two of us were in a fully committed relationship, getting caught fucking in the garden maze at a party might not paint her in a flattering light. Endorsement and deals were rolling in at pace she could barely keep up with and I wouldn't let anything jeopardize it.

So, despite the temptation she presented, I stepped back, using the napkins she'd stuffed in her purse to clean the two of us. After righting her underwear and tucking myself back into my pants, I reached for her hand, which she instantly grabbed.

"Did you mess up my hair?"

"*Fucked it up*."

"Shut up." She shot back, not even bothering to check because she knew I was teasing. "You get on my nerves sometimes, you know that?"

"But you love me."

She tried to hide her smile, but I saw it peeking through as we got closer to the party. "Yeah, I do."

Right before we reentered, I cupped the back of her neck and pressed a kiss against her lips, mumbling words that never failed to make her blush.

"*I love you, too*."

# 30

# EDEN

***3 YEARS LATER...***

NINETY SECONDS.

Ninety more seconds until the end of the second round.

But I was struggling to focus. My mind was all over the place, whirling with the news I'd received earlier.

Our adoption of Jayce had finally gone through.

In the beginning, when I'd asked Madi to sign away her rights, she'd pushed back and gave us a hard time, making shit difficult just because she could.

But this morning, at another court hearing where I'd been prepared for more stalling tactics, her attorney showed up alone with a letter in hand.

In true Madi fashion, most of the contents of it was her gaslighting and refusing to take blame for the problems she'd caused. She'd even accused me of turning Jayce against her.

But I could overlook everything she'd said because the contents in the last paragraph were all that mattered.

She'd given us full custody of Jayce.

The baby I'd raised his entire life would officially be mine. And I'd been an emotional wreck since. Receiving news like that before the biggest match of my career had distracted me in a way that I couldn't seem to shake. But I had to find a way to do so, *fast*. This was my last chance because everything would change after tonight.

My opponent took advantage of my distraction, doing a move that had me flat on my back before I could counter it.

She scrambled to the mat, wrapping her legs around my arm and yanking.

A painful yelp was muffled by my mouthpiece before I pressed my lips together, refusing to release a second screech of pain that wanted to burst free.

Rather than pulling against it, I rolled in her direction, flipping over to free my arm.

We ended up in a weird, standing grapple, where both of us were heaving, refusing to let go in case the other spotted an opening that could land a knockout jab. A quick glance revealed there was only fifty-four seconds left in the round.

I wouldn't be able to go too much longer. Not like this. There was still one more to go and I was breathing harder than her.

Unsurprisingly, considering I was nine years older and had a hell of a lot more miles on my body. My eyes welled with tears, this time having nothing to do with the pain I was in.

This was my last match. Nobody but Hakeem knew but I was officially retiring after tonight. For the last three years, I'd dominated my sport. Contest after contest, tournament after tournament... I battled, I fought, I bled, and I *won*. For three years, I took the PFC by storm and never lost a single fight. Some were ugly and hard-fought, but no matter the obstacle, I was still declared the victor at the end.

I was proud of myself and satisfied with everything I'd accomplished. Everything Eboni promised had come to fruition and I'd had a great run, however short it was.

I'd gotten endorsements, was featured in commercials, and had my face on billboards. I also had way more money than I even knew what to do with. So much had happened during the years that I fought in the PFC—both good and bad—and I'd be forever grateful for the experiences.

But like always, with time, things shifted. My body wasn't responding like it once did. My reflexes were slowing and what were once pesky injuries took longer to come back from.

I was thirty-seven and the oldest person still competing in both the men and women conferences.

For so long, I'd feared the day that fighting was no longer my reality. But now that the day had arrived, all I felt was a deep sense of satisfaction. I had no regrets and was more than ready for the next phase. There were people in my life who filled the voids I'd lived with for so long.

My relationship with my parents and siblings hadn't improved and it probably never would. But where that once would've made me uneasy, I just didn't care anymore.

Because I had Hakeem. I had Jayce and Isaiah. Verse and Garryn. Gia and Israel. Junior. Krystal, Drue, Remedy, Tessa and Lathan.

I had a *real* family, even if they didn't share my last name.

Each of them would fight for me just like I would for them and that's all I wanted. That was all I *ever* wanted.

So that happiness I thought I'd find in fighting, I discovered in others. And not because I was a slave to their desires. It was because it was genuinely reciprocated love. And it gave me everything I needed.

But more than that, I'd found that happiness in myself. I was satisfied and content with who I was as a person so I didn't need to seek validation to feel valued. Anything they provided for me mentally and emotionally was simply a bonus for what I'd found in myself.

And now, I was hanging up my gloves with plans to transition from fighting to becoming a coach.

I wanted to train upcoming MMA fighters, specifically those of color because I knew there were moré of us out there. They just needed someone to foster their talent and not give up on them. They needed someone who understood what it was like to be where they were from. And to understand that their scrappiness and feistiness wasn't because they were bad people.

For some, that anger was a veil of protection and necessary while they tried to survive in their environment.

I wanted to work with someone like that so I could hopefully guide them. Show them what they were capable of so they wouldn't be forced to make the same mistakes I had just to make ends meet or to feel validated.

"*C'mon, Eden*!" My coach yelled from outside the octagon.

My gaze flicked upwards and I saw that only twenty seconds remained.

I had to do it. It was now or never.

I couldn't go out any other way. Though nobody else but the man I loved was aware of my retirement, I wanted to go out with a bang. I wanted to go out at the top of my game. With one last knockout that would solidify my dominance in the sport.

One last time, I drew on that control, focus, and discipline and did what was now known as my signature move.

Like I wasn't hurting in nearly every part of my body, an elbow to her chin got her off me. Immediately, I leaped in the air, pushing one leg off the side of the cage so my other swung in a roundhouse kick. I used the full force of my body to connect with the side of her jaw.

Blood spewed from between her lips and she stumbled backwards, gaze going hazy before her knees buckled and she went down.

I knew I'd won. Even before the referee completed his count, I was a puddle of tears, shoulders heaving as I waited for him to announce that she was out.

When the bell dinged and the crowd erupted, I fell to my knees, cupping my stomach, trying to enjoy the bittersweet moment.

Trying to let every memory, every single thing I'd done for the love of this sport wash over me because I knew it was my last time.

I didn't stop crying after my coach yanked me to my feet, swinging me in the air before lifting my arms.

I didn't even stop as the belt was fastened around my waist, declaring me, once again, the featherweight champion.

The tears didn't stop even as I walked into the dressing room, locking eyes with the man I loved. If anything, I cried harder. Loud, choking sobs as I stopped in the doorway, watching him through my tears.

He smiled, one of those big, rare ones that I loved before he hiked his chin. "C'mere, baby."

I limped towards him, still hurting from the kick I'd taken in the shin early in the fight. "I did it." I said, voice trembling as I walked into his arms.

"You did." My shoulders shook as he rocked me from side to side.

All I could do was keep whispering, I did it, I did it. Because I had and I was so proud of myself.

So proud of overcoming everything that life had thrown at me. I'd made a lot of mistakes. I'd done things that I was embarrassed and ashamed of. I'd let people use, abuse, and hurt me for their amusement because I wanted their approval. Because I wanted them to love me.

But that false love I was seeking for so long? I had the real thing now. Unconditionally. And I wouldn't go back. I'd *never* go back because I had too much to live for.

I had this beautiful man who supported and protected me with a ferocity that sometimes didn't feel real.

I had my sweet Jayce who could still brighten a room with one smile.

I had Isaiah who was driving now. He was back under his mom's roof but since the moment he entered the world, he was still my sidekick even though I had to look up at him.

For once in my life, I was completely happy.

When I'd first met Hakeem, I'd held on to the moments he'd given me because I feared karma would snatch them away one day. I disliked who I was as a person. Who I'd *been.* And thought myself undeserving of the happiness he'd given me.

But those negative thoughts were long gone, replaced by the self-assurance and self-validation that I'd always lacked.

"I love you." I whispered, rising on my tiptoes to kiss his lips. "So much."

His smile softened.

Sometimes he returned the sentiment and sometimes, he did what he did best and maintained his silence. But no matter whether he gave me the words or not, I always *felt* it. I always knew I was loved simply by being around him. It showed in his gaze, in the smile he reserved for me, in the little touches and affection that he never shied away from.

Though I loved hearing it fall from his lips, I didn't need to because being surrounded by it was enough.

And it always would be.

# EPILOGUE

I'd found my happily ever after.

After all the shit I'd been through—all the shit *we'd* been through—we made it.

We might've arrived bruised, battered, and slightly broken but each scar... each knock we'd taken from life only made us more appreciative of the peace we'd found together.

"Tell her she's tripping, Keem. *Please.*"

I turned from the beach, raising a brow at Isaiah. "About what?"

The teenager whose height nearly met mine swaggered out of the beachfront condo we'd purchased a year ago, face contorted in a frown that looked just like his aunt's when she was pissed at me.

"My friends and I want to rent a separate place in the city so we can hang out."

I'd been a teenager once, so I knew exactly what a group of seventeen- and eighteen-year-old boys meant by *hang out*. They wanted a place separate from the family so they could bring girls back without having to sneak them in. Just a few months ago, he'd snuck his little girlfriend in but I'd kept my mouth shut, letting him think he was getting away with it.

The kid had no clue just how much surveillance was on our property. Our place wasn't like his mom's. He might get away with that shit there, but I could see everything he was up to when he stayed with us.

"You and I both know you're just trying to sneak girls in, Isa. Don't play with me."

He sighed, turning to look at his aunt over his shoulder. "No, we're not, Tee. We just want some space, that's it."

My eyes swung to her, lips curving upwards at the sight of our ten-month-old, Noble, on her hip with Jayce right at her heels.

The poor woman was surrounded by testosterone but she handled it like the champ she was, running our household with an iron fist that never failed to bring a smile to my face.

"This place has three extra bedrooms, a whole finished basement with a game room, a damn theater and Olympic sized pool. Not to mention a pool *house*. How much space do you need?"

Isaiah turned to me again but I shrugged, reaching out for Noble who launched out of his mother's arms. "I'm not gettin' in that shit."

He sucked his teeth then rolled his eyes back to his aunt, looking down at her.

Her finger lifted, bringing the tip of it up to his nose. "Don't try to intimidate me. I used to change your shitty diapers, don't forget that."

He chuckled again, then lifted his arms. "You're not budging?"

She shook her head. "Not at all."

His eighteenth birthday was two days away so we'd brought him down during Spring Break to celebrate it and his pending high school graduation. Three of his friends were coming tomorrow morning to spend the week with him. He'd arranged all kinds of activities with a tour guide and we approved as long as he agreed to bring one of my security guards.

He hadn't wanted us hovering over him so Eden, me and the kids would get into our own shit so he could enjoy his friends.

"A'ight, I tried." He said with a shrug before leaning over, pressing a kiss against her forehead, making her blush like always.

Even now, after all this time, my baby struggled to handle open affection because she'd been starved of it for so long.

But each day, we showered her with it, never letting her doubt for a moment how we felt.

Though Isaiah walked off without further argument, I knew that wouldn't be the last time he tried it and Eden more than likely knew it too.

I shifted Noble aside when she approached then spread my thighs to make room for her on my lap.

Playfully, she nudged Noble aside who merely stared blankly at her.

When it was just the two of them, he was a mama's boy through and through, refusing to leave her side. But to Eden's annoyance, if I was around, he wanted nothing to do with her. And he wasn't too fond of sharing me with her either.

Her head lowered to my shoulder as a content sigh sent cool air brushing across my face.

"C'mon, Nob." Jayce said, plucking the frowning infant from my arms. "Let's go inside. I think they're about to start kissing."

"No, we're *not*." She turned to him with a laugh.

"Yes, we are." I countered, grabbing her waist and tugging her close.

His nose scrunched and both of us laughed when he ran off, leaving a trail of Noble's squealing laughter behind them.

Once we were alone, I flicked a quick glance at the house, before slipping my hand between her thighs. She parted them instantly, releasing a soft moan when I brushed aside the loose fabric of her romper to tease her slit.

"You said we were about to start kissing."

I pecked her lips while rubbing her clit, groaning at the wetness coating my finger. "We can go to the pool house, if you want. I promise I'll kiss you down there too."

Her soft laughter was cut off by her ragged moan when I lifted her just enough to push down my trunks and slipped into her from behind.

"The boys..." She moaned despite immediately lifting and lowering herself onto my lap at a slow, leisurely pace.

"Can't see shit." I grunted, plucking her clit between my thumb and forefinger, enjoying her little sounds of pleasure. "And I'll hear them long before they get close." I trailed my tongue along the smooth, mahogany skin of her neck after she tilted her head. "Relax, babe. I got us."

Which I did.

Not just right now, but ever since she'd come into my life and agreed to be mine.

There was no limit to the lengths I'd go and already had gone to for her. Some of which she knew. And others, she didn't. Eden Biggers would never worry another day in her life if I could help it and I'd be willing to go to war to ensure it.

"*Oh, fuck.*" Her movements became reckless and that apprehension from moments ago was gone. Replaced by wild abandon as she bounced on my lap, producing a clap each time her thick ass met my thighs.

"Keem." She pleaded.

And like the love-sick fool I was, her pleas were like a beacon and I became desperate to give her what she wanted. What she *needed.*

Still lodged inside of her, I stood, flipping us until she lay prostrate against the patio table while I lunged behind her, pouring every ounce of my love and affection into the strokes.

"I'm about to... I'm so close..." Then she went stiff, knuckles producing soft popping noises from the tight grip she had on the edge of the table.

Then her legs began that familiar shake and I pressed her deep into the glass, watching her expression in its reflection as I rubbed her clit and fucked us both closer to that blissful end.

Her moans were my torture and peace and I struggled not to explode before she did.

Her pussy clamped down and this time, I was the one going stiff, thanking God above that her walls started spasming around me at the same time heated pleasure shot from my dick, coating her womb with the seeds I hoped would produce a girl this time.

One who looked just like her mama.

"Still got it for an old man." She rasped minutes after we'd finally collected ourselves and collapsed into separate patio chairs. Her returning to my lap would only result in a repeat performance of what'd just happened and we'd definitely be pushing our luck then.

Noble would start giving Jayce a hard time sooner rather than later which meant both of them would be popping up any minute now.

"A'ight." I warned, smiling when that sweet giggle I could never get enough of filled the air at the same time a cool breeze whipped up from the ocean. "Ain't fuckin' old man over here." I grumbled, pretending not to be amused by her familiar jab at our five-year age gap.

"I love you."

"I love you, too." I said instantly because how could I not?

She'd seen the man beneath the silence. Coaxing him out with her sweet words and big heart.

She's shown me a side of myself that I never even knew existed. She'd given me the love and life I'd seen my friends experience but thought impossible for myself.

Eden had been extremely easy to love, even for someone like me. And though our union might not have been picture perfect like Verse and Garryn's. It was ours and I hadn't regretted one minute of it.

Our scars made our love that much more real. That much more *perfect* for us.

"I love you more." She shot back with a smile that could make me take on the world, just to lay it at her feet.

Then she linked her fingers with mine on the armrest, kissing the back of my hand. A tinkling laugh rushed from her lips when I did the same to hers before we both turned our gazes back over the Pacific, basking in what surrounded us.

Paradise.

Love.

Peace.

And sweet, blissful silence.

**The End**

# THANK YOU

Thank you to every single person who has supported me during the creation of this project.

Readers, bloggers, editors, proofreaders, bookstagrammers, reviewers, friends, family, and everyone in between... I thank each and every one of you for supporting me through this *long* process and even longer series.

It means everything to me and I'm forever grateful for the support that's been shown to me by this dope community.

# BEFORE YOU GO...

Reviews are so important, especially for indie authors. They help fuel us to work even harder to provide the content you want to read as well as help other readers decide if they want to check out this project.

If you enjoyed this book (or even if you didn't), please consider leaving a review on Amazon and/or Goodreads.

K.

# ALSO BY K. LASHAUN

**All The Way Series**

Between

Only Friends

**Rewind Series**

By Chance

Second Chance

**The Things Unseen Series**

In This Moment

To Be Loved

Beneath The Silence

With These Words

**The Four Letter Word Series**

Love's Truth

Love's Hope

**Standalones**

Everything & More

Only Gift I Need

# ABOUT THE AUTHOR

K. Lashaun is an adult contemporary author born and raised in the great state of Alabama. Her start in writing followed the typical blueprint for most authors — consuming an insane amount of book at an early age before turning that love of reading into a knack for storytelling.

She enjoys crafting imperfect — *unapologetically black*— feel good, love stories.

She has penned twelve books to date with many more on the way.

K. Lashaun would love to hear from you. Click below to follow her on Instagram and Facebook or visit her website at www.klashaun.com

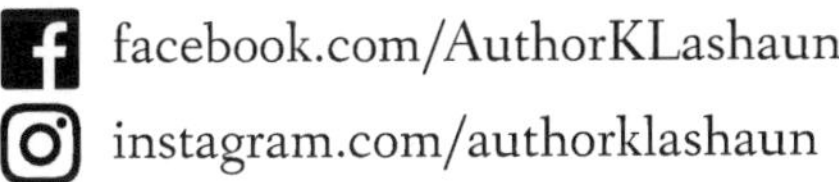

Made in the USA
Columbia, SC
15 May 2025